"They left you alone? Villains! That's like leaving a pearl out on a velvet cushion in full view, with no guards around it. But never fear, I'm here."

Leland's voice stirred the smallest hairs up and down Daisy's arms and on the back of her neck. The breeze brought the scent of warm sandalwood to her nose. She tried to banish the sensations. "Anyone trying to snatch that pearl would lose a hand," she said, without opening her eyes. "I didn't fall down in the last rain, my lord."

" 'My lord?' But why?" he asked in intimate, teasing tones. "You call the earl 'Geoff.' I'm consumed with jealousy. Please feel free to call me 'Lee,' or 'dear Lee,' or 'my darling,' if you will."

"Not likely, my lord."

"I offend you?"

If only he did, she thought. While she knew how to deal with an outright flirt or a lusty boor, she didn't know how to talk with this elegant nobleman. She'd never met anyone like him before.

Somehow he'd been able to bypass her usual defenses . . .

Other AVON ROMANCES

ANGEL IN MY BED *by Melody Thomas*
THE BEWITCHING TWIN *by Donna Fletcher*
SINFUL PLEASURES *by Mary Reed McCall*
A STUDY IN SCANDAL *by Robyn DeHart*
THE VISCOUNT'S WICKED WAYS *by Anne Mallory*
WHAT TO WEAR TO A SEDUCTION *by Sari Robins*
WINDS OF THE STORM *by Beverly Jenkins*

Coming Soon

BE MINE TONIGHT *by Kathryn Smith*
SINS OF MIDNIGHT *by Kimberly Logan*

And Don't Miss These ROMANTIC TREASURES *from Avon Books*

DUKE OF SCANDAL *by Adele Ashworth*
PROMISE ME FOREVER *by Lorraine Heath*
SHE'S NO PRINCESS *by Laura Lee Guhrke*

EDITH LAYTON

HOW TO SEDUCE A BRIDE

AVON BOOKS
An Imprint of HarperCollins*Publishers*
10 East 53rd Street
New York, New York 10022-5299

ISBN-13: 978-0-06-075785-4
ISBN-10: 0-06-075785-X
www.avonromance.com

First Avon Books paperback printing: June 2006

Printed in the U.S.A.

10 9 8 7 6 5 4 3 2 1

To my long lost and newfound
Diamond of a cousin,
Deedee Wolan,
with much love.

Farewell to old England the beautiful!
Farewell to my old pals as well!
Farewell to the famous Old Baily
Where I used to cut such a swell.

My Too-ral li Roo-lal li Laity
Too-ral li Roo-lal li Lay
Too-ral li Roo-lal li Laity
Too-ral li Roo-lal li Lay!

. . . Now all you young viscounts and duchesses
Take warning by what I do say,
And mind it's all yours what you touches-es
Or you'll land down in Botany Bay.

English folk song

Prologue

Port Jackson, New South Wales
1817

"Be damned to all men," the young woman said angrily. "I'll marry and be done with them!" She stood on the dock, her back rigid and her hands closed to fists.

"Oh, Daisy, you don't mean it," her friend exclaimed.

"Well, maybe I don't," Daisy said with the winsome smile that drove half the men in Botany Bay mad with desire and set the other half to lustful daydreams. "But I'm going to leave this place on the next fair tide, see if I don't. I'm bound and determined to marry again. That's the only way to be safe from unwanted attentions."

"There are plenty of single men right here," her friend protested.

"Yes," Daisy said. "But not a gentleman among them. I've friends here I'll miss, true. It's a good enough place to live if you're free. But I'm not free, even though I'm single again. *Especially* since I'm single again." She watched the horizon and the departing ship, and as it became smaller her voice became firmer. "I know what I mean to do and how I'm going to do it. And if a randy captain thinks he can keep me off his ship unless I share his bed, let him. There are other ships and other captains, and not all of them such horn-mad, lusty-guts neither."

"Daisy!" Her friend gasped. "You'll never catch a nob with a mouth on you like that."

Daisy laughed. "Oh, really? I've never heard any complaints from you before." Then her expression grew sober. "But you're right, that's not me; it's the me I became in order to survive. A gentleman wants his wife to be mealymouthed as a parson, no matter what he likes his light-o'-love to whisper in his ear. And the man I'm going to marry is a gent, through and through.

"So, not to worry," she said with resolve. "By the time I get to England, I'll speak so well I'll put duchesses to shame. That's how I spoke before I set sail from England, before I met you. I'd quite forgotten the way of it. It's easy enough to remember and feels more natural, too. Soon it will be habit again, just as will my living like a lady. I won't be traveling in chains in the hold at the bottom of the ship this time, either. And I won't have to marry to get out of the hold. No, this time I'll be up on the top deck, sipping champagne with the Quality. When I get to England, I'll live with them, too. When I thought I'd spend the rest of my life here, I made the best of it. But Tanner was taken so suddenly, by accident, it set me thinking. Life's short.

"So why not dare while we're still above ground? I know what I want and am lucky enough to be able to go after it at last. I'm a widow now, not the frightened girl I was when I got here. So why shouldn't I try? I've been a prisoner and a wife—which is like a prisoner only you eat better—and now I'm free, rich, and still young. It's time to dare."

"But after all that traveling to get to him," her friend protested, "you don't know if he'll marry you!"

Daisy laughed at the disapproval she saw in her friend's expression. "I'm not being vain. I know he liked me well enough. You saw his face whenever he looked at me. He called me 'charming,' didn't he?"

"But you were married then. And he was always a gent."

"You think he didn't mean it?"

"Why not write to him first?"

"Writing's cold," Daisy said, shaking her head. "My father wasn't a lucky man but he knew how to gamble. He always said, 'Play your strongest hand.' I'm not a monster of conceit, but only a fool doesn't know her assets. I know what I've got and it's all face cards, and I mean that exactly. My brain's first rate, but forget that, because men do. All they care about is my face and what's below it. I can't remind him of that in a letter."

"Daisy," her friend said sadly. "You're the belle of Botany Bay and a beauty, no mistake. But there are thirty men to every female here. London's full of beauties, many wellborn and rich as they can stare."

Daisy said nothing, but the morning sunlight spoke for her. It shone through the windows, highlighting the rosy gold hair that tumbled to her slender shoulders, turning her simple muslin frock transparent, outlining her graceful, lithe, lush form. Daisy's tilted, almond-shaped, brown-gold eyes were sober, the feathery brows over them arched in sad surprise.

"I can measure up to any woman in London and go her one better," Daisy finally said, lifting her chin. "I'm rich now, wellborn enough, *and* I have a full pardon, too."

"But he's twice your age," her friend lamented.

"Yes!" Daisy said. "Exactly! He's past the age of all that cuddling and knocking nonsense. Even so, he's not dead, and so I might be able to get a child from him one day. That would be beyond wonderful. But I likely won't, what with his age and my history. I didn't have one when I was married. Still, Tanner never blamed me for it, and he would have if he could have, so I think it might have been his fault."

She shrugged. "Whatever happens, it won't matter much to a man my gentleman's age. He's got his son and heir already, and two more fellows that he calls sons. They're all married now, so he's on his own at last. He's perfect for me. He liked me; I respect him. I can make him happy; he won't ask for much but I won't begrudge him much, either. Don't you see? I could live free with him," she said fervently. "I know I could live safe and in peace with him."

"You could marry anyone here."

"No one here would give me the freedom he would. Wealthy noblemen in England let their wives have their own bedchambers as well as their own social lives. Their own beds! Can you imagine a man here allowing that?"

She gave a theatrical shudder. "Besides, soon I won't have a choice anymore, what with the way Thompson and Edwards are acting and the way that horrible Hughes is talking. I don't dare go out after dark and have to keep my doors locked at all hours. I've no influential male to protect me. No, no matter how much money she has, a woman alone has no power or freedom here. The same's true in England, but at least there I'll have my choice of husband. And I choose Geoffrey

Sauvage: once a convict, now the Earl of Egremont. Who would understand what I've been through better? Who would suit me better? He's old, wise, and kind."

"I wish I were half as brave as you are!" her friend blurted. "But I'm not. Though I suppose I could make a life again in England, I'm not willing to chance it."

Daisy turned, her eyes grave. "I'm not brave. The truth, after all my bluster, is that I don't have the courage to stay here any longer." Her smile was sudden, radiant, warming, like the sun coming out from the clouds. "But I can pretend to be brave, and I will. I mean to take my chances, because at least this time, they'll be *my* chances to take."

"I wish you luck," her friend said. "Though I don't think you'll need it."

"Thank you, but I mean to make my own luck, so please send me off with prayers instead of wishes. I have wishes enough. Now I have to go and make them come true."

Chapter 1

"I'm flattered, my dear, and no mistake," the gentleman said as he gently unlocked the lovely young woman's dimpled arms from around his neck. "But believe me, I'm not worth your time."

She let her arms drop, but didn't move away. She pressed her body to his, put a dainty hand on his chest, looked up at him, and pouted.

"No, in all honesty," he said with a rueful smile, stepping back a pace. "You're such a tempting little delicacy, but I am simply not in the market. Now, Carlton, over there, is," he said, tilting a shoulder toward a short gentleman across the green room. "He's a baron, to boot! Plus he's wealthy, amiable, and very generous when he's pleased. And," he added, raising one long finger to make his point, "I have heard women call him 'cuddly.' Mind, I find that appellation nauseating, but I would. *I've* no desire to cuddle him. But I'll bet he'd want to do just that with you. So," he added, giving her rounded little rump an encouraging pat, "why don't you just go ask him if he's interested in acquiring your so delectable person?"

She looked at the plump gentleman he'd indicated, looked back at the tall, thin, exquisitely dressed gentleman before her, and sighed. Then she winked at him, and turned. She strolled off toward the baron Carlton with an exaggerated wriggle of her scantily clad bottom.

"Good evening, Haye," an older gentleman standing nearby said in an amused voice. "Giving up sweets for Lent, are we?"

"Give you good evening too, Egremont," Leland Grant, Viscount Haye, said in an amused drawl. "Well met. I saw you earlier but didn't have a chance to speak with you. How have you been?"

"I've been fine, thank you, although I hear the latest gossip has me at death's door or up to no good."

"That's what you get for wanting privacy," Leland said. "I've been up to worse and they've said less because my life is an open book."

"A spicy one," the earl commented. "And about as open as a miser's purse. You show only surface; the rest is hidden deep."

"Indeed?" the viscount drawled. "Well, if you say so. However, I agree I've found that tossing gossips warm red meat keeps them full and happy, and not likely to ask for more."

The earl smiled. He was more than a decade older than the viscount, but they'd been friends since they'd met the year before at the earl's adopted son's wedding. The Viscount Haye had turned out to be the long-lost half brother of the illegitimate Daffyd, whose wedding it had been. The earl and the viscount had found much in common and become friends. This puzzled the earl's friends and amused the viscount's cronies, because two more dissimilar men were hard to find.

Leland, Viscount Haye, was a wildly successful womanizer. He loved women and they loved him, but he was resolutely single and lived in high style, entertaining females of all classes and conditions. The earl was still in love with his late wife, and only occasionally formed brief relationships with discreet women.

Geoffrey Sauvage, Earl of Egremont, was bookish, reclusive, a man with a gentle nature. The viscount Haye was said to be amazingly trivial, but also enormously fashionable and in demand, even though he possessed a cutting sense of humor.

They couldn't have looked more different. The earl was a solidly built, muscular, middle-aged gentleman of medium height, who still had his thick brown hair, strong white teeth, and a face that was deemed handsome even though it was unfashionably tanned.

The viscount had just passed his thirtieth birthday. He was tall and very thin, with a long, bony, elegant face, and was languid and affected in speech and movement. But his lean body was deceptively strong. Most people he knew didn't know that, or that he could move with killing force if needed, because most of the time he used only his killing wit.

They were different in age, face, and manner. But the two men got along splendidly.

The earl had discovered that the viscount's care-for-nothing manner concealed a sympathetic heart and a strong sense of justice. He appreciated the viscount's sense of humor, agreed with his politics, and was aware that the younger man hid his true nature except when with friends. The earl's own son and adopted sons were among those few, and since he missed his newly wed sons, the earl was glad for the viscount's company. He found it stimulating.

The viscount thought of the earl as the father he'd not only never had, but never expected to find. He appreciated the older man's experience of the world, compassion, and quiet wisdom.

And so the viscount was surprised to find the earl in the green room at the theater, because that was where men went after the play to make assignations with the actresses and dancers, most of whom were for sale, or at least for rent.

He raised a thin eyebrow in inquiry.

The earl knew what he was asking. "Miss Fanny La Fey, the star of the play, is an old friend of mine," the earl said. "I came to congratulate her. Nothing more."

Leland glanced over at a startlingly bright-haired woman in a gown so flimsy that her modesty was preserved only because of the crush of admirers surrounding her. He raised the eyebrow higher.

"We're friends from the bad old days," the earl explained, "She and I met on a distant shore. She's a rarely determined young woman. I'm happy she also found her way safely back home."

"Ah!" Leland said. Both eyebrows went up. He hadn't known that the actress had been in prison.

The Earl of Egremont had been wrongly accused of a crime before he'd come into the title he'd never expected to inherit. He and his son had been sent to Botany Bay. They, and two young men the earl befriended in prison and took as wards, had served their sentences and returned with him when he claimed his title and the vast fortune that went with it. The earl had already made a fortune for himself through investments, and now was one of the richest men in England. He'd been the talk of the town, and considered slightly scandalous because of his past. But London gossip faded like cut flowers, and now, a year later, he was accepted everywhere.

But he seldom chose to go anywhere that Society did.

"I've congratulated her," the earl said. "I was just on my way out. I won't keep you if you've business here."

"Oh, but that business can't be done here, my lord," Leland said easily. "It can be *arranged*, but not completed. Credit me with some sense of propriety. So if you're going anywhere interesting, I'd be pleased to accompany you."

"I was thinking of a warm fireside, a glass of port, and an early bedtime," the earl said with a sigh. "But I'm promised to Major Reese tonight, for a late dinner at his club. Care to join us?"

"And fight those battles in the colonies all over again with him? Lovely fellow, but I think not. I respect his zeal and regret his lost limb, but there is a limit to how many times I can enjoy vicarious warfare."

"Yes, but he's an old friend and I'm bound to oblige him. How about luncheon at my house, tomorrow? We haven't spoken for a while."

"Not for at least a week! Yes, I'd like that."

"I'll see you then," the earl said, bowed, and asked a footman for his coat.

"My lord!" a sultry, thrilling, voice called. "Not leaving so soon, are you?"

"My dear," the earl said to the star of the evening's play, who had left the group of gentlemen she'd been with. "But you were surrounded by admirers. I just wanted to be one of them and then leave you to your well-deserved applause."

"Old friends mean more than casual observers," she said, but her kohl-rimmed eyes glanced over to the viscount.

"This is my dear friend, Viscount Haye," the earl said. "Leland, may I present Miss La Fey?"

"You not only may," Leland breathed, looking down at the actress intently. "You *must.* Please believe that I am more than a casual observer," he told her, taking her hand in his and raising it to his lips. "I am an enraptured one. As who would not be? Your performance was miraculous. Your presence here, next to me, is even more so."

She smiled. "Are you leaving, too?" she asked.

"Not if you don't wish me to."

She stared up into his amused eyes, and shivered slightly. "I don't wish you to. But I am occupied with well-wishers and can't snub them. Can you wait until I do the pretty with all those I must?"

"I can," he said, one hand on his heart. "If you will be half so kind to me."

"We shall see. I'll be back soon," she promised, and gave him a long, smoldering look before she went back to the crowd of men waiting for her.

The earl shook his head. "How do you do it?"

"I don't know that I did. I think it's this new cologne, actually. . . . My lord?" the viscount asked with an exaggeratedly casual air. "Care to tell me just why she was incarcerated?"

The earl grinned. "No. That should make your

evening more interesting. Just—I wouldn't suggest getting her annoyed. Or if you do, then I suggest you not drink anything that she doesn't. Good night then," he said cheerfully. "See you tomorrow. I hope."

The viscount bowed. "So do I. Good to know you look after me so well," he said with an ironic smile. But it was a wide one.

"Good, you're just in time," the earl said after Leland gave his beaver hat and greatcoat to a footman, and came into his host's study, rubbing his hands together.

"Oh, 'good,' indeed," Leland murmured as he went to the fireside and held his hands up to it. "I've seen cold days in springtime, but this one is ridiculous. I shouldn't be surprised if the Thames froze over again."

"In April?"

"I said I shouldn't be surprised, which is not the same as saying I expected it. It's freezing out there. Still, nothing would keep me from a meal prepared by your chef. The fellow could name his price at Carlton House."

"Yes, but they'd have to take him there in chains," the earl said.

"The way they took him away from London the first time?" Leland asked with a tilted smile.

"Now, now. You know his history is not mine to divulge. He did his time in Botany Bay, and now is free as you or I: past forgotten, future being made. Speaking of émigrés . . . how did you and my old friend get on last evening?"

" 'Now, now,' indeed!" his younger friend said. "I *am* a gentleman. I never discuss my dealings with a lady, *or* a female who aspires to be one. Suffice it to say it was a pleasant interlude for both of us. She'd no reason to be angry with me. And so," he added too casually, "since I never infuriated her, I couldn't tell: Why exactly *was* she sent to the Antipodes?"

"She was there because she was a fair hand with a lethal flying object, or so I was told."

Leland laughed. "Score one for you! I took your bait and ran with it. Though we parted on amicable terms, she must have thought me a strange fellow, because brave I may be, but I didn't dare take wine with her."

The earl sketched a bow, though his eyes twinkled. "Forgive me. Will you accept my apology in the form of a seat at my table? We're having your favorite soup, lobster, squab, beef, and fresh green peas! They've come from a hothouse, but I'm promised they taste as if they came from heaven."

"For half that menu," Leland said fervently, "you could stab me through the heart and I wouldn't complain. So long as you let me sop up the gravy as I fell."

They were laughing when the butler came in, clearing his throat.

"Luncheon ready, is it?" the earl asked.

"Not quite, my lord. But you have a visitor."

"I wasn't expecting anyone."

"The young woman vowed you'd receive her." The butler looked down instead of at his employer. "She said I'd be out on my ear if I didn't let her in." A fraction of a smile appeared on his usually stolid face. "You know her, m'lord," he said, his accents slipping. "As do I. She's from . . . the old country, y'see."

The earl began to laugh. "I think I know who it is." He glanced over at his guest. "You must have impressed her more than you realized."

Leland's eyebrow went up. "I *am* surprised. But maybe she has a complaint?"

"Show her in," the earl told his butler. "I don't know how you do it, Lee," he commented as the butler went to show his guest in. "But you have a profound effect on females."

Leland wore a rueful expression. He shrugged. "Actually I don't know why, either. I see no reason why a lovely creature like that should fling herself at ridiculous, long-nosed, affected creature like me. It can't have been for money. She isn't a courtesan; she has talent and fame and earns a comfortable living. Mind, I do have my ways, and if I set a trap I expect to catch something. If I don't, I start worrying why anyone would want to catch *me*. It's what made me effective in France when I went there on His Majesty's behalf. I suppose it's also why I'm still single."

"I doubt she was angling for matrimony." The

earl looked pensive. "Well, who knows? Maybe she was. Whatever it is, let's settle it. She's a good sort even if she did once make a mistake. After all, it's a long climb from being a penniless orange seller in Spitalfields to becoming toast of the London stage. Maybe she's after another title."

"Then why not you?"

"I'm a lost cause, and she knows it."

"No one knows that but you. Are you so sure?"

"Positive! Ah, here she comes. Courage!"

Both men stood straight as the butler brought the new arrival in. Then the earl blinked, before he smiled in delight.

Leland blinked, too, and for once, with no affectation, he simply stared.

The young woman was something to stare at.

She was more theatrically beautiful than any actress they'd seen on the stage last night, but her face hadn't a hint of paint. The cold and her own excitement had been her cosmetics. Her plump lips were dark pink, the frigid air had turned her fair cheeks coral, and her small nose was pink at the tip. Her long-lashed eyes were golden brown, and bright with emotion. It was cold as ice outside, and she looked like a sunrise in a rose garden. Her rose-colored gown fitted her perfectly: a column of rose silk that showed her high breasts and rounded hips to perfection. Thick, shining gold and red hair was pulled back from her lovely face to fall in a tumble of curls on one shoulder.

She looked at no one but the earl. She hesitated; her smile trembled. A moment later she rushed across the room to fling herself into his arms. "Geoff!" she cried, hugging him. "After all this time and all the miles, I'm back, here—in England!"

"So you are, so you are," the earl repeated awkwardly, patting her on the back. He held himself stiffly, and looked over her head to see if anyone but her maid had come in as well.

"Oh," she said, immediately stepping back. "How rude of me to be so forward, but I forgot myself at the sight of you again. You reminded me of the good times we had together. I didn't have many, and I needed all I could get back then, and thank you for them."

The earl glanced over at his guest. The viscount was watching him with a peculiar, thoughtful smile. "It's not what you think," he said, and turned his attention to his newest guest again. "But where's Tanner?"

She lowered her eyes. "Dead, almost two years. Didn't you know?"

"I hadn't heard from him, but hadn't expected to. We were not precisely friends."

"I thought we were friends though!" she exclaimed.

"Yes, we were," he said quickly. "But what happened to Tanner? He was in the pink of health when I left."

"It was an accident . . . honest!" She laughed

ruefully. "Doesn't everyone in Botany Bay say that when someone they know dies? Habit on their parts, I suppose. But it's truth. He was drunk, he was wagering, he bet Morrissey—remember him? He bet he could take a really high jump. The horse did, but Tanner couldn't stay on it."

She raised a hand as though she was brushing away cobwebs from in front of her face. "No matter, it's over, and long done. I waited to get back on my feet, to get my mind together. Then I decided to come home. Tanner left me rich! Fancy that! He took your advice and invested. You started him off when you were there, but then he scrimped and invested more and turned out to be a hand at it. Never fear that I'm here for a handout. The fact is, thanks to you, I'm rich, Geoff!"

He didn't reply.

She stepped back, looking somehow smaller. "Oh," she said in a stilted little voice, ducking her head. "I beg your pardon. I mean, Your Lordship. I forgot you were a nobleman now. Please forgive me."

"No pardon necessary. But where are my manners? Allow me to introduce you to my dear friend, Leland Grant, Viscount Haye. Leland, this is Mrs. Daisy Tanner."

"Enchanted," Leland said, sweeping her a flourishing bow.

She glanced at the viscount, ducked a curtsy,

and her face went pink again. She looked back up at the earl. "It was bad of me to come without an invitation, but I couldn't wait to see you. I now see that was very rude. I'll return another time, if you wish."

"I wish you to stay," the earl said.

"Should I leave?" Leland asked. "I understand old friends wanting to catch up on old times. I'm the one who can see you some other time."

"Nonsense," the earl said. "Stay. We've no secrets, do we, Mrs. Tanner?"

"No, and it's still just Daisy, please! 'Mrs. Tanner' feels so cold."

"Daisy it is then," the earl said. "And so Geoff it must remain, too, at least in private. Now, have you had luncheon, Daisy?"

"No," she said.

"Then you will, here with us." He looked over her head again. "There's your maid. But where's your companion?"

"I have none," she said. Her hand flew to her mouth. "Another mistake! I've only been in town a few days and I thought—you and I—such old friends. But I see things are different here, aren't they? I'll leave instantly!"

"Nonsense. I think your maid will preserve your name for the space of a luncheon. But you must find a decent companion soon, because a young woman can't stay on in London without one. Are you staying on, and where?"

"I'm at Grillions, which is a good hotel, I'm told."

"It is."

"I plan to rent a house in a good district too, because I certainly want to stay on. Where else should I go? I won't go back to Elm Hill, where I lived with my father. What would I do there alone anyway? I never want to return to that place, too many bad memories, too many bad people, or at least ones that didn't care."

"Then I insist you join us for luncheon. We can try to sort things out for you. I know a realtor in London. We'll try to find you a companion, too. Let's set things in motion for you while we dine."

He offered her his arm. She put her hand on it and looked up at him. "I also need to know where to order new gowns."

"I don't know a fig about fashion," he told her. "But the viscount is an expert on it. He's a tulip of the *ton*."

"Too true," Leland said sardonically, one hand on his chest. "I'm the very pinnacle of frivolous knowledge. All London knows it, and you, lovely lady, may of course rely on me."

She looked up at the viscount and saw amusement in his knowing gaze. Amusement and something more, something she'd vowed to avoid. She quickly looked away. "Thank you," she told the earl, ignoring his guest. "I knew all would be well once I got back to London—and you. That is," she corrected herself with a smile, "when I saw you."

"I'm glad you remembered to come to me when you were in need," he said, patting her hand.

"I could scarcely forget you!" she exclaimed, wide-eyed. "Whether or not I was in need."

"What a delightful luncheon we shall have, my lord," Leland said, as he watched his friend beam at the compliment. "Lobster and squab, and a touching reunion, too. I *am* in luck."

The earl's face became ruddy. "Daisy is an old friend," he said.

"Yes," Leland said with a smile. "What a lot of lovely old friends you seem to have. I can't *wait* to hear how you met."

Chapter 2

She was too nervous to eat, but Daisy knew how to pretend she was enjoying her luncheon. Years of marriage to a man who wouldn't put up with disobedience had taught her that much.

When her heart had slowed to a normal beat after her daring entrance, she sat in the earl's dining parlor and tried to make polite conversation. They spoke about the earl's three sons: Christian, son of his body, and the two adopted sons of his heart. They were all recently married, the earl reported, and doing wonderfully well.

"Marriage was like an epidemic around here last year," the viscount commented with a theatrical shudder.

They laughed at the obvious distaste in the viscount's expression. But Daisy was truly happy for all three young men. She'd liked each of them, and they each in turn had treated her with the same sympathy and courtesy their father did. Now she tried to listen to stories about Christian's new house, his adopted brother Amyas's penchant for Cornwall, and the miracle of Daffyd's settling down at last. But she couldn't stop sneaking glances around at the room she sat in.

She'd lived in a fine house when she'd been a child, but she'd never seen anything like the earl's dining parlor. An elaborate Venetian cut-glass chandelier hung over the dining table, which was set with fresh flowers as well as food. The china plates the food was served on were almost transparent; the glasses looked as though they'd been spun from water; the cutlery was elaborately embossed and pure silver. The walls were covered with patterned stretched green silk; the sunlight that poured in through the long windows made them shimmer. The sideboards and chairs were antique, heavy with age and worth. The footmen were smiling but silent, the food served beautifully. Daisy was awed.

The gentlemen she dined with matched the splendor of the room. They were both well dressed, charming, and mannerly, more so than any men she'd seen in years.

This was her long-held dream, realized at last. Daisy was overwhelmed. She was also suddenly so terrified, she couldn't eat. She wondered if she hadn't bitten off more than she could chew, though she could hardly take a bite of food.

Geoffrey Sauvage, now Earl of Egremont, wasn't as she'd remembered him.

She'd remembered a genial, hardworking older man, usually weary, often sad. He'd dressed in the same rough clothing all the men she knew wore, but he'd worn his with a certain casual style. And, she remembered most clearly, he was always clean. He spoke well and softly, and was always kind to her. Most other men had treated her with wary respect because of Tanner and their fear of his anger if they didn't, because to show no respect to his wife was to insult him. But she'd seen their eyes whenever they thought Tanner wasn't watching. They'd looked her at with appreciation, greedy lust, and calculation. Geoff had never done that.

Nor did he look at her that way now. That wasn't what made her uneasy. It was that he no longer looked sad, or weary, and most of all, now he didn't look that old anymore. He was still dressed casually, but now in fashionable clothes. He looked prosperous, fit, robust, healthy. She wondered why he was still unmarried. She also wondered how many mistresses he had, and didn't doubt he probably had at least one. Because now he looked like a man who would and could use a woman, and not just for show.

That wasn't what she'd been expecting. That

wasn't what she'd traveled halfway across the world to find; it was never what she wanted.

She didn't want to be caught staring so she turned her attention to the earl's guest, and found him watching her. She looked away again, quickly. The viscount was always watching her. But he didn't eye her with any kind of lust; instead he seemed merely amused and curious. She wondered at his friendship with the earl; the two didn't seem to have much in common.

He was years younger than the earl, and far more fashionable, even though his tall, thin frame must have made the perfect fit of his clothes difficult for his tailor to achieve. He had a long face, high cheekbones, and a long nose. Those watchful eyes were dark blue. His light brown hair was just overlong enough to make a fashion statement, and his curling smile was half mocking and half self-mockery. None of this, she thought with annoyance, should have been as attractive as it was.

He was dressed wonderfully well, from his tight blue jacket to his intricately tied neck cloth, to the sapphire pin he wore in it. He wore a quizzing glass, though he never used it to look at her. That, she thought rebelliously, would have been the outside of enough. But it would have given her a reason to dislike him, and she didn't have one, which annoyed her, because he made her uncomfortable and she didn't know exactly why.

She forced her gaze, if not her attention, back

to the luckless baked prawn sitting on her plate. There was only one thing for her to think about now. What about her plans? What was she going to do?

"Don't you find the prawns to your taste?" the earl asked her.

"Oh, they are, but I had a late breakfast," she said, telling partial truth. She smiled an apology. "And a big one. I haven't learned to nibble in the mornings the way I hear London ladies do. I still wake up and tuck in, as though I had a day of work ahead of me."

The earl laughed.

"What sort of work?" Leland asked. "Excuse me, of course it's not my business," he added when she didn't answer right away. "Do forgive my insatiable curiosity."

"No, that's all right," she said, her irritation with him giving her the courage to look him in the eye. Why not tell him? If she didn't, Geoff would. And it would be fun to shock this lazy dilettante.

"My work?" she asked. "I woke at dawn, dressed, ate, and then fed the chickens, gathered the eggs, came back and cleaned the house. We had help, but I had to oversee everything and do much of it myself so it would meet my husband's specifications. I helped wash the laundry, and there was a lot of it. My late husband used his sleeves the way the gentlemen here use napery or towels. He was also a horseman, or fancied himself one, and there was always dust and dirt on his clothing.

"I also tended the garden in summer, knitted and sewed in the winter. I shopped and helped prepare our meals, and cooked them, too. We were well enough off and could have hired more help.God knows servants in the Antipodes were cheaper than dirt. Recently freed convicts are always eager to earn a stake so they can start over with their own houses or businesses, or else they need the money for fare for passage out of there. But my husband became a real skint. I told you that," she said to the earl, with a smile.

If the viscount was shocked at her candor or her history, she didn't catch it. When she looked back at him, he was smiling with appreciation.

"A mighty lot of work for such a delicate-looking lady," he commented. "I commend you."

It didn't sound like that to her. It sounded sardonic. After all, why would such a peacock admire a woman who had worked like a peasant?

"So what are you going to do now?" the earl asked, his real concern clear to see by the furrows on his brow.

She had to make up her mind, and found she had. Things looked different, but nothing had really changed but her perceptions, and they could be wrong. And so she'd change nothing until she saw she had to. She gave Geoff her sweetest smile, and told him most of the truth, which was always best, her father had taught her, because there was less danger of being caught in a lie when you had to lie.

"That's just it," she said. "I don't know. My greatest plan was to get here. I can't believe that I actually did that. Now? I suppose I want to find a place for myself."

"Not a husband?" a cool, amused voice drawled. "That *is* what most single females I know are after."

"But I'm not one of them, am I?" she replied as sweetly. "And you don't know me."

"Alas, my loss, which I feel more acutely each moment," the viscount said, hand on his heart.

"Are you sure?" she asked. "How many ladies do you number among your acquaintance who were jailed and then sent to the Antipodes? Not a whole lot, I'd wager," she said with a roguish wink at Geoff.

She looked at her inquisitor again. "I didn't kill anyone, so you don't have to pick up your knife in case you have to defend yourself, my lord. Actually, all I did was hold a brace of partridges my father brought home for me to cook. They were one brace too many, especially after the trout he'd taken the week before. Because they were poached from the woods of our neighbor, his dearest enemy, as our dinners often were. This time, the squire had my father followed. So we were caught with the goods and removed from the premises, as they put it. We were also speedily tried and convicted of a long string of similar offenses."

She raised her chin, and spoke in her haughtiest accents. "You can do a great many things in this country, my lord, but God help you if you take a ha'penny from a gentleman's purse, or money in the form of a rabbit or a trout from his property. My father, who had been wellborn, was unfortunately overly fond of spirits and not lucky at his favorite sport: gambling. He was also in the habit of lifting his dinners when the spirit moved him, and it frequently did. He also particularly loved to vex the squire."

She gave a pretty shrug. "I suppose the squire had second thoughts at the last. My father *had* been a gentleman in the neighborhood before he drank and diced away his own house and lands, and gentlemen have a code of honor, I'm told. So the squire had our sentence commuted to transportation rather than hanging. And so there I was, and now here I am. *Not* in need of a husband at the moment, thank you very much," she said with a sly smile, aping his exaggerated way of speaking. "Just happy to be home again at last, safe, and," she added with a soft look to Geoff, "among friends."

"You are that!" the earl declared. "Don't mind Lee. He teases unmercifully but there's no real harm in him."

"Gad!" Leland murmured. "That sounds dreadful! Worse than if you thought I meant harm."

"The thing is that you are here now, as you say, Daisy," the earl went on. "I'd like to help you settle in, if you'll let me."

She felt the hard knot of tension ease in her chest. She gave him her best, most winning smile, and the whole truth. "Oh, Geoff," she said on a sigh. "Of course. Thank you. That is exactly, precisely, absolutely what I wanted you to say."

"A lovely creature," Leland commented after Daisy had left them. "Clever, too." He sat back and swirled the brandy in his glass, but kept watching his host, who stood by the fire staring into it, thinking, long after Daisy's coach had gone. "Very clever, indeed."

"She's had to be. Poor child."

Leland's silence was his question.

"No harm in telling you the rest," the earl said. "She told you how she got into her predicament, and if you're going to help, you need to know more. You are going to help, aren't you? You weren't just being polite?"

"I'm *never* just polite. I meant it. I'll send word to an employment agency; she'll have eager would-be companions lining up at her hotel door tomorrow morning, early. And I'll help to outfit her, too. That, at least, will be a pleasure. She really is a charming armful. Her body is exceptional. Slender, but firm and full . . . Oh, don't scowl. I could go on, but I won't. Still, she has spectacular good looks, you know."

"I do."

"*That* sounded very matrimonial," Leland said with interest.

"What? Oh, 'I do'? What? Me, and her? What are you thinking of? She's younger than any of my boys. Far too young for me."

"She's also widowed, I remind you, and of age."

"Yes, widowed, and good for her, poor child."

Leland raised an eyebrow.

"Her husband, Tanner, was a brute," the earl said sadly. "A good-natured brute when things were going his way. But a bully when they weren't. He was a prison guard sent to the Antipodes with the convicts to watch over them in the new penal colony. He did it for the extra pay. He always loved money. Her father—now there was a cad—got her into prison. But he tried to do one good thing for her, at least. Or what he'd thought was good. He urged her to marry Tanner, as asked, so she could be protected from the other guards as well as prisoners on our ship."

"I thought they kept the females separate," Leland said with a frown. "That's what the reformers are always demanding."

"So they do. And so they have, here, or at least at most prisons in England. But once a ship is under way, it has its own law. No one can have a thousand eyes, and the few Bible thumpers who sailed with us were fooled a thousand ways. No question a little beauty like Daisy would have been ill used. So she did her father's will and chose to be ill used by one brute instead of many, and married Tanner."

"A wise choice," Leland said into his glass, though his lips were curled in distaste. "She didn't do too badly, though, did she? She's rich now, or so she says. And she doesn't look the worse for wear."

The earl gave him a strange look. "Lee, you're a clever fellow for a fool."

The viscount sat up, his manner no longer lazy. "I play a fool, my lord, that's true," he snapped. "Lamentable, but true. It is an affectation that amuses me. Are you telling me you now believe me?"

The earl waved a hand. "Relax, please. Forgive me. My experiences in prison are still a sensitive subject. But no man can understand unless he was there. Life's different for a convict. Actually, he no longer has a life of his own, that's the point. He has only his dreams. Someone else owns his body. Many don't survive. Those who do bear scars, some visible, some not, however deep and potentially lethal they may be. Amyas still has nightmares. He's happy now, but I think he will always have them. We all do, because we lived a nightmare.

"Still, if it's possible, it's harder for a woman than a man. Daisy was just turned sixteen when she had to marry Tanner. He was three-and-thirty. He was a robust young man, not unhandsome, but she didn't marry him for his looks. They were wed by a parson aboard ship on the way to the penal colony. Her father told her that if she married a guard, she'd be safer. And so it was. The authorities looked the other way and let her live with Tanner until her sentence was done."

"So her father did try to look out for her? That's good."

"Did he?" the earl asked. "We'll never know. Some of us thought that money changed hands, as did promises of special favors, because though other men wanted to marry her aside from Tanner, he was the only one her father urged her to wed. Whatever he meant or got from it, her father never saw any other gain. He died of a fever before we reached land.

"There's no question living with Tanner helped Daisy survive her time in Botany Bay," the earl went on as he stared at the glass in his hand. "But I think only just, in some ways. Hers might have been just as hard a sentence to serve as ours."

Leland drained his own glass and waited for the earl to continue.

"She's four-and-twenty now," the earl finally said. "I saw her tonight and marveled. She looks and sounds wonderfully well. I don't know how even that valiant spirit stayed so bright after six years of marriage to Tanner. He never spoke when he could shout. He never asked when he could order. He never hit her in the face, because even he could see how rarely beautiful she was, and I suppose he didn't want to ruin that. It was a source of pride with him. But he did hit her, because he didn't know how else to argue or show his displeasure; we all knew that. He struck her for such infractions as speaking up, for not speaking, for being there when he was drinking deep, but mostly, I think, for being who she was. He was as proud as he was resentful of her superior breeding, knowledge, and spirit."

The room was still except for the spitting logs in the fire in the hearth.

"I did not know," the viscount eventually said. "I wouldn't have guessed. You're right. She possesses more than a lovely face and a clever mind. She must be a brave spirit, indeed." He cast a bright eye on his host. "So, what exactly is your part in this now? Do you think you can make it up to her? I wouldn't blame you. You could; you'd be a good husband. And she's very beautiful, and single again."

"God! You have wedlock on the brain. No, and no, and no again," the earl said, pacing in agitation. "I'm happy in my single life. I'm content. My wife was the best of wives; I've no desire to have less. And, sadly, I'd think any other woman was less."

"Oh, you've taken up monkhood then," the viscount commented dryly. "A new order? One that *gives up* abstinence? Interesting. Do you fellows make cheeses or brandy when you're not at your prayers?"

The earl's ears flushed. "I have my diversions, and well you know it. But those good women don't demand more than my company and support. I can't give them more, and don't want more in return. As for Daisy? I always admired and pitied her, and just want to do good for her."

"And if she wants more from you? Because I suspect she does."

The earl stared at his guest.

"Her voice, when she speaks to you," Leland said impatiently. "Her eyes. Good Lord, you could see it if you opened *your* eyes. She wants you, and for more than an old friend."

"You see it, maybe" the earl scoffed. "I don't, and I don't look for it." He stared at his elegant guest. "So. The only question is: Will you help me help her?"

"You trust me with her?"

The earl laughed. "With a beautiful woman? Of course not, unless you give your word not to toy with her, and I won't ask that. Not to denigrate your charms, Lee, but I believe her to be impervious to them. Open *your* eyes, my friend. Didn't you see how she reacted to you? I don't want to hurt your feelings, but for once in your career, you must admit you failed to charm a female. She didn't like you."

Leland gave his friend an odd look. "You thought so?"

"Yes, and I'm glad of it."

"Am I then such a monster?" Leland asked mildly. "A seducer, a despoiler?"

"No, nothing of the sort. You never do real harm. You take a willing female under your protection, or dally with one, and leave her none the worse for the experience."

"And usually a little richer," Leland commented wryly.

"Yes, in funds and experience. But I don't want that for Daisy. Because for all her experience, she's inexperienced with men such as you."

"There are no others such as I," Leland said in mock affront.

"Probably true, but I'm not joking," the earl said. "She doesn't seem to like you, and that's good because it will keep her safe. The only problem with it is that she must work with you if you're to bring her up to snuff."

Leland cocked his head to the side.

"She has to take your advice and follow your lead," the earl said, as he took his friend's glass and filled it again. "You know fashion. You know who is acceptable, and who is not. You're accepted everywhere. My God, you could rule London Society if you wished."

"I certainly do not wish," Leland said. He raised his glass in a toast. "To not being king of the *ton*! Society amuses me. It wouldn't if I took it seriously. Nothing is amusing if taken seriously, and I live to be amused."

"I know it. Now, my plan is to get Daisy Tanner into Society, find a good man to take care of her, and see her well settled. I'll have to think of some way to get her to trust your advice, at least. But that's what I mean to do. Are you with me?"

"Of course," Leland said. "Make a chit from Botany Bay into a paragon of fashion? Create a diamond of the first water from a felon, and marry her to a lord, at least? It would be quite a coup for me."

"You aren't working with an empty basket. This isn't the fable of Pygmalion. You aren't making something of mere clay, building an ideal woman from nothing. She already has breeding and beauty and wealth."

"And a fascinating criminal past."

"It's her future I'm speaking of. I'm serious."

"So am I," Leland said. "I mean it. Count me in. This is something I have to see."

Chapter 3

She wouldn't go back, but didn't know how to go forward. Daisy paced the hotel suite she'd taken for herself and her maid. She'd much to think about and little time to do it in. The rooms she paced were decently furnished, but only that, but they cost so much, she thought she ought to have been gliding over velvet carpets and sleeping in a golden bed. She'd only wanted respectable lodgings. That was what she was paying for, but she didn't know how long she could or should stay here.

Daisy hadn't lied; she did have money now. But what had looked like vast riches in Port Jackson was nothing like it here. Geoff's house had staggered her. There was wealth in every seam and fleck of paint of it. She and her father had lived in a modest home. What she'd lived in while with Tanner was considered good in a raw new colony, but the tiles in Geoff's front hallway probably cost more than that whole house had.

If she'd had another place to go, she'd have left the hotel the minute they quoted her daily rates. In truth, she'd been half dreaming, half hoping the earl would invite her to stay with him. She supposed he could have if he'd a respectable older female relative living with him. But Geoff lived alone, although the strange viscount who'd made her so uneasy yesterday certainly made himself at home there . . .

Daisy halted in her tracks. Was there a reason for that? *Did* the fellow live there?

That would put a different light on everything, one she could see clearly in. She wasn't an innocent anymore, or like most young women in England whether they were experienced or not, for that matter. Living as she had done, in prisons and among convicts, meant she'd seen and heard about different sides of life. Men took love where they found it, and some found it in unusual ways. She'd accepted that without judging it.

Daisy sat down abruptly. Still, that was certainly something she hadn't thought of. She'd never seen a hint of it in the earl when he'd been plain Geoff Sauvage. She cocked her head to the side, considering the matter. It could account for his peculiar friendship with the much younger, fashionable, and oh-so-affected viscount! She sensed the fellow didn't trust her and didn't know why, but if she was right it would make sense. He might be afraid she'd steal Geoff's affections.

She chewed her lip and frowned. It would definitely explain why Geoff was single even now, when he had wealth and title.

But she still admired and respected Geoffrey Sauvage. The more she thought of it, the more she liked the idea of marrying him even if he preferred men. She'd be untouched but not unloved. They could always adopt a child. Hadn't he already taken two boys under his wing, seen them grow into happily married men, and rejoiced for them?

Daisy contemplated the idea of marrying a man who'd never take her physically. It seemed too good to be true after the years of marriage she'd endured. In fact, she thought with rising spirits, if the earl were so inclined toward his fellow man, it might be the best solution of all for her.

But she didn't know if he was. She didn't know much of anything yet except that he was here, he still liked her, and he was still available, in one way, at least. She'd have to see about the rest. If he didn't want to marry, maybe he had friends his age or inclination who did. She didn't plan to marry for love or money, just for security and a place to belong, a place where she could stay on in peace, unmolested. She'd never be free until she was married, and then if she had a husband who simply cared for her like a father or a friend, it would be bliss.

She roused herself from dreams. Money, the here and now of it, was her most pressing problem. She wasn't as cheap as Tanner had been—no one could be. But she'd learned to worry about funds going out, and they'd been draining at an alarming rate since she'd gotten here. At least she'd been smart enough to hire a maid in New South Wales. That cost was small enough; the girl had been eager to go home to England.

But what about the hotel charges, the house she had to rent? The clothes she had to buy? And the "respectable" companion she had to hire?

Respectability, Daisy thought bitterly, looking around her spare, expensive room, came dear. She'd bet whomever the earl recommended would come dearer. If her plan didn't work, how long would her investments continue paying off? She had money, but not the golden touch Tanner had. How long could her money last and grow if she had to keep paying out at such a clip?

Daisy shot to her feet. She wouldn't go back. Whatever happened, she wouldn't go back. That left her only one way to go: forward.

She walked to the door to her maid's room and called. "Amy? Please go downstairs and tell the hotel manager that he can begin sending up applicants for the position of my companion now."

* * *

Life with a father always looking for money and with a husband always looking for a fight had taught Daisy unusual skills. She could read faces the way other women read books, and she was a fast reader who seldom missed a nuance of meaning.

She soon discovered that some of the women she interviewed pitied her for being alone and without family, and some felt superior to her. In turn, she pitied some of them, and some frankly frightened her. Only one thing was plain, and that itself was a little frightening. There were too many respectable women who needed jobs in London Town.

Daisy was ready to halt the flow of prospective companions because the interviews had taken up most of the morning and she was getting hungry. She was heartily sick of her dreary room but planned to eat in, even though it made her feel like an outcast and a prisoner again. The hotel dining room had looked splendid from afar, with its glittering glassware and clean white tablecloths and well-dressed, merrily chattering patrons. But she couldn't eat there. She couldn't dine alone, or with a maid; she had to have a respectable companion with her before she could dine in public.

"You have recommendations with you?" she finally asked the last woman she interviewed before she sent for her luncheon, after the woman recited her qualifications.

"Yes, of course," the woman answered. She held out a sheaf of papers.

Daisy pretended to study the letters, but watched Helena Masters instead. She saw a woman some years older than herself. Seven-and-thirty, her papers said, but she looked older because of the barely concealed worry on her face, and the plain, sensible, drab clothing she wore. A sailor's widow with two children who lived with her own widowed mother in the north of England, she had to work for her keep.

She seemed well bred and had a pleasant voice. Mrs. Masters's brown hair was neat, as was her figure. Her face, with its sincere blue eyes, was plain but promising, because she had laugh lines, which meant that at least she sometimes laughed. The letters from former employers extolled her. She'd never lost a position so much as had to move on because of circumstances beyond her control.

But not all the words on those letters or the woman's own softly voiced history impressed Daisy as much as the fact that her hand trembled when she handed over her excellent references. And the glove that covered that hand had a tiny darn in it. She needed the work, badly. Need was a thing that Daisy never missed. She knew it too well.

"I plan to buy a house in a good district and stay on in London," Daisy said, returning the papers to her. It was also time to put her cards on the table. "Your duties would not only be to accompany me, but to advise me on current manners and fashions. I've been out of the country for years, you see."

Light sprang to the woman's eyes. "I could do that," she said. Her hands knotted together over the papers.

"Starting immediately."

"I could do that as well."

"And the salary pleases you?"

The woman nodded; Daisy realized she was too tense to speak.

"If you'd like, I could give you two days off every three weeks, so you could visit with your children. Since they live so far we could see about more if you needed," Daisy added, and then frowned, realizing she was gilding the lily because she wanted this woman to stay on with her. Need called to need, and so this woman didn't frighten her. She took a breath. If it was going to hurt, she'd best get it over and done with.

"I came from New South Wales," Daisy said bluntly. "I was a prisoner there, then a wife, then a widow. I was convicted with my father, and that because he poached once too often on a neighbor's land. But I was a convict, and that is who I am." She held up her head.

Mrs. Masters's eyes widened. "Oh, you poor child," she exclaimed. Her hand flew to her lips when she realized she'd said so bold a thing to a prospective employer.

Daisy's eyes searched her face; she could see no recoil as realization of what she'd said about being a convict sank in. The pity she'd originally seen was gone in an instant, replaced by sorrow, and the woman's obvious distress at her outburst.

"Yes, well, it *was* bad," Daisy said. "Now, I want only good. Can you help me, Mrs. Masters?"

"You will have me?" the other woman asked, as though afraid to believe her good luck.

"I will. So. When can you begin?"

"Now. At once. What would you have me do?"

Daisy hesitated. Then she heaved a small heartfelt sigh, and voiced her present dearest wish. "Would you come downstairs and have luncheon in the dining room with me?"

It was the loveliest gown Daisy had ever seen up close. Red, with rose ribbons at the waist, gold ones trimming the flounces on the skirts and on the puffed sleeves, and a beautiful needlework rose climbing up the bodice and blooming at the breast. The model wearing it looked magnificent. Daisy turned a glowing face to the earl to see his reaction before she said she'd take it.

"No, not for you," Viscount Haye drawled before she could. "A gown need not be beautiful in itself; it must make the woman who wears it beautiful." He waved a hand. "There's too much gown there, madame. Show us another."

The modiste nodded. "Trust you, monsieur," she said with a little smile. She clapped her hands to signal the next model to come out.

Daisy turned a militant face toward the viscount, but the look of approval on her new companion's face as she gazed at him stopped her from saying anything.

"It *was* a work of art," the viscount murmured to Daisy. "That's the problem. Do you want people to notice the beautiful gown they see, or the woman in it?"

She subsided.

He nodded. "And red, my dear, can be a striking statement for a woman with your coloration. But a little goes a long way, and that gown went much too far."

The earl laughed. *"That,* Lee, is why you're invaluable. See, Daisy? I told you he'd be your best guide. I don't know a thing about fashion. He's right. I can't even remember what the woman wearing that concoction looked like, and I usually have an eye for a pretty young girl."

Daisy grinned at him. "Then if you say so, so be it. I don't know much about fashion, either, and will be guided by you."

The earl sat back, looking pleased. The viscount's midnight blue eyes were half shuttered. He looked bored, but then, Daisy thought, he usually did.

The blue gown and the silver one that came out after it were deemed suitable. The coral walking dress was roundly approved, but the green gown was frowned at. Though Daisy had loved it, she held her tongue. But when the model came out in the gold gown, Daisy actually sighed aloud, in appreciation. The gold cloth was sleek and tissue thin; every curve, every indentation on the model's slender body showed. It was shocking, but even though the girl looked sensual, she also looked elegant, sophisticated, classical, like a Greek statue dipped in gold.

Daisy smiled when the earl said, "Why, that color ought to look good on you, Daisy!"

Before she could agree, the viscount spoke. "Yellow for Mrs. Tanner would work, yes," he said lazily. "Not gold. And not in such thin ply. Much too daring for her. You don't want to lie about her background, of course. But do you want to flaunt it?"

Daisy spun around to stare at him. She was insulted and indignant, even though she realized what he said might be true. Insult won out. "But if Geoff, I mean, if the earl likes it," she declared, "it's good enough for me. I'll take it."

Leland shrugged a shoulder.

"Really, Daisy, he's the expert," Geoff said.

"Well, if you think I'd look bad in it," she said, "then I'll change my mind."

The earl's face turned ruddy, but he nevertheless looked flattered. "I liked it, yes. Still, what do I know?"

"Enough for me," she said firmly.

Leland's eyebrow went up, but he mimed a slight bow to Daisy from where he sat. "Of course. Opinion's a relative matter," he said negligently. "The most important opinion is that of the person who'll be wearing the gown; a dress made of spun silver would look bad if she didn't believe in it. But if you believe your figure and your confidence is firm enough for the gold, why not? If you want it, Mrs. Tanner, so be it."

Daisy didn't answer. The mention of silver and gold turned her thoughts in unpleasant directions. It suddenly occurred to her that she'd ordered up four gowns, and yet hadn't been told the price of one. That was bad trading, poor practice, and very foolish of her. Even her father would have frowned. Tanner would have . . . well, it was best not to think what he'd have done. Bad enough that realizing what she'd done took the joy out of the morning for her.

She'd been having a wonderful time until now. Mrs. Masters had told her to wear one of her best gowns to go to the dressmaker's shop, and she'd laughed, thinking it ridiculous. But she was paying for that kind of knowledge and so had put on a tasteful long-sleeved violet walking dress she'd had made up especially for the trip to England.

She was glad she had after she got to the dressmaker's shop. It didn't even look like one. It was so luxurious, she felt more like she was paying a morning call on a fashionable lady of the *ton* than ordering new gowns. The place was furnished like a sitting room; the dressmaker was called a modiste and spoke with a French accent. There were comfortable couches to sit on, and she was given a little cup of dark coffee to drink. There were patterns to muse over; and lovely young women came out modeling the gowns for sale. And there hadn't even been a sign above the door!

Everything had started off well this morning. The earl had complimented her on her good looks when he'd come to call for her in his elegant carriage. He'd met Helena Masters and roundly approved of her, Daisy could see it in his eyes and hear it in his voice. Even the viscount had seemed impressed by her choice of companion.

Daisy had even found the viscount amusing, at first—until he'd turned dictatorial. She'd had enough of men ordering her around. In truth, she realized now, she'd been getting so angry at his increasingly domineering attitude that she'd have insisted on buying a dress made of paper if she'd seen one, if he'd disapproved.

She'd been lulled by all the luxury, but now worried, wondering if she could afford her new wardrobe, at least enough for her peace of mind.

"You know?" she said in a bright, tight, little voice. "I think I've bought enough for one day. So I won't take the gold gown, after all. My goodness! I've never had so many new ones at once."

"Oh?" the viscount purred. "So you don't intend to go into Society?"

She stared at him.

"You've bought enough for one morning visit, one afternoon's walk, one afternoon tea, and an evening soirée," he explained. "That will do for one day. No one ever wears the same garment twice in a week."

"Maybe you're right," she said, whispering in a fierce under voice, keeping one eye on the modiste to be sure the woman wouldn't hear. "But do we have to get them all at the same place? I mean, we should shop around, see if there are some for sale at a better price . . . and perhaps," she added, seeing his surprise and trying to make it sound like she meant something else all along, "we could find better styles at well."

"Better than at Madame Bertrand's?" he asked, amazed.

Mrs. Masters's eyes widened. Daisy realized she'd made a mistake.

"I think," the earl said, "what Daisy means is that she's not used to buying so much, and certainly not at one place, without comparing prices. She's just in the habit of being frugal."

"Yes," Daisy said in relief. "That's it exactly."

"Not a bad habit, either," Leland said. "But not one we're used to here in London."

"Does that mean I have to squander my money to be accepted?" she asked angrily.

"It means you must never talk about money," he said, holding up one long finger the way a teacher would if he called for silence. "But I will talk about money now, if only to tell you that many of the ladies who buy here don't pay their bills for years, if ever. No one in the *ton* does."

"Except you, Lee," the earl said, smiling, "and me. Me, because I never want to be in debt for any reason. I've seen too many poor souls in prison because of it. And you, because you love to be contrary."

"Thank you for noticing," the viscount said, as he got to his feet and slowly uncoiled his long body. "I do try. But I also know that too many merchants who cater to the rich have to run their businesses like gamblers, and too often lose because of it. They think serving the nobility is good advertising, but what good does it do them if they only attract more rich spongers? The upper classes can be debtors because of the ever-present promise of their money, at least as shown by their inherited properties. But I think they really can do it because of all their friends in high places. If you own the legal system, you're not likely to be bitten by it."

"Very republican talk for a nobleman," the earl commented, suppressing a smile.

"Yes, good that I'm not from across the Channel, isn't it?" Leland agreed. "I'd have taken my last ride in a tumbrel years ago."

"Of course," the earl commented to a wide-eyed Daisy, "you know he may say the opposite tomorrow if it amuses him."

"So I may," Leland agreed. "Now, I'll just have

a word with madame, and then we'll have luncheon, shall we?"

"Yes," the earl said, "and tell her to have at least one gown made up and ready to go by tomorrow evening."

Leland stopped and looked at his friend curiously.

"We want to take Daisy to the theater, don't we?" the earl asked.

"Do we?" Leland answered, as though fascinated.

"Well, I do," the earl said. "Sad stuff to sit around a hotel room while all London is amusing itself outside your window, but you don't know the city enough to venture out on your own. In Daisy's case, it's even worse, because she can't go anywhere at night by herself."

"Indeed," Leland said expressionlessly. "I'm to be included in all this merrymaking, am I?"

"If you'd be so kind," the earl said. "You know London better than I do."

"So I do," Leland said, bowed, and strolled away.

Daisy watched as he sauntered over to talk with the dressmaker. He was so tall and thin, she'd have thought he'd be awkward, but he moved with the same lazy, effortless grace he spoke with. Today he was dressed in black and dark gray, except for a splash of crimson in his waistcoat. The gentlemen she'd seen in fashion plates were tidy men, neat and precise. He was much too tall, thin, and careless for fashion, but he *was* Fashion. It still amazed her.

He spoke with the modiste, and Daisy's eyes narrowed as she saw him amble over to the model wearing the gold gown she'd wanted. He stopped and smiled down at the woman. For one mad moment, Daisy thought he was going to arrange to buy the gown for her, as an apology for how disagreeable he'd been about it.

The model was tall and slender, but she still had to look up at the viscount. She was striking, with classical features. Her sleek black hair was pulled back tightly in a bun, as all the models' were, so as not to interfere with the presentation of the gown, or so the viscount had said.

The earl rose to his feet, too, so Daisy did as well, but she kept her eyes on the viscount. As she watched, she saw him lift one long white hand and run the back of it lightly across the model's cheek in a careless caress as he whispered to her. He'd been right. The material of the gold gown was thin. Daisy couldn't help but notice that the nipples on the model's small, pointed breasts rose in peaks when he touched her cheek. She'd bet they weren't talking about his purchasing the gown.

She was confused. It wasn't really an intimate gesture; it couldn't be, especially coming from a man like Viscount Haye. But it suddenly seemed like one. She frowned.

"Don't mind Lee," the earl said, seeing her expression. "He means well."

"I'm just surprised," she murmured, without thinking.

The earl saw the direction of her gaze. "Surprised?"

"I didn't think he was interested in . . . " She suddenly realized what she was saying and her face colored up.

"In what?" the earl asked with interest.

Well, in for a penny, she thought, in for a pound. There was no time like the present to find out about the earl.

"In . . . females."

The earl's eyebrows shot up. "*Lee?* You wondered that about *him*?"

"I didn't mean to offend," she said quickly. "It's none of my business. But the way he talks . . . I mean," she said, backing off the subject when she saw his obvious astonishment. "Forgive me! You must remember how it was back at the colony: What you think is what you say and devil take the hindmost. I've been gone from England too long, I need to retrain my tongue as well as my manners."

The earl became thoughtful. He looked over at the viscount and the model who was now staring, as if mesmerized, up into his eyes, and a slow smile dawned on his own face. "Well," he said slowly, "there's a thought, indeed. How amusing," he murmured as if to himself, his eyes sparkling. "How ironic. I'd share it with him if it weren't impossible."

He looked back to Daisy, and then said sincerely, "All I'll say is that you needn't worry about Leland's attentions, my dear."

"Oh," she said. So it was true. But then, what about Geoff himself?

"Whatever else he is, Leland is entertaining, good company, and a good man under all his affectation," the earl went on, "which is why I like to spend time with him, as do my sons."

"Doesn't living with him become trying, though?"

"Living with him?" The earl laughed. "Daisy, the fellow runs tame at my house, but he doesn't live there!"

"Oh," she said, and beamed her vast relief at him.

"So, shall we?" he asked, smiling down at her in turn as he offered her his arm.

"Thank you, yes," she said, taking his arm and looking up at him as though he'd presented her with a gift, and so not noticing that the viscount was now watching them, or the slight concerned frown he wore as he did.

Chapter 4

"You haven't come to see me in too long, my lord," the woman said dramatically. "At last, in far too long a time for me. I must know, so I can try to go on. Have you found another?"

She lay back on the couch, her filmy gown in artful disarray, one knee bent, her skirts rucked up to show her long legs. Her long dark hair was the only thing covering her shapely naked breasts.

"I seem to recall you said those exact lines the night I met you," Leland answered, eyeing her with a smile.

She looked puzzled.

"You were in *The Lady's Surprise* that night. The

supporting role, too," he added, "and you were very good."

She was diverted. "Yes, I was. Fancy you remembering that! And not even at the Haymarket, but at that little theater in Brighton. You never said! Is that why you looked me up when I came to London?"

"No. In London, I looked up at the stage, saw you again, and knew Fate had been kind," he said, his hand on his heart.

"Aye, well," she said, sitting up. "It was a good line, and it applies now though, don't it? You're done with me, are you?"

He shrugged. "Not 'done,' surely. That sounds so fatal, so *culinary.* But yes, our time together is ended, I fear. Come, I haven't hurt you in any way. It was a brief but lucrative fling for you, wasn't it?"

She grinned. "Aye, that it was. But for all that, the truth is that I liked being with you. At first I didn't know what to expect, because you act so fancy. But you're funny, and fun to be with, and clean, too. And you know your way about a girl, in every way, don't you? Some gents are a trial, and some are just rude pigs, but you made sure to give as much as you got, and I'm grateful for it. I know a likely lad or two willing to keep me company when I'm not working, so I like meeting a gent I can imagine might be one of them. Combines business with pleasure, so to speak, but it's rare. So thanks."

He smiled. She'd never said so much at one time before, and her new, less theatrical personality was charming. It was too bad she'd decided to be herself with him only when he'd decided to be rid of her. But her few weeks were up. He never kept a mistress longer. It became too hard to forget he was paying for her company. That was why he didn't visit brothels, either.

But he did so enjoy sex with a warm, willing partner. There was nothing like the feeling of a female body pressed to his own, nothing to make him feel more connected to another being, and not just in body. Ecstasy was the goal, but so was the feeling, for a few minutes, that he was no longer alone, that he was part of something more.

He had few acceptable outlets for such intimacy. Though he loved the act, he was fastidious. A stupid woman with a magnificent body attracted him no more than a fine-looking filly might. He didn't desire a healthy animal; his partner had to have brains as well as beauty. If a woman was educated, he was willing to settle for less beauty. But most educated women were of his own class, and they weren't available to him. He wouldn't conduct affairs with married women, as so many men of his rank did. Nor could he with his social inferiors, however smart or beautiful they might be. They needed marrying, it was only fair, and he always tried to be a fair man.

He didn't want to marry, certainly not after

what he'd seen of the institution of marriage in his own life. Even so, he'd loved once or twice, and lost both times: once to a fellow with a higher title, and once to one with worse intentions. True, he'd never actually asked either lady to be his wife, but he'd been working up to it.

He had the reputation of a predator. He agreed with that, because he'd read that wolves spent more time looking for prey than actually devouring any. It was a wonder they survived. He often thought the same about himself.

"Want to stay for a cuppa, at least?" his soon-to-be ex-mistress asked perkily. "I've got a tea-kettle; I'm not the only thing here that's hot, you know." She laughed. It did wonderful things to her half-clad body.

His smile changed. He cocked his head and looked at her with interest.

She saw it. "Ah, why not?" she asked, reaching her arms out to him. "You've paid enough. This one's my treat, my lord. Let's see how different that makes it."

It was late afternoon; he'd come to settle matters with her because he'd seen someone more interesting. But her smile was genuine, and her welcome was as well. That was a novelty, and therefore, irresistible.

"Yes," he said as he sat. He ran a slow hand through her glossy hair and watched it slide through his fingers. He felt the peak of the silken breast beneath the silken mane rise to his hand.

"Yes, thank you very much," he breathed as he bent to her.

"My lord," his butler said as Leland came in the door "You've a guest waiting for you, in your study."

Leland looked up with interest. His butler was trying to conceal a smile. Then his guest had to be someone he knew well. Geoff? He strode to his study and saw the young gentleman who was waiting for him: a lean fellow of middle height, with regular features except for his long, aristocratic nose. His hair was jet, his smile was a startling slash of white in his face because he was dark as a Gypsy, though his eyes were as cobalt blue as his host's.

"Daffy!" Leland exclaimed.

"Lee!" the young man said, rising to his feet. "About time you came home! What have you been up to? Oh, the devil, who cares? Good to see you!"

The two men embraced, then thumped each other on the back.

"Sit, do sit down," Lee said, stepping back and examining his guest, "Lord! Look at you!"

"Look at what?" the other asked, confused.

"You're *happy,* Daffyd. My God! You *ooze* contentment from every pore. Marriage has been more than a tonic for you, it's been a cure." He walked a circle around the other man. "No question about it."

"Yes," Daffyd said with a lopsided grin, "for once, brother, I won't argue. If I'd known what a wedding would do for me, I'd have done it years before, if I could have, but I only met my lady by luck, so I couldn't . . . Good God! Listen to me, I'm babbling."

"Good," Leland said. "Now sit. Babble to me. Tell me everything, the how and why of being happy."

Daffyd did, at length. He talked about how the renovations on the estate he'd bought were going, the way his lady was planning her garden, the problems with servants, from masons to housemaids. The only reason Leland's eyes didn't assume their familiar half-lidded bored expression was that he was genuinely happy for his half brother. Born of the same mother, Leland was an eldest son and heir to title and fortune. Daffyd was the illegitimate result of his mother's fling with a wandering Gypsy, abandoned by her at birth and heir to nothing but hard work.

The two had met as adults and found they shared more than dislike for their mother's coldness. They had the same quick wit, and for all the different upbringings, the same scruples. Both could also summon irresistible charm if needed: they'd had to in order to survive their equally difficult childhoods.

Finally Daffyd stopped talking and smiled sheepishly. "I'm a dead bore now, right? Serves you right for asking."

"No, I let bores know when they fill me with ennui. It's my specialty. I was actually listening. I'm pleased things are going well for you and Meg. Where is she, by the way?"

Daffyd's smile was brilliant. "You're the first to know. She's home because she couldn't stand traveling; she's too busy being carriage sick on land that doesn't move. Lee, she's expecting our baby in the summer! That's really what's got me babbling. Me, a father! Can you believe it?"

"I can, and a damned fine one you'll be. Congratulations!"

"Not yet!" Daffyd warned him. "Too soon. My Gypsy grandmother would have your head for saying that. When the babe cries out for the first time, telling us his name, *then* I'll take your congratulations, and gladly."

"I'll be sure to be there to hear it, if I'm invited."

"As if you wouldn't be! I came to London to tell you and Geoff. I'll ride out into the countryside to tell Amyas and Christian, when I'm done here. Letters are for you *gadjes*; I needed to see faces. I want all of you to come visit with us as soon as the house is finished. Why the frown? I thought you were happy for me."

"When did you last hear from Geoff?" Leland asked quietly.

Daffyd's eyes flew wide; he sprang from his chair. "What? He's sick? I didn't know!"

"No, no, sit down. He's well. Gads, what a firework you are."

Daffyd sat, but the viscount didn't. He began to pace. That was so unusual that Daffyd frowned as he watched the tall figure range the room.

"No, Geoff's healthy, wealthy, and wise, as always," Leland said. "It's just that . . . Damnation, the thing is that he's lost his heart, if not his head. He's met a female, Daffy, and he seems to be in love with her."

"Well. Well, well," Daffy said, sinking back into his chair. "What do you think of that?"

"Not much. Which is why I'm telling you before you see him and meet her. Although I think you may know her already. She's from New South Wales."

Now Daffyd scowled. "Not *Millie Owens*? Damnation. She's the only one with enough gall to pursue him, unasked. She has the sensitivity of a brass monkey. Of course she'd follow him over the rainbow if she heard he came into money. But why would he choose her? It was only a brief affair, and I think he must have been drunk as a monkey at that, to start up with her in the first place . . . "

"It is not Millie Owens."

Daffyd scowled. "Not Mrs. Parsons! No, it couldn't be. She took up with Stanley Burns and was happy with him."

"No," Leland said. "He had no affair with this one; I believe she seeks to remedy that now. I didn't know Geoff then, but I do know he'd never take up with another man's wife—which this female was when you were there. Her name is Daisy Tanner."

"Daisy?" Daffyd yelped. "Daisy Tanner? She's here? Good for her. But wait—where's Tanner?"

"Dead, and unmourned, I gather."

"Of course not. What a thorough bastard that one was. But Daisy, she's a darling, and just a girl! Her, and Geoff? Never. He was always kind to her because he felt sorry for her, but who didn't? No, you've got windmills in your head and marriage on the noggin, brother, if you think anything would come of her and Geoff." Daffyd chuckled.

"Whatever she *was*, she's four-and-twenty now," Leland said. "And extremely beautiful, charming, and, I understand, also now rich. Oh, she has a slight physical disability, too, which perhaps you don't remember?"

"Daisy, disabled? Oh, too bad. I don't remember anything like that."

"Yes," Leland drawled. "It seems she can't stand without Geoff's arm to support her, or see anyone else in the room if he's there. At least, she seems unable to take her eyes off him. Her hearing is fine, though. Anything *remotely* amusing that he says makes her laugh. Geoff *has* noticed this debility. It appears to please him very well."

Leland sat down opposite his guest and leaned forward, his eyes dark with concern. "Daffy, you and I are half brothers. Our fathers were different and neither of us was lucky enough to have one like Geoff. He *is* wise. But men of his age are known to let youthful lovers fool them into thinking they themselves are young. Sometimes such liaisons work well. Too often, they don't. If she's merely looking for a father, that mightn't be too bad. He's good at that, and even though I think he could have more from a wife, if that's what he wants, there's no harm in it. But is she after something else? Why would a young, rich, beautiful woman travel across the world to London, arrive, leave the docks, and then immediately—and I do mean immediately—seek out and try to captivate a man twice her age?

"I wonder, and I worry," Leland said, frowning. "Because if she traps him in marriage and then finds a more suitable mate, for her bed, it would be devastating for him. You know that. We both have had experience with an unfaithful wife, if only at second hand. Our mama showed us how much joy there was in it for the innocent, didn't she? We know too well the havoc unfaithfulness can cause. I worry, and wonder if this chit plans the same for Geoff. So, you know her. What do you think?"

"She's not married anymore, Lee."

"No, but she was, and she's not an innocent by any stretch of the imagination, being both a widow and a convict. Her smiles and guiles are all for Geoff. He seems to love it. So, I ask you: What can be done? Should anything be done?"

"How long has she been here? Looks and smiles

aren't a contract." Daffyd's words were clipped. "Why do you think it's serious?"

Leland shrugged. "She's been here a week."

His half brother interrupted him with a shout of laughter. "A week? She's a daisy, in truth. But only God can achieve anything that serious in a week!"

"A week of luncheon together every day and dinner together every night; and the theater or the opera or the ballet every other night as well?" Leland said calmly.

Daffyd's smile faded.

"She hasn't gone out without him yet," Leland continued, "because she says she doesn't know anyone in Society, and he says he wants to make her comfortable until she does. She's making herself very comfortable in his pocket, that's certain. She's delicious; I will say that for her. Her figure is nothing short of sensational. That golden red hair is spectacular, but somehow she manages to look more like an angel than a trollop. She has wit and charm. She'll be your stepmama if this continues, I'd bet on it."

"Not my stepmother," Daffyd muttered. "He's not my real father, though I wish he were." He sat thinking. Then he studied his half brother for a moment. "And you? Have you been there each time, all this time?"

"Yes."

"Oh. I see," Daffyd said with a dawning tucked-in smile.

Leland waved a long hand. "You don't. I'm there because Geoff begs me to be. He doesn't want to ruin her reputation by seeing her alone, because even with her companion there it will look like they are à deux. He was the one to remind her that she needed a respectable companion, by the way, and I had to send her applicants for the position. Thank God I was visiting at the time she landed herself on Geoff, after stepping off the docks and into his life with only a maid in tow. I knew a good employment agency, or who knows what she may have accomplished by now?

"Geoff says he doesn't know who to introduce her to yet. He says his other friends are too stodgy and opinionated to take her at face value, and friends from the old days in prison would want to take her for far more, whatever he said. He'd rather not bring her into Society until she has a full wardrobe *and* has been coached in the finer niceties . . . there being few practiced in New South Wales, I gather."

"But she knows her manners. She was wellborn and well bred," Daffyd said. "That was why Tanner insisted on marrying her soon as he clapped eyes on her. Pretty females are rare on a prison ship. He could have used her and passed her along for profit. That was done. But beautiful, innocent, *and* wellborn? If her damned fool of a father hadn't alienated his family years before, she'd never have been there at all. Tanner seized the opportunity. He grabbed her and wouldn't let go. He knew what he had. A real rarity."

"Yes. Precisely," Leland drawled. "She may have fallen into some sloppy speech patterns, but she knows how to speak and behave. Still, Geoff's like a mother hen with her. If he were merely paternal, I wouldn't worry. I'm not at all convinced that's it. And if you were secretly amused a moment ago because you think I am slain by her big brown eyes," he added too lightly, "I assure you I am not. She never turns them on me anyway."

Daffyd's eyes searched his. "And does that rankle? You're famous for your taste in females, and as you say, she's tasty. Are you annoyed because she ignores you?" The haughty look he received in return made him laugh. "Don't give me your famous offended camel look. I don't understand her overlooking you. I don't know how you do it, but you usually get any female you want. And she doesn't notice you at all? Really? Wait. Have you been nice or have you been your famous 'Viscount Too Cruel,' as that caricature put it? Be honest."

"That ridiculous caricature?" Leland asked. "Really, *no one's* nose is that long! Well, Wellington's maybe. But Rowlandson drew that because he owed me money and was angry about it. The man's a genius with his pen, but he should never bet on anything when he's drunk. Actually, that means he should never bet. At any rate, I haven't been cruel or kind, and it wouldn't matter if I were. As I said, her eyes slide off me. She can only see Geoff."

"Then it's time for me to have a look," Daffyd agreed. "I'll get to the bottom of it. I doubt she's up to anything underhanded, but it's impossible to fool another old flimflammer, which is what I am."

"Was," his half brother corrected him. "And I'm not?" he added, sounding offended.

"You have some scruples, Lee. They'll be the ruin of you, too, if you don't watch out."

They laughed. But they looked pleased, too. They nodded at each other, because whatever the outcome, at least they would be working together.

Chapter 5

"I want a gold gown," Daisy told the dressmaker. "Not the one you showed me the other day. Not precisely, that is. I loved it, but I don't want Viscount Haye sneering at me all night. You heard how he felt about how revealing it was, or at least how it would be for me. But I've been invited to dinner with him and the earl tonight. They said they have a surprise, an old friend come to see me, and so I want to look wonderful! I know there isn't much time and so I thought if you could alter a gown that was already made up? That one was so lovely. Oh, please, madame, say you can somehow make it acceptable for me!"

This one, Madame Bertrand thought, as she

saw the doting look the lady's companion bent on her charge, could charm a mossy rock. And money is money, and Haye brought her here. *That* one's approval could make her rich.

"I could, I think," the modiste said. "I haven't sold that one yet. I could make . . . alterations. But in a day? I don't know."

"Oh, please. Surely you could add an underskirt, or something, to make it more the thing for me. Price," Daisy said, and paused as she swallowed down her fear, "is not an object."

She waited, half hoping the answer would be no. Price was always an object, and spending money frightened her. But if the viscount had been telling the truth, and the earl and her companion agreed that he was, then it would be some time before she had to pay her bills. If it was true that creditors gave ladies special favors, then time was on her side, and timing was everything in life. By the time she absolutely had to pay she could be married, or her investments could have made more money. And so far, everyone thought she was a lady. So she had to act like one and run up debts, though it went against the grain.

She'd taken a hired carriage to the dressmaker's as soon as Helena said the shops would open. She was delighted to find that, as Helena had also said, no lady would be up at this hour. It was easier to play the lady of leisure when there weren't any real ones around.

"Please?" she added, smiling at Madame Bertrand.

"Let me see," the dressmaker said. She clapped her hands. "Margot!" she called. "Put on the gold cloth gown and come out here at once, if you please."

A few moments later, the same tall, dark-haired model she had seen the day before came gliding out in the daring gold cloth gown. It still looked wondrous to Daisy.

Madame Bertrand walked around the model, muttering. "A train would add elegance," she murmured. "*Oui.* But it must be rose-colored, a gauzy spray of rose spread out in a train, floating behind the gold, moderating it, like a sunrise seen through clouds. And an underskirt, *mais oui.* We raise the neckline and add a chemise so the gold cloth doesn't lie like a second skin. Add long sleeves, puffed at the shoulders . . . *Oui.* And rose ribbons; gold is too harsh for you, mademoiselle, the viscount was right. But a touch of rose here, a dash of it there, to tame the gold, and you will glow.

"Yes," the dressmaker added. "We can have the gown looking proper enough so that even the Viscount Haye won't be able to say it is daring, though daring it would still be. But it will not be audacious. It's beautiful as it is," she added with regret, "but he's right. Such gowns are best left to those women who know how to use them, and who can. But yes, mademoiselle, it could be done."

"Thank you! Then do it!" Daisy said, then added, "And it is *Madam* Tanner, madame. I am a widow. I know how to use such gowns, too, you see, but alas, I'm a lady, and so I cannot." Her grin was nothing like a lady's.

This one, the dressmaker thought appreciatively, will go far. "I must find the right gauze, and begin," she said, and marched back to her workroom. "Margot!" she called over her shoulder, "Please return the gown to me, and put on the blue one. The countess is coming, and we know how she loves blue."

Daisy didn't need the rose gauze in order to glow; she felt triumphant. Whatever surprise Geoff had planned, now she could meet it with equanimity. She had a proper companion and would wear a wonderful gown, and whomever she met from the old days would have to forget the shame and degradation of her marriage and see only the success she'd become.

She was smiling when the tall model in the gold gown approached her.

"Congratulations," the woman said in a cool, low voice. "The gown will look beautiful on you. It is only too bad you can't wear it as it is. Viscount Haye was much taken with it, you know."

"He was?" Daisy asked. She had to look up at the model, and got the feeling that the woman was looking down at her in other ways, too. She was smiling, which somehow made it worse. The woman was slender and long-limbed as a boy, with only her small breasts and a hint of supple hips to show her gender, but she nevertheless exuded female sensuality. Daisy wasn't surprised. She'd met too many kinds of women in jail to ever make the mistake of comparing the size of a woman's breasts or hips with the size of her sexual appetites or inclinations.

She also knew when she was being taunted, and she'd been oppressed long enough to know too well how people who couldn't speak freely could still voice their opinions clearly. She waited because she wanted to know more.

The model understood. "He offered to buy the gown for me," the model said, nodding her sleek head. "But I have no use for it, and so I told him. Anyway, he liked it even better when it was off." Her smile grew wider; she nodded again and glided away, looking as though she'd accomplished something.

Her words could be taken several ways. Daisy was no fool and took them each and every way they could be. She'd been warned. That much, she was sure of. She just didn't understand what she'd been warned of, or off.

"What did she mean by that?" Helena asked, frowning.

Daisy had known Helena Masters for only the week since she'd hired her, but already knew she was a dear person. Her new companion was an educated woman who'd been married for a decade before she was widowed. But she'd been married to a decent man and had always lived among decent people, and so was still an innocent at heart.

Daisy laughed. "She could mean that the viscount likes to wear gowns, or that he likes women who don't wear them. It doesn't matter. Really it doesn't."

But it did; it mattered to her plans for the future, and she was still thinking about it as she left the shop.

The light at sunset showed the glorious sunrise of Daisy's new gown. It was silken and it slithered, scintillating with every step; it flowed and glowed gold, moderated by a pink that looked as innocent as the underside of a rose petal. The dressmaker delivered it in plenty of time to dress for dinner. But Daisy had to try it on right away to be sure it was what she wanted to wear tonight.

She wanted to wear it; in fact, she never wanted to take it off. It glorified her; it flattered her, and made her feel both rich and right. She stood in the center of the bedchamber of her hotel and gaped at the magnificent creature she saw in the long looking glass. She was, she thought, a long, long way from Botany Bay, and a universe distant from the stinking prison ship that had brought her there. The elegant beauty in the mirror could never have set one silken slipper's toe in such a place, or ever dreamed of it. Nor had she dreamed she could look like this. And Tanner! If he'd ever seen her in such a dress . . .

Daisy's eyes went dark and blind to the moment as she saw something that wasn't in the mirror.

Tanner would have stopped and stared at her the way he always did when he saw her looking good, or in a different light—the way he did if he chanced to see her rising from the tub after a bath, or with her arms in the air as her gown slid down over her body while she was dressing, or even outside, hanging up the wash, with the sunlight silhouetting her body.

His mouth would get loose; he'd grin and grab for her, and she was never ever allowed to say no. It wasn't a great hardship, not really; she didn't know why she never got used to it, why she never stopped dreading it, her skin crawling, her stomach in a knot whenever she saw him looking at her like that. What he did took only a few minutes, after all.

But it always took too long for her. And she hated that she gave such pleasure to him when she didn't want to. That was why she dressed in the dark, and bathed only when he was out of the cottage, and . . .

Daisy drew a deep, shuddery breath. He wasn't here now. He'd never be here again. She could dress like a princess and bathe in the light, and no one would ever be able to touch her if she didn't want him to, no one.

"Daisy?" Helena asked. "Is there something wrong with the gown?"

"No," Daisy said, returning to the present. "It's perfect."

"It's magnificent," Helena said. "More than that, you look so beautiful in it. The fit is perfect, the color brings out your hair, your eyes—you'll astonish them. But is it a very grand dinner? Because that is a very grand gown."

Daisy blinked. She saw Helena's reflection behind her in the mirror. Her companion and her maid were staring at her with identical expressions of wonder. But the gown now looked wrong to her, theatrical and overdone compared to what they wore: the maid in her simple gray frock, Helena in one of her usual modest, high-necked lavender day dresses. The maid looked dazed, and so did Helena. But her new companion, Daisy thought, also looked a little wistful. She realized why. She'd spent too many years wanting what she couldn't have not to know what she was seeing.

Daisy shook her head to clear it. Then, to make her audience laugh, she overdid it, shaking her head like a puppy coming out of the water. She grinned. "Too right! Trust you to put your finger on it. It's too magnificent! I can't wear this tonight. I don't know if I ever can, unless I'm invited to a coronation—as the queen. I'll wrap it in tissue and put it away until I do have a reason to wear it, some very special occasion. Tonight I'll wear a gown I had made up before I came here. It's rose-colored, too, and very pretty, actually, and I have a gold paisley shawl to make it livelier. But this?"

She raised her arms and held them straight out from her shoulders. "I'm afraid to move in this! I feel like a frog in a silk purse, mucking it up just by letting my skin touch it. I don't want to get it dirty or damp, I don't know how to live in it! The viscount was right: It isn't for me, no matter how it's dressed up or down. And you know what?" She snapped her fingers. "*That* for the viscount's taste! I have to live my life as well as be fashionable. We'll go back tomorrow and pick out some simple gowns that I can wear without worrying."

"But you've already ordered some," Helena pointed out.

"Well, so I have, but we also have to get something else. You need new gowns, too!" She saw her companion's face grow still and added quickly, "Not that there's anything wrong with what you wear, but if I'm to look splendid—and every gown Madame Bertrand makes is splendid—then you must, too. I'm paying for it," she went on, raising a hand. "Think of them as uniforms. Well, a fine thing if I go wafting in prinked to my ears, and let you look plain. I'll look like a terrible vain creature, trying to keep you from being noticed, because you're very pretty, you know."

Helena laughed. "How could anyone look at anyone but you? With your face and hair? No one sees any other female when you're in the room. And anyway," she added more quietly, "a companion isn't supposed to look dashing."

"Why not?" Daisy asked, putting her hands on her hips. "That's ridiculous. Why shouldn't you look well? Please don't argue." She raised her arms again. "But please help me out of this beautiful thing right now, because I'm afraid to take a step in it!"

Daisy was afraid to step into the earl's house that evening, too, but she wouldn't let anyone know it. She wore a fine gown, if not a spectacular one. Her hair was drawn up in a cluster of curls, a simple cameo that she'd bought the other day hung on a spiderweb-thin chain at the base of her throat; her slippers were new, too. From her new underthings to the new cape on her back, there was nothing to be ashamed of.

"You hesitate?" Helena asked her.

"Well, I don't know who'll be here," Daisy whispered. She smiled. "Expect the worst and get the best," she said with false bravado. She raised her head and the hem of her cape, and walked into the earl's front hall, Helena Masters a respectful two steps back. Geoff had been in Port Jackson. He knew how she'd lived. She doubted he'd ask any of Tanner's friends here. Geoff Sauvage had been a popular fellow, with a smile for everyone, but he and his boys had been close to the nicest people there. Not one of Tanner's cronies had been that.

Even so, apart from a few female friends, there was no one Daisy yearned to see, and a lot more she hoped never to lay eyes on again. She wondered again why it was that a woman who was treated badly by her husband attracted men who wanted to treat her badly, too. She'd have thought they'd have wanted to rescue her. The only times she'd ever been glad of being married to Tanner was when she'd seen that desire in his friends' eyes when they looked at her after he'd punished her.

She'd dealt with them after Tanner died, she remembered, her mouth settling into a flat hard line. She could again. But she didn't like doing it.

"Daisy!" the earl said as he strode into the hall to greet her and saw her expression. "What's displeased you?"

"Nothing," she said, as a footman took the cape she slipped from her shoulders. She gazed at the earl and felt the tension ease as she studied his familiar, kindly face. "Well, something," she admitted. "I don't like surprises." She shook her head and set her red-gold curls trembling. "Who the devil is it that you have for me to see?"

He laughed. "No roundabout about you, is there, Daisy? Not to worry. It's someone you like."

She placed her hand on his arm and looked

up at him with solemn eyes. "Straight truth, Geoff?"

He nodded, biting back his smile. "Cross my heart, Daisy, s'truth."

She glanced across the hall to his salon. "Then lead on," she said. "I'll deal with it."

She followed him to the door to the salon, Helena behind her. Daisy saw two men rise from their chairs as she entered the room. One was Viscount Haye, looking sardonic as usual, as he bowed to her. The other was a shorter man, dark and handsome, dressed like a top of the trees young gent about town. But she didn't know any gentleman except for the earl and the viscount. Daisy frowned. This impudent fellow was laughing at her as she stood and stared at him, his slash of a smile white in his dark face.

"Don't know me?" he asked. "There's a blow to my vanity. Thought you'd remember me, Mrs. T."

Her eyes widened. "Daffy!" she yelped, and raced up to him. She stopped short and looked up at him. "Of course I remember you. Always had a good word for me even on the hardest days, and weren't there too many of those for both of us then? But I never saw you rigged out so fine. Lord, get a look at you!" she said, shaking her head. "A gent from your nose to your toes!"

"That I look, but that I'm not, I'd swear you know me better," Daffyd said. "But you! You're a lady, Daisy."

"That," she said, "I'm not. But I reckon you know that, too. Gawd, look at us, won't you? A pair of rooks got up like swans."

"A trio," the earl said.

"No!" Daisy said, swinging around to look at him. "You're a gentleman born, Geoff, and that you always were."

"You, too," he said soberly. "You were born a lady. Have you forgotten?"

She hesitated. "I'm trying to remember," she told him sincerely.

His smile was so full of sympathy and understanding that for the first time since she'd left New South Wales, she felt she'd done the right thing to come here and find him so she could make a life with him.

Then she looked up to see the viscount's face, and doubted herself again. The expression she'd glimpsed was gone in an instant. But Daisy always looked for insult and distrust and knew it when she saw it.

"Lord," she exclaimed, "some kind of lady I am! Where are my manners! I've forgotten most, you know. But I'm trying. Here's my companion, Mrs. Masters; she's here to remind me of them. Helena, here is Daffyd, the earl's ward, one of the nicest fellows ever to be sent to Botany Bay by mistake."

Daffyd laughed as he sketched a bow. "That's what every lag in the colony says, and in my case it was no mistake. But you don't have to watch your purse, Mrs. Masters. I gave up that life after I met the earl. So, Daisy, tell me about your trip and how things are back at Port Jackson."

"My trip here was much better than the one out," Daisy said with a wry smile, "as you may imagine. Still, I'll be happy if I never set foot on a ship again! And I don't think you really want to know how things are back there. Well, and if you do, all I can say is that we get more citizens by the day. You must be emptying all your jails here." She frowned. "I don't mean 'we' anymore, do I? You? We? Which do I mean? Lord, but it's hard living between two worlds. Do you find that so?"

"Aye," Daffyd said. "But it fades like a bad dream after a while."

"In time, you forget," the earl agreed in soft and thoughtful tones. "But never altogether, and that's not altogether bad, you know. It's good to recall bad times when you feel sorry for yourself for whatever reason. I promise it makes anything look better."

The three smiled at one another.

The viscount watched them, and then looked at Helena Masters. They exchanged a knowing glance.

The earl saw it. "This will never do," he said. "We're excluding Leland, and . . . ah"—he searched for Daisy's companion's name—"Mrs. Masters. Come, dinner's waiting. We can talk then, and share reminiscences, except, Daffyd, please remember that I also have guests with tender sensibilities."

"I live with a lady, remember? My wife's got sensibilities, too. I won't horrify Mrs. Masters," Daffyd promised.

"Oh, but I'm not easily horrified, sir," Helena protested.

"I meant the viscount Haye," the earl said.

He won the others' laughter, and a mocking bow from Leland.

Daisy sighed. Geoff's surprise had been a good one. Still, she fervently hoped there'd be no others. Her course was set, and she wanted only smooth sailing from now on, all the way from here on up the aisle, where she'd join her new husband, Geoff, at last.

Chapter 6

Damn the wench for being so pretty, Leland thought sourly, and double damn her for being saucy, because pretty alone was never enough to snare a man like the earl. Leland picked up his wineglass again, all the while never losing sight of his host and his lovely guest.

Bright, vivacious, with a charming smile and an equally pretty wit, the woman was a dazzler. That red-gold hair was spectacular, and unlike many with similar hair, her face didn't disappoint. She had a sprinkling of light freckles on her little nose; they might not be fashionable but they were certainly kissable. And her figure was fetching, to say the least. At least, it fetched his attention. She was not his sort of course . . . Leland paused. He was always honest with himself. Of course she was his sort. She was any live male's sort.

His eyes narrowed as she laughed at a joke the earl made. Hers was rich, full-throated laughter that made a man want to join in. That wasn't the only thing he wanted to join in, he noted, watching how her laughter made the tops of her high, firm breasts jiggle. No sense saying she was wearing an indecent frock, either, he thought moodily. All women's clothing was indecent these days: made of thin fabric, low at the neck, and styled with a high waist that accentuated the bosom. Hers didn't need accentuating.

But in spite of the womanliness of her figure, she was slim and graceful; even her hands were slender. So was her neck. He noticed things like that. He noticed everything, looking for something to find fault with. The only fault he could find was her unseemly fascination with a man twice her age. As for her looks, her skin was clear, her eyelashes long, even her earlobes were shapely. Her hair wasn't the fashionable brunette that was all the rage this Season. She wasn't a classic beauty, even though she reminded him of a Venus on a seashell on a cresting wave in a painting he'd once seen. She was too small and piquant for that. But she was perfectly adorable.

So what was she doing hanging on the earl's sleeve, watching his lips for the birth of his every new word, laughing at his slightest jest, looking sad if he said a somber thing, and expectant when he so much as cleared his throat? There was a limit to being a good audience. Sarah Siddons herself never held an audience as enraptured as Daisy Tanner seemed when the earl so much as spoke to a footman to ask for a new fork, Leland thought moodily.

Now, the Earl of Egremont was a good man and a kindly one, not unhandsome, and in fine condition for a man his age. But even so, he wasn't the type to set any female's heart beating faster. Leland knew to an inch what sent a woman into raptures, if only because he himself didn't—until he got to talk with her awhile and made her forget what she had wanted in a man.

The earl, for all his virtues, wasn't an irresistible male, either, or even a seductive one. His fortune definitely was both, though. Was that why the Tanner woman acted as though the earl was the only male at the table, in the room, and in the whole of England? She'd *said* she was rich now. That certainly bore investigating, Leland thought.

Leland glanced at Daffyd, to see if he noticed any of this.

But Daffyd was laughing at something Daisy had just said. Leland sighed. She had a bubbling personality and enough charm to fill three young ladies' finishing academies. She was, in fact, too good to be true. Especially since she'd been a convict. Of course, the earl and Daffyd had been convicts, too. But they'd been innocent men.

Leland had doubts about Daisy's infatuation with the earl. It seemed too complete. He himself wasn't considered a dullard, yet his own most clever comments weren't met with half the appreciation that the earl's dullest ones were.

"And so, what are your plans now that you're back in England, Mrs. Tanner?" Leland asked into a brief conversational silence.

They all stared; his voice had been unintentionally sharp. Daisy's smile slipped as she looked across the table at him.

"That is to say," he added in a fashionable drawl, so it would seem he wasn't that interested in her reply, "one can understand the joy of coming home again. As for myself, when I've traveled abroad for any length of time, I'm so *consumed* with relief to be home, I can't even think about what I'll do the next day. But after a week or so, the old familiar tedium does set in again. So, what are your aims? How do you intend to stave off ennui?"

The earl answered for her. "We didn't worry about 'ennui' back in Botany Bay, Lee. Or 'the old familiar tedium.' We worried about the next day. Being there to see it, that is."

Daisy laughed. "There's truth. Only after I married, I knew I'd be there, all right. But that wasn't much better." She saw Leland's expression grow chillier, and added, "I know it sounds bad to say anything rude about my deceased husband, my lord, but everyone at this table knows it was no love match. It wasn't a match at all, actually, just an unhappy circumstance, at least for me. So I didn't worry about ennui, either, just escape. And now I've done that . . . " She paused, thought a moment, and then said, "I suppose what I want is something I'm not used to thinking about. Peace, I guess, and happiness, however I find it."

Which was, Leland thought, a very good thing to say, except that she said it to the earl, and her sad smile was for him alone.

"You must make a list of things that will make you happy and bring you peace," Helena Masters said unexpectedly.

"Why, so I will," Daisy said with one of her sudden grins. "And the first thing on my list, I think, would be more of that lovely soup I just had."

"You're too easy to please," the earl said, as he signaled to a footman. "Although my chef isn't, and he'll be in ecstasies to hear that his art made the top of your list."

They all laughed, but there was no laughter in Leland's eyes as he watched Daisy, only calculation and rising interest. Her answer had been a masterful parry to an excellent thrust, and he loved a good duel.

"No sense in the three of us gents having our port while you two ladies sit by yourselves," the earl said when they'd finished dinner. "Let's all remove to the salon together. Do you play, Daisy?"

"Cards?" she asked. "Yes, very well. My father taught me."

"Then not very well," Daffyd said dryly.

She grinned. "There's that. But I learned things from him he didn't teach me. I know how much it hurts to lose, so I don't lose my head when I play."

"I meant the piano, or the harp," the earl said. "But we could play cards if you like."

"Oh," Daisy said sheepishly. "I used to play the pianoforte, and I did enjoy it, but it's been years. That will be next on my list: learning to play music again."

"I'd be happy to play for you now," Helena said softly. "And teach you later, Mrs. Tanner, if you'd like."

"Daisy!" Daisy exclaimed. "Please, call me that and forget the other; I'm trying to."

"Even in company?" her companion asked.

"Everywhere," Daisy said vehemently.

They left the table and walked down a long hall until they came to the salon. A fire was already blazing in the hearth, the draperies had been pulled across the long windows, and the lamps had been lit. The servants obviously listened to what their master said as much as to what he asked of them, because several lamps had already been brought to the ornate pianoforte that stood in one corner.

The earl saw Daisy comfortably settled on a couch and went to the piano. "This came with the house. It's decorated with gods and goddesses," he said, indicating the intricate gilded paintings on the ebony wood. "But I don't know when it was last tuned, so I can't say if it still sounds heavenly."

Helena Masters strummed her fingers along the keys. "Some notes need adjustment, but I think something good can come out of it. It's a fine piece."

"Then let's find a fine piece for it," he said. He opened the top of the bench, took out some music sheets, and began to discuss them with her.

"I'll be back in a moment," Daffyd told Daisy. "I'm off to the necessary, not that I'm supposed to tell a lady that," he added, lowering his voice. "But you know me, Daisy, and I didn't want you thinking I'd deserted you."

"And you know me, Daffy," she said. "I'm no lady."

"You are, and time you started thinking of yourself as one," he said. "Here, Lee," he told his half brother, standing nearby, "entertain the lass until I get back, will you?"

"My pleasure," Leland said. He ambled over, sat next to Daisy, settled back, stretched out his long legs, put his arm across the top of the settee, and smiled down at her. "So," he said. "Music is at the top of your list. After soup, I suppose. What comes next? I hope it's me. Please don't break my heart by saying no, at least not right away."

He was smiling, such a snug, comfortable, friendly smile that Daisy could hardly believe it belonged on the face of the tall, cold nobleman she'd just passed the last hours with. It made him look years younger, and entirely approachable. This close she could see his teeth were even and white, his skin clear; the smile was wide enough to show a crease in the side of his left cheek, making that long, thin face look rakish and attractive. The smile spoke volumes. Without a word, it told her of his understanding and fellowship, and complete interest in her answer.

But the most fascinating thing was what the smile did to his usually cold, bored eyes. It turned their dark blue to the shade of warm tropical waters as they gazed at her with all-encompassing concern. She was embarrassed and didn't know where to look, which was just as well, because she couldn't look away.

As he focused on her, she realized he seemed to emanate a growing warmth that she could feel in every pore. He positively radiated a subtle heat. His gaze gentled, and she realized he was now looking at her lips, but not as though he was expecting to see her answer there. Her mouth tingled as though he'd touched it. So did other soft parts of her body, to her utter astonishment. But she couldn't help it. He was no longer chilly, or aloof. Neither was there anything foppish or feminine about him now; he seemed entirely, intensely masculine, although he didn't smell like the men she'd known. Instead he gave off the heady scents of soap and spice and sandalwood, warm sandalwood.

He was something she'd never known, a man who desired her in a way she'd never encountered, but with great lust, nevertheless. That, she knew. He made her remember he was a man and she a woman and what he wanted had nothing to do with the rough invasion she hated, and yet everything to do with it.

She caught her breath. Her skin felt damp, her heartbeat picked up, she felt trapped and frightened, and yet fascinated. She wanted to answer; she wanted to get away from him. But she couldn't remember his question.

"So, do you like Papa Hayden this evening?" the earl called from across the room.

The viscount turned his head to answer in his usual laconic tones. "Yes, if Mrs. Masters would be so kind. Always a treat."

Daisy looked away and swallowed hard. She gave herself a mental shake. She didn't know what had come over her; this was the same effete nobleman she'd met days before. Was she mad? His interests lay in what she was wearing, not the body beneath. She'd probably had too much wine. They'd likely slipped brandy into the sauces, too. As for the viscount? He probably just lusted after her gown, she told herself, and felt much better.

"Singing lessons," she said, making him turn his head to her again. "Finding a house for myself is first. But singing is next on my list. Because I can't play as well as Helena, and won't even try."

"You don't know how good you are at anything unless you try it," he said softly, smiling as though he knew exactly what she'd been thinking.

But she'd been caught in his web before, and she learned fast. She would not amuse him at her own expense. She rose to her feet. "Then I'd better go watch her fingers for a start," she said.

Then, as though she'd narrowly escaped something fearful and still worried about being caught in its clutches again, she made her way over to the piano to join Helena and the earl. She could swear she felt the viscount's gaze, as if he'd placed a large, warm hand on her back, so she moved smartly while trying to look as though she were only strolling there.

"They make a nice couple," Daffyd said as he settled down on the settee next to Leland, inclining his head to where the earl, Daisy, and her companion were gathered at the piano.

"The earl and your Daisy?" Leland asked wryly.

"Geoff and Helena Masters," Daffyd said. "But he don't see her at all. She might as well be the piano."

"Charming woman, but she's just a companion," Leland said. "He's a nobleman; he's not supposed to see her."

"Not Geoff. Class and rank don't matter to him," Daffyd said, slipping into slum argot as he sometimes did when he wanted to make a point about his origins. "Nothing like being locked up with the riff and raff as well as the toffs to learn that a man or a woman's worth ain't in their class or rank. No, he doesn't see the companion only because he's too busy seeing Daisy. She sees to that. You were right. She's after him. I don't know why, and it don't make me happy. It wouldn't exactly be a mismatch, but it wouldn't be right, neither.

"She's had a hard life, and Tanner was a right bastard," Daffyd said. "But that's no reason for her to try to snare Geoff now. He needs a mature woman. Whatever else she is, Daisy ain't that. It isn't that I'm afraid of being cut out of the will if he breeds a houseful of kids with her, because I won't be. I'm not his son and heir in the first place, and anyway, I don't need his money. I've done all right for myself, and I think and hope he'll live forever. It's because I'm not sure she's right for him. You were right about that. It doesn't fit, and I don't like things that don't fit. Means somehow something's askew. So, what's to do?"

"Talking to him won't help," Leland said, watching how Daisy hung on the earl's sleeve, this time literally. "Warn a man about something and he has to look at it more closely. Once he concentrates on it, it may be he'll decide he wants it even if he didn't before. By the way, do you think he wants her?"

Daffyd shook his head. "Dunno. Hard to tell with him. But he's available and male and he breathes, so he must. I'm as faithful to my Meg as the sea is to the shore, and glad of it, but even I can't stop looking at Daisy. She's an eyeful, ain't she? And it won't do any good to talk to her, neither. She's learned to keep her thoughts to herself; we all did, but her, especially. If she'd ever told Tanner what she wanted, he'd use it against her, and she isn't stupid."

They stared at the trio at the piano.

"Have you investigated her finances?" Leland asked. "She says she's rich, but she was only a prison guard's wife, after all."

"Aye. Still, Tanner was the cheapest man I ever met. He squirreled away every bit of bribe he ever got, and he took every one he could squeeze out of his job. But that wouldn't make him rich. He did invest with Geoff, and that made rich men of many of us. I'll look into it. Don't think she's lying, though. She knows it would be too easy to find out the truth. That's the thing about dealing with a woman like her; she knows every angle. Doesn't mean she's up to no good, just means she has her wits about her, because she's had to." He looked at Daisy and sighed. "Won't be the end of the world if he does marry her,

I suppose. Just not the best thing for either of them, I think."

"So do I. But it's early days. Don't go and buy a wedding gift yet," Leland said, stretching his long body as he spoke. "There's a long road to travel before we get to sit on either side of a flower-draped aisle. Geoff's not a rash man or a fool. I don't know what your Daisy is. But I mean to find out."

"Well then, good. But Lee?"

Something in his half brother's voice made Leland turn his head to look at him.

"Whatever you do, don't hurt her. She's a game 'un, and she's been through hell. Maybe all she does want is a little peace."

"Maybe," Leland agreed. "Who doesn't? I won't hurt her. I hope to merely educate her."

But Daffyd didn't smile. "She's a friend, Lee. I mean it."

One thin brow went up. "Indeed? You're very serious. Very well, so am I. I won't hurt her, I'll promise you that. I don't think I'm capable of it anyway, in any sense. But you have my word on it. I just want to find out what's happening."

"And your vanity is wounded," Daffyd said.

"Of course," Leland agreed so pleasantly that Daffyd didn't know if he meant it or not. But it didn't matter to him. He was content. He had Leland's word, and no bond was stronger.

"Well, that was an evening!" Daisy said as she shed her cloak when she got back to her hotel room that night. Her maid took it. "Thank you," she told the girl. "Now go to bed, it's late. Look at that," Daisy told Helena with a crooked grin, as the maid scuttled off to do her bidding. "Me, ordering a maid around as though I'd done it all my life, when my father couldn't afford help at home for years before we were arrested. I feel good and bad about being mistress to a servant, I can tell you."

"If your father had been more cautious, that is to say, more temperate, you would have had scores of servants," Helena murmured.

"Aye," Daisy agreed, as she sank to a chair. "But 'cautious' isn't the word. Nor is 'temperate'; he didn't know the meaning of either word. Thing is, he was a damned fool, poor fellow. He drank and gambled too much, had no regard for the future, and thought too much of his ability to slip out of trouble. I can't even say he got that way because he missed my mother when she died, as I'd like to. Because as I heard it, his drinking and gambling was one of the things that sent her to an early grave."

She looked at Helena and added, sadly, "I grieve for what he might have been, but not for him. No, I can't. He sold me to Tanner to get himself better treatment on the ship, you see."

"You said he wanted to protect you. You said he did it to save you from further indignity," Helena reminded her gently.

"So he might have done, if he'd known he was

dying," Daisy said, pulling the ribbon from her curls, laying her head back, and staring at the ceiling. "I don't think he did, and I'm not sure he would have even if he had known. I tell folks that so they won't think worse of me, because people do judge you by your parents. If they think he was a rogue, what will they think of me? We both went to Botany Bay, and they say the apple doesn't fall far from the tree. I didn't fall—I was thrown," she added. "But now that I know you better, I don't think I have to lie anymore."

"You don't," Helena said. "You aren't responsible for his actions. But think about it; you may have been right all along, he might have given Mr. Tanner your hand for your own protection."

Daisy turned her head. She was sleepy and mussed, but still looked charming. Helena thought her new employer could do nothing to change that. She was a remarkably radiant creature, inside and out.

"I don't think so," Daisy said. "He told me I had to marry Tanner right away or we'd really be dished. I didn't want to, but I obeyed. Well, I was only sixteen and frightened to death of the life I saw in jail, and it was worse on the ship, if that's possible. So I did what he said. My father never said it was just to protect me, and he would have if he'd thought he'd done something noble. He loved praise. No, he was just a man. You can't count on any of them."

Helena gasped.

Daisy looked up at her.

"What a thing to say! It's not true," Helena exclaimed. "My father, my dear Vincent . . . they were men, and they were wonderful people. They never tyrannized or drank or gambled; they put family before themselves, always. Poor Vincent even gave his life for his country and the men under his command. Sacrifice came naturally to him. I can only hope my son grows up to be such a man. The men I've known have mostly been valiant and brave.

"Sometimes men are vain creatures, that's true," she added wistfully. "Even Vincent preened when I told him how good he looked in his uniform. But so are women vain, some notoriously so. We're encouraged to be. Men can be irresponsible, too," Helena continued, as Daisy watched her with a darkening expression. "But so can women. It's true men seem to love adventure more than we do, but that may be because we can't have adventures the way they can. I believe many of us would, if we could. There's not that much difference between the sexes except that men are trained to responsibility, and so we're surprised when they're not trustworthy."

"We don't force men to our pleasures," Daisy said flatly.

Helena was silent a second. Then she shook her head. "But, Daisy, most men don't, most don't even want to. It isn't right to taint a whole gender because of experience with one wicked representative of that sex."

"That's true," Daisy said, the darkness leaving her eyes. "Look at Geoff, I mean, the earl. He's noble and kind, and I never saw him do a cruel thing to a woman, or heard of him doing anything like, neither. I can't imagine him doing that, and don't believe he ever would."

"Of course not," Helena said.

"Yes," Daisy said with a sigh of satisfaction. "That's why he'd make a perfect husband: he's a kind, noble, and considerate gentleman."

Helena frowned. "It's forward of me to even ask. But it would make things easier if I knew. Daisy, are you contemplating him for your next husband? Are you setting your cap for him?"

"Of course," Daisy said in surprise. "That's why I came to England. He still thinks of me as another man's wife, but I hope to change his mind about that soon. The sooner the better."

Helena was still.

"You don't approve?"

"It's not for me to approve or disapprove," Helena said, knotting her hands together. "But he is twice your age."

"Yes, but men like young wives. I know he doesn't need an heir, and that's fine with me, too. If we don't have any babies, I'll have lots of grandbabies to play with. You heard that Daffyd's wife is anticipating. Well, so is Amyas's wife. All the earl's sons are in the same boat. From what Daffyd said with a wink, I think Christian's wife will be popping out a babe soon, too. I'll be up to my ears in babies if I marry Geoff!"

"And the process of begetting them?" Helena asked, her eyes wide. She knew she was risking her position, and a fine one it was, but she couldn't restrain herself. Was this glowing young woman actually saying she didn't want a vibrant young man in her bed? She remembered her own youth and her young husband and the sensual joys they'd shared. She herself was a mother now, and she wouldn't want her own daughter to make such a match when she came of age.

Helena hoped that was the only reason that the idea of the earl and Daisy together in a marriage bed seemed so wrong to her.

"You don't mind missing that?" she asked Daisy, her face coloring up. "It's not mine to say, but however hale he is, it's a universal truth that an older man is not as . . . vigorous as a young one."

"Exactly," Daisy said. "A man can't perform as regular when he gets older, and he loses the inclination, too. That's what all the whor— Lord! I have to watch my mouth. I mean that's what all the tarts in jail said. It's harder work for them enticing older men. They have the money but not the honey. That's what the girls used to complain, because they needed traffic to keep their rents paid. But a husband like that would suit me fine. One like that, or like Viscount Haye, who doesn't want females in the first place!"

Helena gasped again. "What? Viscount Haye? Are you mad? Excuse me. This whole conversation is irregular, I know it," she murmured, as if to herself. "But if you're going to dismiss me, it might as well be for honesty." She drew herself up, folded her hands, and announced, "Haye is one of the premiere rakes in London."

"No!" Daisy said in surprise.

"I'd have warned you about him right off," Helena said. "But I thought you knew, and anyhow, I didn't believe he'd ever set out to seduce a friend of his friend. Gentlemen have their scruples, and that, I believe, is one of the foremost among them."

Now Daisy's eyes were wide. "The viscount? But all he cares about is clothes. And he minces and . . . " She hesitated. That wasn't true. The viscount didn't mince. She thought of how he walked, with long easy strides, and the way he moved, with supple grace. "Well, he doesn't seem interested in females," she concluded weakly, "only in what they wear."

"He's interested, believe me," Helena said. "He's famous for it."

"But he drawls . . . and acts the man of fashion."

"He *is* the man of fashion, and not the least because he's a rake. Oh, dear," Helena said sadly. "And I thought I'd like it here with you. But I know I've been too outspoken. Please give me a second chance. I won't be so bold again. Please forgive me."

"Of course not," Daisy said. "There's nothing to forgive. I need someone I can talk with who'll be honest with me. Now, don't be foolish, please. Just, promise, always be honest with me, and I'll be happy."

"I'll try," Helena said, turning her face away. But she didn't promise. Because there were some things she would prefer never to mention. Such as the fact that she thought the Earl of Egremont would be a wonderful husband, just not for Daisy Tanner.

Chapter 7

Leland and Daffyd had their eyes fixed on Daisy, as did every male they'd passed so far. They were strolling through Vauxhall Gardens behind Daisy, the earl, and Helena Masters. It was sunset, and the park was beginning to be thronged with fashionable people as well as commoners there for the evening's entertainment.

Daisy was hard to miss. She was wearing a low-cut green gown, enlivened by a green and yellow patterned shawl thrown over her shoulders. Her vivid hair was done up with white ribbons, and she wore a crystal rose on a silver chain at her neck. The crystal caught the last sunlight and danced rainbows on the white skin of her breast. She shone like the setting sun, and her radiance made the earl, dressed in a dun jacket, dark breeches and boots, and high white neck cloth, fade into the approaching twilight.

"Do you know?" Leland finally told Daffyd in a soft under voice. "I believe watching and waiting is foolish. You're leaving Town soon, and besides, you don't know how to ask her. I think *I* should see just how serious she really is about Geoff."

Daffyd turned, his eyes grave. "You said you wouldn't harm her."

"Gads!" Leland said in annoyance. "What do you think I mean to do? Kidnap her and force the truth from her? I only thought to try a little friendly persuasion. She's a grown woman, a widow, and one who's been in darker places than I'll ever know—you said so yourself. I simply meant I'd throw out lures and see if she took any. I may be a beanpole, with a nose that's a caricaturist's delight, homely as an old boot, in fact, but I have been known to attract a female or two in my time, you know."

"I do know," Daffyd said. "Too well. You almost stole my Meg from me."

"Oh, yes," Leland said sarcastically. "If I'd half a chance, you'd be visiting her in *my* house today. But she couldn't see me once she'd met you."

"She saw enough. She still says you're madly attractive. I don't know how you do it, but you do. All right. Daisy can take care of herself. She survived prison, Tanner, and Botany Bay. I guess she can deal with you. See what you can find out.

If she really loves Geoff—then good luck to her. I don't know her that well, but as I said, she's a good sort, in all. Oh, by the way. She is rich. I asked someone who would know. It's true."

"I know," Leland said. "I asked, too. But she's not as rich as the earl is; few in England are. That's always a lure. Some people never have enough money. Well, then, let's see what happens, although there's not much I can do if she keeps hanging on his arm like a bracelet. But there's always dinner. She'll *have* to let go so he can eat. Not that there'll be much of that. Dinner here means watered wine, shaved ham, and bits of fruit, for a huge price. What a delightful evening," he said too brightly. "Going to a fireworks display. What fun. You know, Daffy, if you and Geoff weren't such good friends, I could think of many more interesting things to do."

"Your virtue will save you money and the possibility of a nasty rash."

Leland laughed. "I don't have to pay *all* my flirts, you know. And thank you, Mother, but I listened to your lectures and I'm always very careful . . . " The laughter left his voice as he saw who was approaching the earl. "Oh my God," he breathed. "Speak of the devil and there she is."

They stared at the elegant woman who had paused to speak to the earl. She was a tall, beautifully dressed woman of middle years, with fair skin and fairer hair, and eyes that were dazzlingly deep blue even from a distance. Everything about her was impeccable; even her smile seemed to have been measured for a fit before she tried it on.

"Our noble parent," Leland said. "I thought she was still in Bath. I didn't know she was back in Town. Did you?"

"Why should I? "Daffyd said with a shrug. "She only calls on me when she needs a favor, and doesn't acknowledge me to the world at any time. No surprise there; after all, she left me a week after I was born, and didn't speak to me again until I surprised her by turning up again last year. Remember? Much I care. But you're the heir."

"Much that matters. She left me when I was three to run off with your father, and only came back a year later because he beat her. Remember?" he echoed mockingly. "Well, you wouldn't. That's when she got you. One of the few things she's done that I approve of. I didn't at the time, of course, because your advent was a fact she neglected to share. Actually, I wouldn't mind a few *decades* without her now. Neither would my baby brother, but he's lucky. He's in school and almost never has to see her. I, unfortunately, run into her at social occasions more often than is comfortable for either of us."

"God!" Daffyd said. "What do you suppose she'll make of Daisy?"

"Mincemeat," Leland said, and walked over to greet his mother.

"Dear Haye," the dowager viscountess Haye said, greeting Leland and offering the right side of her cheek to the air at the side of his left cheek. "Daffyd," she said, nodding her head in a slight bow. "Heavens. Is this some sort of family excursion?"

"Mrs. Tanner is an old friend of mine and Daffyd's," the earl said. "As the viscount Haye is also a friend, we're all taking her out on the Town to see the sights."

"And you have never seen fireworks?" the viscountess asked Daisy, taking her in from her hair ribbons to her slippers in one long sweeping glance, pausing only to stare at the low neck of her dress, one eyebrow moving ever so slightly upward as she did.

Daisy had been smiling, but her smile stiffened when she saw how the older woman was weighing her up, and managing to criticize her without so much as saying a word. She felt the tension in the air around her, slowly let out a breath, and then smiled again.

"Fireworks? I've seen some when there was a celebration," she answered. "But never what they're supposed to have here in London. I hear their displays boggle the mind, and I've a mind to have mine boggled."

She laughed. The men did, too, but the viscountess only smiled her cool smile.

"I see. And you are visiting from . . . ?" the viscountess persisted.

The earl didn't leap in to answer the question. Neither did Daffyd or Leland. So there was nothing for it but the truth, Daisy thought resignedly. Might as well know now as later how she'd fare in high society. Men might accept her, but women ran the *ton*, and if this female wasn't Society with a capital "S," she knew nothing at all. Geoff might marry her whatever anyone said, because he was that sort of fellow. But how much easier her road would be if she were accepted first.

She smiled her usual wide, radiant smile, an inch short of laughter. "I was raised in Sussex," she said. "Then I went to London with my father. We stayed a while on Newgate Street, and then took a sea voyage halfway 'round the world. My poor papa never left the ship, at least alive. I settled in Botany Bay, where we'd been bound, and now I'm free, I just decided to come back home to England."

The older woman didn't blink. "Ah. A friend of the earl's from the old days, indeed. And your husband, did he come with you?"

"He'd love to have done," Daisy said. "But he's dead. And so I'd be all on my own if the earl, and Daffyd, and the viscount Haye hadn't taken pity on me. They're very kind to widows, as you must know."

"Do I?" the viscountess said softly. "I'd no idea they were so very charitable. How good for you to have such friends. Was your husband a companion of the earl's in those days; is that how you came to know each other?"

"What a surprise," Leland drawled. "You didn't tell us you were applying for a job with my mama, Mrs. Tanner. In what capacity, may one ask?"

"I merely wished to know how such a lovely young creature like Mrs. Tanner came to befriend a man of the earl's age and condition, Leland," his mother snapped.

"My condition is fine, my lady," the earl said, bowing. "Thank you for worrying."

"Lord, how the gentlemen do rush to slay dragons for you, don't they, Mrs. Tanner?" the viscountess said with a thin smile. "Although I hardly qualify as one, I promise you. But I was ever an inquisitive creature. Do forgive me if I seemed to be prying. And my lord," she told the earl, "I never meant to imply you were in anything but fine fettle. One only needs to look at you to see that. Still, I must admit I wondered until I saw you just now. I'm relieved to discover all's well. One never sees you at the usual social occasions, after all."

"I fear one never will," the earl said. "I'm not much of a hand for balls and musicales . . . though I suppose I'll have to learn to be, won't I?" he asked Daisy. "At least if I want to show you all of London's gaiety."

Daisy's smile was relieved. "I don't want to force you to do anything," she said. "I can live without balls and musicales. After all, I've done it all my life."

"No, you shall have it all," the earl said, patting her hand where it lay on his arm. "Especially because you haven't seen them before."

The viscountess didn't blink an eye, but those eyes looked keener now as she watched the earl and Daisy. "One hesitates to ask," she said, "but there are times when one must. Would she have gone to such affairs had she not left England?"

Total silence fell over the people before her. Leland's eyes narrowed and his lips grew tight.

His mother didn't look at all perturbed. "I ask in order to spare Mrs. Tanner's feelings," she went on calmly, "not to wound them. London is one of the best cities in the world to visit, I understand, and a foreigner can get much pleasure from it. But there are some places that can only be visited for pleasure if one is considered fit to be there."

"Or," Leland said coldly, "if one is good at disguises, and can dress and speak like a lady or a gentleman."

"I've done it many times myself, my lady," Daffyd said. "And well you know it."

"Yes, I do," she said. "It's done. How else does the footman get to elope with the duke's daughter, or how is a jealous mistress finally able to see her gentleman friend's wife up close? But I thought a lovely young woman like Mrs. Tanner wouldn't get much pleasure out of being an incognito, especially on the Earl of Egremont's arm. There'd be such gossip and tattle, after all."

The others fell still, in shock. None of these things were proper to say in front of any young woman who might be Quality, even if she was a widow. Daisy knew that, too.

"They can gossip and tattle all they want, my lady," Daisy said, taking her hand off the earl's arm and stepping away from him. "And I'd give them good cause to. I *was* a prisoner at Botany Bay, transported for my father's crimes. But I think it would be stale gossip. Papa was Sir Richard Searle of the Sussex Searles, one of the last of an old family. Everyone knew he poached on his neighbor's grounds one too many times. It was the talk of our little town, at least.

"Papa hadn't a penny left to pay anyone off. He'd gambled everything away and alienated whatever family remained, lost all his friends and made new enemies, and was a scandal in the neighborhood. He couldn't be hanged, understand. Not for stealing dinner, at least, like any commoner would be. There are some benefits to being wellborn. But they wanted him far away, so they transported him, and me with him. As it turned out, he went farther away than they'd thought he would, because he died before he got to Botany Bay, and by then, no one cared but me."

She shrugged, and well dressed as she was, looked very lost and vulnerable standing there in the growing twilight.

The earl lifted her little gloved hand to his lips. "That you were punished was a worse crime," he said.

She looked down in pretty confusion.

"Well, that's done it," Daffyd murmured to Leland as they finally parted from the viscountess. "Attack an honorable man's escort and he'll find himself married to her in no time."

"Not *that* honorable man, at least not if she's not equally so, I promise you," Leland said. "I said, leave it to me. Now pretend you're having a wonderful time. Or go have one. Find an old friend to talk to, or a nice quiet place to compose odes to read to Meg when you get home. But let me see what I can do."

"I doubt even you can budge her now. Looks like Geoff took the bait and the line and will run with it."

"Perhaps. Perhaps not. I can, at least, find out why the chit is so in love with Geoff. *If* she is. And if she isn't, then why she wants him to think she is."

Daffyd looked at him strangely. "And you're doing all of this for Geoff's sake?"

Leland smiled. "You know me well. Generosity isn't *always* its own reward. There are always ancillary benefits, if a man is lucky."

"I hate to leave you alone," the earl told Daisy an hour later, hesitating as he stood by their table.

Daisy laughed. "Alone? There are hundreds of people here tonight."

"Thousands," he said. "But you'll be alone at the table."

"Not for long," she said, smiling. "Helena said she'd be right back. And you won't be far away. Anyway, it's nice to just sit back and relax. I can't wait to see the fireworks but they won't go off until it's full dark, and night's slow in coming at this time of year. I'm safe enough, Geoff. You said the fellow in the Bath chair was an old friend; you'll look no-account if you just keep waving to him. I have nothing to say to him, so it would only be awkward if you took me to his table. So, go. Don't worry. I'll be fine."

The earl wavered. Daffyd had gone to visit with a friend he'd spied at another table; Daisy's companion had excused herself, obviously to find the convenience, and Leland must have done the same because he'd also vanished. The outdoor dining area in the park was set up for the brief English summer. It was a circular area outside an enclosed rotunda that was open on all sides. This dining section was quieter, it had small tables and chairs, and an ornate railing enclosing all. There was an airy canopy on poles stirring over the tables, but it didn't keep out the soft spring breeze. Not only the breeze was free to roam; anyone could enter the place. The prices kept the rabble out.

Musician played soft music in the background,

there were lit torches everywhere, and urns filled with flowers lent more beauty to the place. Londoners knew how to make money from any spectacle, and a night of fireworks drew in huge crowds. The wealthiest came here; the common man ate food brought from home or from one of the many roaming vendors. The earl knew Daisy would be safe enough. And his friend Roger Crandall couldn't walk too well, so it was only right that the earl visit at his table. Daisy didn't know him, and in truth, he was an old bore, so it wasn't fair to either of them to drag her along. Still, the earl hesitated.

"Do go," Daisy said. "He keeps watching you, and I feel guilty. I've been alone in a colony filled with hardened criminals and took care of myself very well. I don't have to here. I'll just rest and wait for you."

"Very well," he said. "But if anyone troubles you, call a waiter."

Daisy smiled. If anyone troubled her, she'd give the troublemaker a thing or two to think about. But she nodded, and watched Geoff leave. Then she closed her eyes at last. She sat back and felt the night breeze stir her hair. She relaxed, feeling safe and content. She was in England again, and entirely free. Geoff liked her, and he was still the warmhearted, generous man she'd known. She thought lazily, considering her options. In time Geoff might come to love her, or at least maybe want to adopt her, as he had the boys.

Except in her case, he'd probably be willing to marry her instead. Things were finally going her way.

It didn't take much to make her happy. New clothes delighted her; just being in London did, too. The opera and the theater were lovely, but it was also been great fun to come here tonight and stroll along, meeting people, being treated like a lady. But being alone and feeling safe while being so was in itself a rare treat for her, and she relished it.

"Fie!" a familiar voice purred by her ear. "They left you alone? Villains. That's like leaving a pearl out on a velvet cushion in full view, with no guards around it. But never fear, I'm here."

Leland's voice stirred the smallest hairs up and down her arms and on the back of her neck. Her nostrils flared, the breeze brought the scent of warm sandalwood to her nose. She tried to banish the sensations. "Anyone trying to snatch that pearl would lose a hand," she said, without opening her eyes. "I didn't fall down in the last rain, my lord."

She heard him settle in the chair next to her.

" 'My lord'?" he asked in intimate teasing tones. "But why? You call the earl Geoff and Daffyd Daffy. I'm *consumed* with jealousy. Please feel free to call me Lee, or Leland, or even Haye, if you must. Or dear Lee, or my darling, if you will."

"Not likely, my lord," she said, and kept her eyes closed.

"I offend you?" he asked softly.

If only he did, she thought, and said, "No, but I don't know you."

"Easily remedied," he said. "Just talk with me awhile."

He'd been much easier to talk with when she'd thought he didn't desire females. Now she felt wary and uncomfortable with him. It wasn't only that. He'd changed. He'd been ironic and distant before, languid, amused, and disinterested. Now, maybe because she knew the truth about him, or maybe because he'd changed when he was with her, he was definitely interested.

And now he was too close, and she realized he was trying to get closer. While she knew how to deal with an outright flirt or a lusty boor, she didn't know how to talk with this elegant nobleman. He was friendly and charming, but everything he said was overlaid with innuendo and invitations that could be taken many ways. She'd never met anyone like him before. The only thing she could do was to be herself, and watch her step while she was at it. That was why she couldn't look at him. The last time they'd spoken together, when he'd looked into her eyes, somehow he'd been able to bypass her usual defenses.

"Talk to you?" she asked. "If talking told a person true things about the other person, there'd be no wars."

"A very wise saying," he said.

"It's not mine; my father used to say it," she said. "But as you know, he wasn't very wise."

"Which, I suppose, proves your point," he said. "Are you going to open your eyes? Or did the sight of me strike you blind?"

"I'm trying to get accustomed to the dark," she lied. "Daffyd said that if you close your eyes first, then when you see the fireworks they look brighter."

"Very true. Except that they aren't going off for an hour. If you keep your eyes closed, you may be asleep by then."

"Not if you keep talking to me."

He laughed in what seemed like genuine delight. "But I must. I'm sitting here, and I get lonely. Anyway, the earl has seen me return. What will he think of me if I leave again? I'm an English gentleman, and I can't leave a lady alone in the night."

"I'm not a lady," she said.

"You know," he said in a flatter voice, "at the risk of being rude, I have to tell you that *does* pall, after a bit. You were born a lady, and raised one. What happened after doesn't change that. It can't."

Her eyes snapped open. She glared at him. "What happened changed me forever, my lord. *You* try living in Newgate, being shipped out on a prison hulk, living with the lowest and trying to stay alive at all costs, and so then marrying . . . Well," she said, swallowing hard, as she forced down more bitter words, "all I can say is that it *does* change you, forever. I can't think of myself as a *lady* anymore."

"And so you don't think of the earl as a gentleman, either?" he asked with interest.

"That's not what I meant. Of course he's a gentleman. He always was and always will be."

He tilted his head to the side, and smiled. "Yes. And so it is with you. Now, there are some ladies born who will always be common, and some commoners who will always be ladies, in spite of what those of my class might say. That can't be changed. You can't help it. And you ought to stop denying it. You don't want the earl to start believing it, do you?"

The torchlight showed his eyes to be the color that lingered on the edges of the twilight sky as the day gave way to night. But they were warm, and human, and seemed to search her soul.

She shivered, finding she wanted to move closer to his compelling warmth, until she reminded herself that he was a virile male, and so no better than any she'd known, and perhaps even a bit worse because he could make her forget it, even for a minute.

"Geoff knows me," she said, tearing her gaze from his, and looking down at her lap. "I don't try to deceive him. I don't think I could. So if he thinks I'm a lady, that's fine. I'll try to be one."

"It isn't a matter of trying. Or of airs and graces," he said. "It's to do with honor and heart, this matter of ladies and gentlemen. But of course in Society, it's only semantics. My own mama, who thankfully is too busy or pretending to be at her table to bother with us, is deemed a great lady. But she's not, far from it. The earl *is* a gentleman, and not only one born so. And you *are* a lady, even if not born to a title. There it is."

"And you?" she asked, looking up at him because she couldn't help herself.

"Oh, me?" He seemed surprised. Then his smile was sad. "I don't know. I *try* to be a gentleman. I really do. It's a thing I can't know. Perhaps you could tell me when you get to know me. And you will, Mrs. Tanner, I mean to see that you do."

She didn't know if that was a promise or a threat, and in spite of everything she planned and felt and knew, she was threatened and challenged—and thrilled by it.

Chapter 8

"Ready to go see the fireworks?" Geoff asked Daisy when he returned to their table.

"Go?" Daisy blinked and turned her head from the viscount's steady gaze, feeling her face grow warm. Geoff's words cut into the strange daze she'd been in as she'd gazed into the viscount's eyes. She felt as though she'd been caught doing something illicit.

"Oh. Yes," she said, snatching up her wrap and bolting from her chair as though it had started burning. "But why go?"

"Because though they can be seen from here, they can be seen better from elsewhere," the earl said. "I didn't mean to rush you, but I saw Daffyd and he said he'd be here directly. We have to wait for your companion though. By the way, shouldn't she be back by now?"

"Blast me for a fool!" Daisy exclaimed. "She should be! She went to the lady's withdrawing room, wherever it is, and didn't come back, and I didn't notice. Give a dog a good meal and it forgets the streets," she muttered. "No female ought to walk alone at night, here or anywhere. At least not one as gently bred as Helena. What was I thinking? Come, who'll go with me to find her?"

Leland looked at her with surprise. "I would if you had to. But you don't. Don't worry. They keep the rabble out of this place; she'll be fine."

"The rabble isn't what I'm worrying about right now," Daisy snapped. "You gentlemen do your share of mischief, you know. And Helena's a fine-looking woman. Let's go."

"I'll come with you," the earl said. "What was she wearing?"

"Lavender, she always wears lavender," Leland said.

Trust him to know that, Daisy thought, and said, "Not as of tomorrow, she won't," she said, scowling fiercely. "She's got a lovely saffron frock coming, and a red one, too."

"Wait," Leland said, raising his head to see over the top of the crowd. "I see her coming now."

Helena walked into the torch-lit circle, and Daisy immediately rushed over to her. "Where have you been?" she demanded, hands on hips.

"I'm sorry I took so long," Helena said breathlessly, and then, seeing them all standing, looking at her, her face flushed. "There was such a long line. Pardon me if I delayed you."

"No need to ask pardon, just don't go alone again," Daisy said gruffly.

"You're not angry?"

"Well, I was," Daisy said as she pulled on her gloves. "But not at you. I'm sorry I let you go alone. I don't know what I was thinking. Forgive me."

"It's not my place," Helena began, but Daisy cut her off sharply.

"Bother. It is so. You work for me, but really with me, and I should look after you."

The earl smiled to see the diminutive Daisy claim she was looking after her taller, older companion.

Leland didn't. He stood watching Daisy, head to the side.

"She's wonderful, isn't she?" the earl asked him softly. "After all she's suffered, still fresh as the daisy she's named after."

"So it would appear," Leland said. "Ah, here's Daffyd. Shall we go?"

They strolled away from the outdoor café.

"Wave 'ta' to Mama," Leland told Daffyd. "She's watching us go."

"She's watched us all night," Daffyd grumbled, but nonetheless raised a hand in farewell.

"Nicely done," Leland said. "You made her look away for the first time in an hour."

"Why the sudden fascination with us, do you think?" his half brother asked.

"Us, or Mrs. Tanner? Or Geoff, or the fact that we're all together? One never knows what interests her, or why, except for the fact that whatever it is, I'd bet that it's something she thinks will benefit her. Never mind, she won't follow us. She only spies if she can do it casually. I know a good place to watch the fireworks from," he said more loudly to the earl and Daisy, who were walking ahead of them.

"Lead on then," the earl said.

"No," Leland said. "Let's keep to protocol. An earl leads this pack. We trail behind. Mrs. Masters, take my arm, if you will."

"Thank you, but it isn't necessary," Helena said.

"I must differ," Leland said, offering her his arm. "This is a public place, and the public, as you know, comes in all guises. Once out of the charmed circle of torchlight, anything may happen. I like to playact as a hero, please indulge me."

Helena put her hand on his arm and they paced down the path.

Leland had been right, Daisy realized. The paths were crowded with Londoners of all classes and conditions. The fireworks display was free, and always spectacular. But that wasn't the whole lure. As with fairs and public masquerades, many came because of the rare chance for all the classes to mingle. It wasn't only that the poor wanted a glimpse of the rich; some in the upper classes also enjoyed the opportunity to freely mix with those they never could meet socially in ordinary circumstances.

That accounted for the legion of prostitutes patrolling the grounds tonight in all their tawdry splendor. They weren't the only ones looking for spontaneous employment: pickpockets were there, along with cutpurses. And there were those who were there in hopes of other, less obvious ways to make money from the event.

Footmen who had spent their quarterly wages on clothes were there, openly ogling unfortunate-looking wealthy young ladies famous for holding up the walls at Society dances. They were looking for a chance to pluck a wallflower off the wall, take a stroll down a dark lane with her, and then maybe for a ride up to Gretna Green and a walk down a different aisle. Fortune could smile on anyone here. Young, overly pomaded clerks were openly eyeing aging Society dowagers, and often being considered with interest in return.

Satisfying lust or making money wasn't the only attraction. Saving it was, too. Young gentlemen who had gambled away their allowances sought shopgirls they might impress, and in return receive romance for nothing.

Families were there for a rare treat of an evening out. Vendors carrying merchandise on trays hung around their necks offered sweets and meat pasties, hot chestnuts, and flavored ices for their pleasure.

"Hands on pockets, gentlemen," Leland said. "As the crowd thickens, so do the pickpockets."

"Yes," Daisy said. "And many we knew in the old days, eh, Geoff?"

"Too many," he said. "Poor fellows. It's a chancy occupation. If they get a gold coin instead of a penny, they hang instead of cooling their heels in Newgate."

"Some of them," Daffyd commented. "Some are lucky, like me. They get a chance to tour Botany Bay."

"At least we won't see anyone we know from there tonight," Daisy said. "That's a world away." She stopped walking abruptly, and shuddered, her hand flying to her mouth.

She'd seen a shape of a man in the crowd that reminded her of a nasty fellow she'd known in Port Jackson.

"What is it?" the earl asked. The viscount and Daffyd tensed and looked at the crowd.

"Lord!" she said, her hand on her rapidly beating heart. "I could swear I just saw Oscar Wilkins. Tanner's friend!"

"It's because of what we were talking about," the earl said.

"Aye," Daffyd said. "Couldn't be Oscar. He wouldn't have wasted a second before he said hello. You're traveling in good company now,

Daisy, and he was ever one to seize the moment."

"Well, he tried that already," she said nervously. "Wanted to marry me when Tanner passed, could you believe? I said no and then had to shout it. He gave me the shakes just looking at him. I told him not to pester me again, and that I'd have the law on him if he came back to bother me. I could count on Lieutenant Lamb at the jail to chase Oscar if I asked him to, if only because he himself had a fancy for me."

She saw Leland staring at her, bemused. Her chin went up. "There aren't enough females in Port Jackson," she explained. "A mare could get a marriage proposal if she wore a rose behind her ear."

Leland looked at her, standing there, a slender figure glowing in the dim light, her skin pale as moonlight, her sunset hair sparked by torchlight. "My dear," he said sincerely. "They could have had females from coast to coast standing three feet deep in rows, and still you'd have gathered proposals."

Daisy heard the admiration in his voice, and her heart rose because of his praise. But she didn't believe it, or him. "Maybe," she said. "But remember I had money, too, after Tanner passed. That's rarer than looks, wherever you are."

"She doesn't know," the earl said with a touch of pride, "and won't hear of it."

"Know what?" Daisy asked suspiciously, afraid she was being mocked.

"You're lovely," the earl said, "and Lee here was only saying that."

"That, and that you're charming and clever, too," Leland said. "A rare combination, in any country."

Daisy tossed her head. Compliments annoyed as much as flattered her. They came too easily to most men to impress her. But Geoff seemed sincere. She wouldn't have trusted what the viscount said if he'd told her her name was Daisy.

"Let's move on," Leland said in amusement, as though he knew what she was thinking. "Mrs. Tanner wouldn't believe me if I told her she was standing on this path. And we must move smartly now because night's falling, and the fireworks will soon be rising."

Daisy put her hand on the earl's arm and walked at his side again, just as she had in her dreams all the way to England. But now she couldn't ignore the man who walked behind them. She wished she could. His presence addled her. When he was pleased, he was as easy to talk with as any female, and fun to be with. But now that she knew he liked women, he also made her feel like one—toward him. That alarmed her.

"Go toward that enormous tree straight ahead," Leland said, "then down the lane to the left. It's dimly lit and keeps turning, but keep on and we'll be at the lake. The reflections in the water will make the fireworks look even more spectacular; the torchlight everywhere else will ruin the view. I know they don't light up the sky, but they diminish the effect. It won't be as crowded there, either, if anyone's there at all. The lane doesn't look as though it goes anywhere, but it leads straight to the water's edge."

"Trust you," the earl said. "I wouldn't have thought of it, but of course you're right. How do you know about it?"

"I live in London," Leland said simply.

"Yes, but I can't picture you roaming the parks at night. I thought you spent most of your time with the *ton*, at balls and the theater and such, or at private parties. How do you know so much about good places to see fireworks?"

"I don't spend all my time at high-minded *or* expensive activities. Some of the *best* treats are the most common ones."

The earl laughed. "Lord, talk about common! How do you make the most common things sound salacious?"

"It's his talent," Daffyd said. "Close your ears, Daisy. Pardon him, Mrs. Masters. I don't know how he does it, either. But he can make a butterfly sound lewd if he tries."

"Butterflies *are* salacious creatures," Leland said mildly. "All that flitting from flower to flower, pouncing on a beauty, staying on long enough to sip sweet nectar, then flying away to a brighter blossom? Don't get me started or I'll make poor Mrs. Masters blush."

Helena laughed. "I didn't know you studied insects, my lord," she said.

"He knows everything," Daffyd said. "Or so he wants you to think."

"Well, maybe he does. Would you look at this?" the earl exclaimed.

They'd come to the end of the lane and found themselves standing on a closely cropped lawn that looked out over the lake. The view across the water was clear, or would be if there was anything to see. Twilight had finally ceded to nightfall, and it was a dark, starry night. The moon was a sickle; the only light came from torches across the lake and their mirrored reflections dancing on the water. The only sounds were those of far-off music drifting on the air.

"Lee, my hat's off to you," the earl said with admiration. "This is the best place to see fireworks in all of London, I think."

"No," Leland said. "The view from the balcony in back of the palace is perfect, marred only by the host. It's difficult to watch fireworks or anything else from there because Prinny hates attention being paid to anything but him. So. Everyone comfortable? There's only one bench, and we'll have to wipe off the dew to spare the ladies' gowns, but at least no one is occupying it. Ladies?"

"I'd rather stand," Daisy said. And then, as a comet suddenly launched from the earth across the lake and soared up to splinter into golden pieces high in the sky, she clapped her hands and cried, "Oh! Look!"

Soon, silver shells were bursting in air, and green ones, scarlet and blue, some thumping and pounding like artillery, some screaming as they ascended before they burst into sparks and flowers and sizzling spinning wheels high in the sky overhead. The night was shattered with explosions of light, and the dark lake below glittered, echoing the spectacle.

Daisy was thrilled. Her upturned face was rapt. At one point, each of the three men was looking at her when they noticed the others doing the same, and they couldn't help exchanging small secret smiles of pleasure at her obvious enjoyment.

The last shell had exploded and its sparkling lights long since faded into the blue haze of gunpowder that hung in the air before anyone spoke again.

"That," Daisy said with enormous satisfaction, "was worth the price of admission."

"It was free," Leland reminded her.

"Not for me," she said. "I had to travel across an ocean, and I'd sworn never to set foot on a ship again. But that made it worthwhile. Well. Thank you, gentlemen. When are they doing this again?"

"We'll find out, and go," the earl promised her, laughing.

"Good," she said.

Leland raised an eyebrow, and then exchanged a look with Daffyd.

"I can't," Daffyd said, "I'm going home tomorrow. Fireworks are fine, but my Meg's finer to my eyes. When you come visit us, Daisy, I'll order up some for you. Until then, you're on your own."

"Not at all," the earl exclaimed, "She'll see more. Spectacles are common in the summer in London."

"Oh," Daffyd said. "So, you're going to skip your usual trip to Egremont, stay on in London for the summer, and be her constant companion here, are you, Geoff?"

There was a significant silence, and then earl smiled down at Daisy. "Why not? Does that suit you, my dear?"

"Oh yes," she breathed.

"Lovely," Leland remarked sourly to Daffyd when they reached the main road again, and Helena Masters had thanked him and went to stand by her charge. "That's set the seal on it. Well done. Or was it *quite* enough, I wonder? Maybe you'd prefer to come right out and say, 'She's all alone, will you protect this beautiful, vulnerable creature forever, Geoff?' "

"Damn," Daffyd said. "I just wanted to know. Suppose I could have been more subtle. Well, what can you do?"

"*You,* my dear little brother, nothing. But *I'll* continue to try. Her getting Geoff is like trapping a fish in a barrel. The man's lonely, and she's done everything but move in on him. I'll be here to find out why and perhaps prevent that from happening."

"For his sake?" Daffyd asked.

He got no answer.

The earl paused at the end of the lane, at the edge of the crowded road. "Here we are in the thick of things again," he said. "What a mob. Shall we wait, and have an ice or some such?" he asked Daisy. "That way we can let those in this crowd who are bent on leaving right away do so. Most of them have to work tomorrow morning; we don't. We can let them go first if you'd like. My carriage is waiting. We don't need to hurry."

People crowded the paths, moving forward like a living river, the crowd surging toward the exits to the park. Daisy hated being jammed in with a crowd. Anyone who'd been in Newgate prison would feel the same. She looked up at the earl. But before she could answer, she saw movement from the corner of her eye. The viscount came lunging toward her. She gasped and shrank back.

Leland had seen a man plunging toward Daisy and dived forward to intercept him. He felt a shove as the fellow pushed against him, and reached out to grab him. But the man ducked and spun, and ran away too fast for him to get hold of.

Daisy felt a sudden lightness on her arm. "My purse!" she shouted, looking down, "the bastard cut the strings and nicked my purse! Stop thief!" she shrieked. "Stop him! The bloke with the red kerchief 'round his greasy neck. The bloody bugger clipped my purse!"

Then she picked up her skirts and plunged

into the steam of humanity, shouting as she ran after him.

If there was anything Londoners liked better than a fireworks display, it was a chase, especially one in defense of a gorgeous lady. This lady cursed like a trollop and ran like an athlete, but that only added to the theater of the moment. They loved theater, too.

Leland usually enjoyed a spectacle, but not tonight. His long legs ate up the distance between him and the thief, whose red bandana was like a beacon urging him onward. Too soon, Leland felt his strength draining. Still, he kept on, frowning as he did, pushing people aside with no ceremony, wasting no breath on apologies.

The culprit heard the ruckus behind him and looked back to see a sea of Londoners chasing him, shaking fists and shouting curses. The little beauty whose purse he held ran after him, screeching. He put on a burst of speed, leaving her behind. The tall, lean gentleman who had been with her cut through the mob, bloody murder clearly written on his face.

The thief flung the purse he'd cut into the crowd, causing them to part and scramble, fighting like spinster bridesmaids to be the one who grabbed the bouquet. He bent double and barreled through the crowd ahead of him, pushing any hapless people who blocked his passage. When he came to a thicket at the side of the road, he ran away down a dark path.

"That's it, oh, thank you," Daisy managed to pant when a rumpled red-faced fellow who looked like a grocer on holiday proudly presented her with her reticule.

The earl came along a few minutes later. He was clearly winded, but recovered his breath enough to delight the crowd by presenting a golden guinea to the fellow who had retrieved the purse.

"He's gone," Daffyd said in disgust, as he emerged from the dark path the thief had taken. "There's another path it led to, and a few hundred people on it, but not a sign of him."

"Let him go," the earl said. "No sense pursuing now. He did throw it back. Anyway," he said, still catching his breath, "wouldn't want to see a fellow face a noose for trying, would you?"

"Aye, you're probably right," Daffyd said regretfully.

After much mutual congratulation, the crowd slowly melted away, and went back to pushing toward the exits again.

"Don't brood. You almost had him, Lee," Daffyd said, seeing a peculiar expression on the viscount's face. "He was ahead by a long shot but you were gaining on him. Then you slowed down and he took off. But it was a near thing."

"Well, yes," Leland said. "It's hard to run in evening shoes. Had I been wearing my boots, I'd have gotten him."

"You look very pale, my lord," Helena said with concern. "Are you all right?"

"Pale as a sheet," Daisy pronounced. "Sit down."

"No," Leland said. "I'll do better standing." He put a hand to his heart in his usual gesture of sincerity, but then lifted it, looked at it, and frowned. His hand was covered with blood.

Daisy gasped as she saw the widening stain on the front of his jacket.

"I see the fellow was after more than your purse," Leland said as he stared at his gory palm. "It appears he tried to take my life as well. If I sit, I doubt I'd stand again. So, shall we go?"

Chapter 9

"You should lie down," Daisy told the viscount.

"If I did everything I should, I'd be a very different man, and a much unhappier one," Leland said. "Don't worry," he added more gently, "not only is there not enough room in this carriage for a maypole like myself to lie down, there's no need of it."

The viscount had gotten a knife thrust in his chest, and no one could be sure he was as well as he insisted he was. He sat in the carriage, head back, the earl and Daffyd close on either side of him so he wouldn't be shaken by the ride. Daisy worried because he was so pale, and because of the amount of blood she'd seen. She sat opposite him, alongside Helena, and they stared at their wounded companion.

"Nothing vital's been punctured," Leland reassured them with a faint smile. "Or I couldn't be sitting here arguing with you. Nothing's bubbling or spurting—sorry, but you force me to be graphic. How can I say it politely? However I put it, I'm not in distress. I've got handkerchiefs and my neck cloth binding up the wound, so I won't be shedding any more blood. My only concern is being seen in public with a bare throat. *That* I'd never live down. I ought to have taken your neck cloth when you offered," he told Daffyd, "because I'm convinced you wouldn't have cared *half* so much as I do."

"You're right. I'd have just tied a handkerchief 'round my neck like the Gypsy I am," Daffyd said. "Don't worry about being seen. No one will see you but the doctor. He's already been sent for."

Leland peered out the coach window. "This is not the way to my house."

"No," the earl agreed. "It isn't. You're coming with me. I don't trust you to care for yourself, Lee. You're too casual with your life. You get a knife in your chest, diagnose the wound, whip off a neck cloth to blot up the gore, and pronounce yourself fine. That won't do."

"Worse if I pronounced myself dead," Leland muttered. But though he joked, his voice was fainter, his pallor pronounced, and those in the coach with him exchanged worried glances. "Any rate, even if it were bad, it's always best to greet the devil with a quip. I hear he likes that. . . . Only jesting," he said into the sudden silence. "Would you rather I moaned?"

"I'd rather you took it seriously," the earl said.

"I've survived worse," Leland murmured. "My poor heart must be impervious to insult by now, what with all the fair maidens who have rejected me, and the rivals who stabbed me in the back. But thank you, Geoff. I think I will take advantage of your hospitality, because . . ." He paused, and his eyelids fluttered down.

Everyone in the coach stiffened.

Leland opened his eyes, and laughed. ". . . because my valet would surely suffer a heart attack if he saw me in this state."

They waited in the earl's salon, not saying much because they were too anxious. Daffyd paced and Daisy looked out the window, while Helena sat quietly waiting. They relaxed when they saw the earl's expression as he came into the room.

"He'll do," the earl told his guests. "The doctor says he's lucky, the knife missed heart and lungs, but we guessed that. He might run a fever, and that would be another story. I've sent for his valet. Lee's agreed to stay on here until I'm sure he's well, but not with good grace, I might add. He'd still be complaining if the doctor hadn't given him a draught so he'd sleep."

"I'll postpone leaving in the morning, as I'd planned," Daffyd said. "I'll stay on, too, if you don't mind. At least until I'm sure he's better."

"Do that, and he'll rage himself into that fever we don't want to see," the earl said. "In fact, he mentioned it to me just now. 'Send Daffy on his way,' he said. 'I'll be fine.' "

"He'd say that if his head was cut off and on a pike," Daffyd grumbled.

"If he could, yes," the earl agreed. "He's a remarkable man. He dresses like a dandy and carries on like a fop, but he's pure steel beneath. He fences, rides like a demon, and spars with the Gentleman himself," he told Daisy. "You wouldn't know it from his conversation. He even worked with the government in secret when Napoleon was marching toward Paris again; dangerous work, too. Did you know that?"

"Aye," Daffyd said. "What's more, the little emperor has no hard feelings. Rumor says Lee's visited him on Saint Helena since."

The earl smiled. "The man could talk rings around anyone."

"He's a master of flattery, even I can see that," Daisy admitted.

"It's more than that," Daffyd said. "He never says what he doesn't mean."

The earl shook his head. "Let's not go on like this, it sounds like we're at a wake. Lee's very much alive, and I hope to keep him that way. So," he said seriously. "Time to get down to nasty details. Do you think the knifing was an accident? A cutpurse who got frightened when Leland lunged at him? Or do you suspect something else?"

Daisy frowned, Helena looked surprised, but Daffyd nodded approval.

"Good question," he said. "Could have been a mistake: The fellow was trying a simple slice and run, and that don't make for accuracy. And Lee's big and he was going at him like a charging warhorse. He could have just frightened the filching cove so much he struck out and cut by accident. I don't know. Now, I do know we're a pack of old lags, so we always have crime on our minds. If it was something else, was Lee the mark, or one of us? We'd be fools not to think about it."

He stared at Daisy. "No one's angry at me at the moment, that I know of. Anyone mad at you, Daisy? I'm not saying it was you the cove was after; think of the risks he took when he knifed Lee. If he'd nabbed a purse and thrown it away before he got caught, he might have got clean away. Even if he was caught with it, he'd have got off light if your purse was light, too. And ladies don't carry too much lolly. But flashing a blade at a gent? Everyone knows it's the nubbing cheat for attempted murder, if the victim's a gent. Did he mean it or not? Was he just a rattle pate, or a murderer? We've got to think of everything."

"Too right," Daisy said. She saw Helena's expression, and translated for her. "Pickpockets have to be careful they don't nick too much money, or they'd be hanged if caught. And it's certain hanging for trying to kill the gentry. We don't know if the bloke was out for money or blood. Was he such a fool that he tried to stab anyone who might catch him? Or was he sent to do murder?"

She looked thoughtful. "As for me having any enemies . . . I've got some who are vexed with me, true. But they're all back in Botany Bay, and far as I know none of them mad enough to be after my head. It was my hand they wanted. Although I think I see them everywhere, I've never really seen them anywhere."

"Did Tanner have any relatives who disputed his will?" the earl asked.

Daisy made a sour face. "He had no kin, or so he said. That's why he took a job in the Antipodes. And he had no will. He couldn't write. The judge gave everything to me, because I was all there was. And I think, because the judge knew Tanner, he thought I deserved it."

"And you, Geoff?" Daffyd asked. "Anyone angry with you these days?"

"The man who hated me is in his tomb, Daffyd.

I don't know of any others. But I'll think on. I'll also send word to some of our old friends who did settle here in London and ask them. And I'll call in Bow Street. I'll have to ask Lee, too," he added unhappily. "But not today."

"Don't worry," Daffyd said. "If I know my man, he's already dreaming on it. He doesn't miss much. In the meanwhile, it's late. I'll see the ladies back to their hotel. While I'm out I'll get some old friends to watch their rooms tonight. Never fear," he told Daisy.

"I don't," she said simply. "I've got my own blade up my sleeve. I didn't think to flash it tonight, because it happened too fast. I've got a barker, too. I should have brought it with me, but I thought it was safe in London."

"A barker?" Helena asked, frowning.

"A pistol," the earl translated.

Helena gasped.

Daisy turned and rounded on her, her eyes flaming. "Yes, I carry a pistol, Mrs. Masters. I learned in a hard school. Lessons for living, they were, and they served me well because here I stand, don't I? If it distresses you, then we'll just have to part company."

"I didn't mean that," Helena said, eyes wide.

"Aye, I know." Daisy sighed. "Don't pay attention to me, Helena. I'm tired and angry, but not at you. See how anger works? Likely it *was* a cull who got too excited and panicked who cut the viscount. He looked like murder on wheels when he came at the cove," she told the earl. "But even if it wasn't that, I'm ready. Who knows what enemies a person can make just by breathing? Tanner had dozens who wanted him dead, so I learned from him. He always went armed, hand and foot. And you, Helena?" she asked suddenly, "anyone mad at you?"

"My friends are all in the countryside," Helena said nervously. "And I've no enemies. At least, so I think."

"There it is," Daisy said impatiently. "So. What time can we come back tomorrow?"

The earl and Daffyd stood looking at her, the earl with a slight smile, Daffyd with a wide grin.

"Heart of oak, no fainting or wailing, and no retreating," Daffyd said with approval. "That's the daisy, all right! You know what? I think all girls should go to Botany Bay instead of finishing school."

The laughter that greeted this made Daisy feel better. But nevertheless, she looked into the shadows when she left the earl's house a little while later.

Daisy was up early the next morning, even though she had not slept much, or well. That, she thought, was Leland Grant's fault. She had gotten into bed and thought about his wound, wondered at his stoicism, and then, in the small hours, worried about his survival. He was such a cool, sardonic man, it was difficult to picture him helpless. And he was young and strong. But she'd seen death come to young and healthy people too many times. And so every time she'd closed her eyes, she'd thought of the possibility of seeing his knowing blue eyes closed forever. She'd only drifted off to sleep at last by promising herself she'd see him in the morning.

The man was an enigma; she was both attracted and distracted by him. But whatever he was, he'd offered his life for hers, and she didn't forget a debt. At least, that's what she told herself when she'd realized how upset she was by the attack on him, and how much he dominated her thoughts.

She dressed in shades of pink today, from her bonnet to her walking dress, colors carefully chosen to brighten a sickroom. She'd also bought a bag of sweets and a book the bookseller promised her was all the rage with the gentry these days.

She and Helena got to the earl's house just in time to see Daffyd leaving it. He'd only had time to say good-bye to Geoff and tell Daisy that Leland was feeling better before he left London. That reassured Daisy. She knew that as much as he wanted to get home to his wife, he wouldn't have gone if his half brother was in danger.

She picked up the hem of her skirt to go up the stairs when Helena stopped her with a light touch on the arm.

"A lady can't visit a gentleman in his bedchamber unless they are related, however ill he may be," Helena said apologetically.

"You hold with that, Geoff?" Daisy asked the earl, tapping a toe on the floor of his marble hall.

He bit back a smile. She looked ready to explode, her patience clearly held by a thread. He looked at her companion.

"I was hired to keep Mrs. Tanner company as well as to tell her how things were done in London," Helena said helplessly. "I can't approve what I know Society would not."

Daisy looked mulish. "I know what's proper but I can't and won't desert a friend in need. The viscount got cut trying to help me, didn't he? Fine thanks if I let him rot away alone upstairs without so much as a thank you, because 'a lady doesn't go into a fellow's bedchamber unless they're related!' I keep telling you—I'm not a lady! And if I were, I wouldn't want to be that kind of one. Anyway, if he's in bed with a knife wound in his chest, and I'm fit as a fiddle, I don't see how he *could* compromise me! If he even wanted to, that is," she added.

"Anyone would want to compromise you, Daisy," the earl said gallantly. "Though I doubt even Lee's up to it this morning. He's not exactly rotting away upstairs, by the way. He's well attended and is doing fine, but yesterday took a lot out of him and the doctor's draught slowed him further. He's no danger to anyone but himself, if he insists on doing too much."

"What say you, Mrs. Masters?" he asked Helena. "Daisy clearly will have her way. I don't want her climbing in the window. Why not agree and look the other way—metaphorically, that is. I won't tell if you don't."

Helena frowned. "But the servants . . . "

"Don't gossip, they're loyal to me, to a man and woman," the earl said. "I trust them implicitly." He saw her hesitation, and took pity. The woman obviously had morals and didn't want to take her salary if she couldn't provide what she'd promised.

"If Geoff thinks it's all right, then, *certainly,* so do I," Daisy announced.

Helena saw the fond look on the earl's face as he looked at Daisy. "Very well," she said with resignation, "What can I say?"

They went up the stairs, into the long hallway, and finally paused outside an oaken door.

The earl eased the door open. "Lee?" he called, "are you ready for company?"

"I was from the moment I heard they were here," Leland's voice said. "I'm decently dressed and delighted to receive them. Show them in, if you please."

Daisy followed the earl in, but had eyes only for the man in the huge bed. Leland was lying down, propped up on pillows, but otherwise she'd never have guessed he was in any way hurt. He wore a maroon dressing gown over a white shirt and gray breeches, and if it weren't for the fact that he wore morocco slippers instead of boots, he needed only a neck cloth to look ready for a stroll down the street.

It was true he was pale, but that only made his eyes look bluer, as he looked at her. She caught her breath as she met that calm regard. "Welcome," he said, "I'd bow, but my bandages are so tight, I might sever my body at the waist, and I think I've treated you to enough gore already. Thank you for coming; I'm glad the sight of my blood didn't put you off me forever. How are you this morning? I love your gown, Mrs. Tanner; the color brightens my day."

It hardly needed brightening, Daisy thought. The drapes had been pulled back from the windows and the room was flooded with morning light. It was a handsomely appointed room, with rich carpets and ornate furniture. Her nostrils twitched. There was no stale, medicinal smell of a sickroom here; instead the room bore a slight familiar and delicious scent of soap and warm sandalwood.

"I got you a book and some sweets," she said, ignoring his compliment. "But it looks like you don't need for anything."

"Oh, but I do," he said. "I needed company *des-*

perately. Not that Geoff isn't delightful, but he's woefully short on gossip."

"Well, so am I," Daisy said, as she took a chair the earl moved to the side of the bed. "All I can tell you is that it's a beautiful day."

"Then let's *make* some gossip," Leland said with a tilted grin.

"I'm only here because they promised me you couldn't," she said.

She heard Helena take in a breath, and the earl laugh. Daisy smiled as she realized how much easier it was to talk with the viscount when he was safely confined to his bed.

He laughed. "They can't promise what they don't control, Mrs. Tanner. But never fear! I'm on my best behavior. That's not difficult this morning. Did you know I creak when I move, like Prinny in his corset? Very distracting. But you, Mrs. Tanner, tempt me most awfully. And speaking of distractions, Helena, I see you're wearing the gown Mrs. Tanner told me about. I'm so pleased. You look splendid in it. Not that the lavender didn't suit you, but you glow in saffron, just as Mrs. Tanner promised."

As Helena smiled and thanked him, Daisy tilted her head to the side. So it was "Helena" so soon, and no correction offered, even when her companion was such a monster of propriety? And *four* "Mrs. Tanners" in a row? She doubted it was an accident. A glance at the light dancing in the viscount's dark blue eyes told her it wasn't.

"You can call me Daisy," she told him grudgingly. "Save yourself some breath that way, and I guess you need it today."

He put one hand on his heart. "I'm moved almost to tears. Thank you, Daisy. *Is* that your given Christian name, by the way?"

Daisy's face flushed. "My father always called me that, so everyone else did, too. But I was given the name Deidre. He thought it was too formal for"—*"a little redheaded sprite"* was what her father had said all those years ago, but that she wouldn't share—"a little girl. Daisy suits me, though. I don't think I'd even answer to Deidre if I heard it."

" 'Deidre of the sorrows,' " Leland quoted thoughtfully. "Yes, I can see it doesn't fit a little sprite like you. Have I said something wrong?" he asked when he saw her start.

"No, it's just that was what he said. Anyway," she said, trying to collect herself, "sometimes a name you get by accident is the one you keep. Funny, that. Even my father forgot Daisy wasn't my name. Years later, I asked if the fact that it wasn't my *real* name on my marriage lines made them invalid, but the magistrate said no, since everyone knew me as Daisy." She sighed with remembered regret. "Well, it was a long shot, but I tried. So it seems if you use a name long enough, it's yours to keep."

Leland watched her, seeing how bleak memory brought sorrow to her face. "Why, yes," he said. "In many ways. If I suddenly turned to nothing but acts of charity and repaired to a monastery, I'd still be called a rake. Not that I plan to do that!" he said in mock horror, to make her smile again. "My injury didn't frighten me *that* much. I'd need to be struck by an axe, not a knife, for that kind of repentance."

She smiled at him as his lips quirked in a real smile, too. Their eyes met in acknowledgment of the joke. It was a curiously intimate moment for Daisy. She liked the feeling she was sharing something amusing with another person who understood; she hadn't done that since she was a girl and had shared secret jests with her best friend. When she realized that a second later, her eyes widened.

What was it about this man? He wasn't handsome, not by half. But she found herself increasingly appreciating his arresting, angular looks. She'd passed so many years in a place where females were in the minority that she'd thought she'd met every kind of male. But she'd never met one like him, so full of manners and yet also filled with mirth and clever wickedness. He spoke as lightly as he moved and seemed to take nothing seriously except fashion. And yet he was strong and virile.

He was a novelty. She thought that might be it, entirely. At least she hoped so. In time, after meeting more fellows like the viscount, she might come to regard him with fondness, not the disturbing mixture of pleasure and alarm she felt whenever she met his gaze. As now, when she felt like squirming because of how he was watching her with rueful amusement and yet with sympathy.

He looked away, releasing her. "Any new ideas about my assailant?" he asked the earl.

"No. And you?"

"None," Leland said. "I pride myself on my enemies. After all, it isn't only one's friends that are the measure of a man. My enemies are superior, too." When they stopped laughing, he added, "At least my enemies are outspoken and would never hire anyone to do their dirty work. The more I think of it, the more I think it was an accident. London's full of thieves; they can't all be expert. But Daisy," he added, meeting her eyes again with a steady, serious gaze, "you be careful, at least until we're sure."

"I'm prepared," she said, holding up her chin.

"I'll bet you are," he said. "But I don't want to see you tested. Now, I should be ready for a public viewing by the end of the week. Shall it be at the theater or a party? Or a ball? I've invitations to a delightful ball; it will be a mad crush. I haven't sent in my card yet."

Daisy considered it. She wanted to go anywhere the earl could, to find out if she'd fit into his world.

She just wasn't sure if she was ready for such a big test. It wasn't a matter of suitable gowns. Because if she found she was a total scandal, she'd have to leave Geoff, with regrets. She wanted him as her husband but it wasn't fair to saddle him with a wife who could never be accepted. She knew too well how it felt to be an outsider, and wouldn't wish it on anyone she liked.

"But surely you aren't ready to dance," the earl protested.

"No, but I never am," Leland said. "I do it only to be obliging, but I don't care to caper, I'm just not cut out for it. I look like a scarecrow in the wind if I join a country dance, and like I've also got a broomstick up my breeches if I try a minuet. Excuse me," he said, with a look at Helena, seeing she was trying to suppress her laughter. "I'll try to be more sensible of my guests' tender ears, ma'am.

"Still, I *could* dance by then, if I wished," he added. "And if not, then surely flirting won't use up my strength, and that's what I do best. Another benefit is that I'll be such a sensation after my mishap that we can slip Daisy into any fashionable party without anyone looking at her with undue scrutiny. They'd be too busy goggling at me. Would you mind not being the belle of the ball?" he asked Daisy.

She could swear he'd read her mind. "No," she said, with relief, "not at all."

"I'm not sure the doctor will let you," the earl told him. "But if you want to try, we have to leave you now, so you can be up to it. The doctor said rest, and that's what you'll get until his next visit."

"Alas!" Leland said, sinking back on his pillows. "You're not going to let any more lovely ladies come up to my bedchamber? *That* might kill me. But I will survive, if only because I'll be readying myself for Saturday evening. Save a waltz for me, Daisy, will you?"

His voice asked for more than a waltz; his eyes did, too. She found herself unable to say yes, because of the sudden vision of herself in his arms. How could she resolve her uneasy feelings about him if she got that close to him?

"I haven't danced in years," she said truthfully.

He waved a hand. "You'll remember when you hear the music. And I'm infinitely patient. So?"

"Thank you, yes. I'd like that," she lied.

He grinned, and she knew that he knew that, too.

Leland lay back and closed his eyes after Daisy left, seeing the red of his inner eyelids in the sunlight, and the red-gold of her hair in his mind's eye; feeling the warmth of the sun on his face, imagining the warmth of her body next to his. He didn't know if he'd ever feel that in reality, because for some reason he'd frightened her today. He didn't know why.

He had the reputation of a rake, that was true.

But why should she fear that? Especially coming from where she'd been? After all, with all he was, he *was* a gentleman. She had to know he'd never force her to do anything. In fact, he wasn't sure he was that much of a libertine; it was only that he'd gotten the name and it amused him to keep it. Many gentlemen had just as many lovers, but he was more open about it than most; he'd concede that.

The truth was that he loved to love. The joy of a woman's body was a miracle in which he could always forget himself, and that was no small miracle in itself. He liked more than their bodies; he numbered women, even though many were unobtainable, among his friends. Unlike other men he knew, he didn't believe a person's body shaped her mind, at least not entirely. Yet he'd never loved the way poets said a man could: once and forever and with a burning desire that was more than passion. Since he hadn't, he didn't know if he could. But the game of love, flirtation and challenge, acceptance and pleasure, always delighted him.

He didn't know whether Daisy Tanner knew she'd been flirting with him. She'd done it beautifully, though, until he'd frightened her. That surprised him. Did she have a guilty secret? Did that have something to do with why she was wary of him and making a dead set for Geoff?

It was important, for Geoff's sake, that he find out. He laughed aloud.

"My lord?" his valet, who had been cleaning the room, asked. "Are you all right?"

He opened his eyes. "Nothing," he said. "It's nothing. I laughed because I was so amused by lies I was telling myself. It must be the effect of the medicine the good doctor gave me for pain. I tell you what, give me some more to make me sleep. I have to be ready to dance."

Chapter 10

Daisy took one last look in the mirror. She was going to pay another call on Geoff and Viscount Haye after breakfast, and so had tried to look both elegant and cool this warm summer's morning. Her hair had been tamed, drawn taut and smoothed back from her face, allowing ringlets to riot only at the back of her head. She had on a yellow gown, sprigged with tiny pink flowers and green leaves. There was even a parasol to match, but she regretfully left it in its wrapping tissue. She still didn't feel enough of a lady to sport one, never knowing when to use it for shade, rest it on her shoulder, or twirl it flirtatiously, in the easy way ladies of fashion did. That, along with the use of a fan, was like using another language, an art she meant to acquire.

She picked up a pair of yellow kid gloves. "I can't look better," she said. "Let's have breakfast. I'm starved."

Helena sighed but held her tongue. A lady wouldn't have said she was starved, but she wouldn't hurt Daisy's feelings by correcting her for something that minor.

But Daisy had seen her expression. "I mean," she said puckishly, raising a hand to her forehead, "I vow I am fairly *famished.*"

Helena laughed. "No. You said it right the first time, because you said it the way only you could."

"I may never be styled a lady, you know," Daisy confided as they walked to the door.

"You'll be called 'charming' and 'candid' and 'refreshing,' and that's much better."

Daisy stopped and looked at Helena. She was frowning. "Do you really think they'll do that? That they'll accept me?"

Helena didn't have to ask who "they" were. "If the earl does, they will," she said diplomatically.

"Good," Daisy said in relief. "I can change, but only so much. I mean, I suppose I could, but I've had enough of being someone I'm not in order to please a man."

It was Helena who was frowning slightly as they went down the stair. But Daisy didn't notice, she was too intent on getting downstairs to eat and then see Leland. And Geoff, she reminded herself.

"Go right on up," Geoff said when Daisy and Helena arrived. "I've a visitor, my man-at-law; our business won't take long. Leland's still upstairs, but only because he can't get down here on his own yet and refuses to be carried."

"I'm on my way," Daisy said. She saw Helena's face grow pink. She hoped there wouldn't be another objection to her seeing the viscount in his bedchamber.

But Helena turned to the earl. "May I be excused for a moment?" she asked in embarrassment. "And have you a withdrawing room?"

Daisy suppressed a giggle. No question that good breeding complicated things. Few people in Port Jackson would have known what Helena was talking about; they'd a much simpler way to say they needed a chamber pot. But Daisy had seen how much tea Helena had drunk at breakfast, and the earl was used to good manners.

"It's just down the hall," Geoff said, and indicated the direction.

Helena nodded. "I'll be there soon," she told Daisy unhappily, because though she clearly didn't want Daisy to go up alone, she knew she wouldn't wait.

This time, Leland's door was open. This time, too, he sat up in a chair by the bed. He wore a robe over a shirt and breeches. His face wasn't as pale as it had been the day before. His eyes were just as intense and blue, but she thought she saw pain in them.

"Why look at you!" she said. "Out of bed already. That's very good."

"So it is," he said, and sat back, letting out a gusty sigh of relief, as though talking had exerted him. Then he smiled. "And look at you! You're wearing one of Madame Bertrand's gowns today. Very lovely, the color suits you. Take a chair, please. If you continue to stand, I'll feel I must, too."

She looked around. There was a chair near the window, far from him. And there was one right next to his. Too close, she thought, and too awkward. But how stupid she would look sitting on the other side of the bed! She'd have to shout to talk to him. She sat down, gingerly, next to him.

He saw her hesitation, and she saw amusement in his gaze. But "Tell me about the world outside" was all he said.

"You've only been here a few days," she scoffed. "And you read the newspaper. I don't know anything that's happened that you don't."

"Oh, do you not?" he asked softly. "I think you know much that I want to know. What do you think of me now, for example?"

She blinked.

"You thought I was a fop and a man milliner, or worse, when we first met. Don't deny it," he said, raising a hand. "But now," he said, watching her intently. "What do you think now? I ask because you are so very wary of me. Surely you know I mean you no harm?"

"Well, of course I know that," she exclaimed. "You took a knife in your chest in my defense."

He cocked his head to the side. "Any gentleman would have done that. What is it about me that frightens you, Daisy?"

Well, there was plain speaking, she thought with a little panic. She cleared her throat for time. "You say such flirtatious things, my lord," she finally said. "And flirtation is a thing I'm out of practice with."

"It isn't all flirtation, Daisy," he said softly. "I mean everything I say. You are beautiful, I do desire you, and I think I could make you very happy. But don't be afraid. I am a gentleman, and would never do anything you didn't want me to. That's a solemn promise."

"What do you want to do?" she asked without thinking, mesmerized by his soft voice and the intimate mood. Then she squeezed her eyes closed and shook her head. "No, no. Stupid question!" she said, and shot up from her chair. "I know very well what you want."

He smiled. "Good. I hoped so."

She didn't know whether to laugh with him or rail at him, but didn't have to do either.

"What the devil are you doing up and out of bed?" the earl said as he marched into the room, Helena at his side.

"Recovering," Leland said gloomily. "Terrorizing Daisy and frightening you. Seeing if I can move at all. Oh bother, I'm sick of lying in bed. In fact, that's it. I *will* be sick if I stay there."

"The doctor said bed rest," the earl said.

"The doctor also wanted to regale me with leeches," Leland said on a barely concealed shudder. "And that *after* he'd let blood. I decided to save some for my veins. There are some things I still do control, you know. And look at me, I'm in fine fettle, and up to all kind of mischief," he added, with a private smile for Daisy.

She couldn't help smiling back at him. The dark, erotic mood he'd established was gone. He was Leland Grant, the trifling nobleman, again.

"I promised the doctor," the earl said, crossing his arms.

"Oh, very well," Leland said ungraciously. "I'll do it to please you." He started to rise, and faltered. His company darted forward. With the earl on one side and Helena on the other, they helped him walk the few steps to his high bed, and into it, so he could lie back on his pillows.

"I confess," Leland said when he was settled, hand on the bandage over his heart, "This does feel better."

"There's a concession!" the earl said. "Do you want us to leave?"

"Never," Leland said, and sounded as if he meant it. "I'm really feeling much better and I enjoy the company, believe me."

"Good," the earl said, "because you've another visitor coming. A lady who asked special permission to see you even if you were in bed."

Leland's eyebrows went up. "And you *agreed*? I must be corrupting you, Geoff."

"Not that kind of visitor," the earl said. "It's your mama."

Leland's smile faded. "Unfair," he said softly. "You ought to have asked me first."

"No, I couldn't and wouldn't," the earl said. "Because refusing wasn't an option for you or me."

Both men fell still.

"Would you like us to leave?" Daisy asked.

"Good God, no!" Leland exclaimed. "Finding me with a room full of young beauties may well speed her on her way. So please stay. You brighten my day. I'm a most unnatural son," he added because of the shocked look on Helena's face. "And she, a most indifferent mother. Still, if I greeted her with exclamations of profound joy, she'd believe me about to depart this life. We haven't the warmest relationship," he explained. "And everyone knows it."

"Well, I can understand that sort of thing," Daisy said with a shrug. "I loved my father, but I always knew he didn't feel the same about me. He didn't dislike me," she added hastily. "Or treat me badly. He just didn't think of me at all, is what it was."

Leland narrowed his eyes against the blaze of

color that surrounded her where she sat, in a pool of sunlight at the side of his bed. Or was she the light that dazzled him? he wondered. She was radiant; her hair, her gown, her frequent smile, her laughter.

Again, he wondered why she was attaching herself to a middle-aged recluse and his wounded friend, when she could have all London at her feet. It was true that with her past she might not attract a man who was a stickler for propriety. But this was the nineteenth century, after all. She was wellborn and well funded. Her wit and beauty, the novelty of her, could lure any normal male to ask for her hand and yearn for the sumptuous rest of her to follow as soon as possible.

Dangerous things to be thinking while lounging in bed, Leland realized, feeling his body stirring in reaction to his thoughts. He struggled to sit up straighter, but the high featherbed defeated him, embracing him and sinking him deeper every time he tried to move. "My lord," he pleaded when he couldn't manage it, punching one of the pillows behind him. "See how helpless I am. At least let me sit in a chair again."

The earl lifted an eyebrow. Leland subsided.

"I don't want your blood on my hands, literally or figuratively," the earl said.

"At least tell the viscountess that I'll see her another day," Leland said. "I feel far too vulnerable this way. She hasn't seen me in bed since the day I was born."

The earl shook his head. "I can't. She's already on her way."

"Damn!" Leland said, and then quickly said, "I meant 'drat,' ladies. Mark it down to my distress and forgive me."

Daisy wondered what he was apologizing for, until Helena spoke up. "It's nothing, my lord," she said. "Or at least nothing we never heard before."

The viscount apologized for saying "damn"? Lord! Daisy thought, what would he have made of how they talked back in the colony? Her eyes met the earl's and they smiled at each other, obviously both struck by the same thought.

"My dear Leland," a cool voice exclaimed from the doorway. "So it was true! You were injured, attacked in public by a cutpurse."

"Hello, Mama," Leland said in an equally cool voice. "No saying it was a cutpurse. It could have been anyone with a grudge against me, as you always said might happen if I didn't reform my way of life."

His mother paused in the doorway, looking at him. Here, in the unrelenting light of day, Daisy could see that the years had left their mark on what was probably once flawless beauty. But signs of age—the few wrinkles at the eyes and around the corners of the mouth, and the gray in the golden hair—didn't detract so much as point up the fact that she was still remarkably handsome. And cold.

From her voice to her smile, Viscountess Haye was a model of composure. She didn't look like the sort of female who had once kicked over the traces and run off with a Gypsy. Or like the kind who had conducted countless affairs afterward. Daisy couldn't imagine this woman showing any kind of passion. But then Daisy remembered a murderess she'd known who had poisoned three husbands and yet looked as though she was incapable of pouring a guest tea that was too hot.

Daisy saw that cool blue gaze fall on her, and looked away. The woman made her feel guilty, and she wasn't sure of what.

"Mrs. Tanner, good morning," the countess said as she stripped off her gloves and came into the room. She glanced at Helena, but only gave her a brief nod, because servants weren't acknowledged, and if Helena wasn't precisely a servant, she was in a paid position, and so, of no account.

Then that piercing blue gaze found the earl, and the countess smiled. "My lord," she said. "Thank you for taking Haye in after the incident. It was very kind of you."

"No kindness involved," the earl said. "Leland's a friend, and I wouldn't have it any other way. But, please, have a seat and stay as long as you wish. Mrs. Masters, if you'd be kind enough to come with me? I've a few questions to ask you about just that incident that I ought to have asked before."

"I'll come, too!" Daisy said, springing up from her chair.

"Please stay," Leland said, "Or my mama will think she's frightened you away."

"Indeed," the viscountess said. "Do stay, Mrs. Tanner. We hardly had time to get acquainted before, and I see you are already a fixture in my son's life."

"Lud, no!" Daisy blurted. "I mean to say, I'm not. That is, I'm an old friend of Geoff's, I mean, the earl's, and since the viscount's a friend of his, we're thrown into each other's company a lot, is what it is."

Daisy's face flushed. Gracelessly said, and not what she meant, it made the viscount laugh and the viscountess's gaze grow sharper.

"Absolutely true," the earl said with a chuckle. "And just like Daisy to say it that way. Come along, Mrs. Masters. We'll be back in no time."

"Don't look so anxious," he murmured to Helena as they left the room. "I've just a few questions, because the man from Bow Street said everyone present that night should be interviewed, and I wanted to spare you the ordeal of having him do it."

Once they were gone, Daisy sat back, feeling uneasy and out of place. Surely mother and son needed some private time together. So she sat quietly, trying to disappear by her silence.

The viscountess sat upright in her chair and put her hands in her lap. She turned toward

Daisy. "So you are in England to stay now, Mrs. Tanner?"

"Yes," Daisy said, wondering why she didn't ask her son how he felt before she chatted with his visitor.

"I see. And where will you live?"

"I'm staying at Grillions, on the park, for now."

The countess's brilliant blue eyes grew larger; that was the only way Daisy could read any reaction. "Surely you don't mean to stay in a hotel forever?"

"Well, no. But I don't know where I want to settle yet."

"Mrs. Tanner will probably settle down with a husband before long," Leland said. "So there's little sense in her buying or renting a house now."

"I see," his mother said, without looking at him. "Have you anyone in mind, my dear?"

"My lady!" Leland said with an exasperated laugh. "Bow Street wouldn't ask her such personal questions."

"Would they not?" the viscountess asked. "So what *have* they asked?"

Daisy sat up straighter. The lady might be elegant, and far above her touch, but her conversation was presumptuous. She herself had been raised to act like a lady, and if the countess wasn't behaving like one, she would.

"Bow Street hasn't asked me anything yet,"

Daisy said calmly. "If they do, I'll tell them all. The thief that stabbed your son was after my purse, and when the viscount here rushed to protect me, he got stabbed. I wish he hadn't had to; it wouldn't have happened if I'd my wits and remembered I had my knife about me. But not my barker. I usually carry one, too, but I'd left it home that night. That won't happen again."

"A *knife*?" the viscountess asked, her brows going up.

"And a pistol," Leland said with amusement. "Don't worry about me, Mama, if you are, that is to say. I'll be perfectly safe now that I've got a bruiser like Mrs. Tanner to protect me."

Daisy laughed. The countess didn't. Daisy wondered if she could.

"Of course I worry about you, Haye," the viscountess said without a trace of emotion. "I understood the wound was not serious. At least that's what the message the earl sent to me said. So why then are you still abed?"

"It's his wish," Leland said. "He feels responsible for me when I'm under his roof. I'm getting up tomorrow and going home soon after."

"That relieves my mind," she said in the same cool tones. "Even so, I will ask for a personal interview with him. You always make light of everything, Haye. I want to know what he really thinks."

Daisy felt chilled. The woman called her son by his titled name, and scarcely looked at him.

There seemed to be no emotion in her. Yet she'd produced a laughing, exuberant son like Daffyd. Daisy guessed that must have been because he'd gotten more of his Gypsy father's blood. But how could this cold creature have produced a merry care-for-nothing sensualist like Leland, Lord Haye?

The viscountess turned her penetrating gaze on her son and asked him how he felt, at last. He told her. And told her. She sighed at his long list of ridiculous mock complaints. She didn't tolerate them for long.

Soon, she arose. "I don't want to tire you, Haye. I'll just go down and ask the earl a few more questions, and then will be on my way. Stay well. Good morning, Mrs. Tanner, until we meet again."

And then she left the room.

Daisy finally let out her breath.

"Tingling toenails is *not* a disastrous symptom?" Leland asked. "Pity. If I'd known, I'd have told her that one first."

Daisy didn't answer.

"Touching, wasn't it?" he asked her in a tired voice. He laid his head back against his pillows and seemed infinitely weary, and maybe in some pain.

"Are you all right?" Daisy asked immediately, coming close to him. He looked paler than he had when she'd first arrived. "Is there anything you need?"

He turned his head to look at her. He had the same color eyes as his mother, but they seemed gentler even in that severe masculine face. Unlike his mother, his eyes didn't pierce, they sparkled. He smiled, and those larkspur eyes danced. "What I need, Daisy," he purred, "is not what I can have here and now."

She stepped back and frowned at him.

"My dear," he said softly, "I'd have to be two days dead not to say something like that to a woman like you. Actually," he said in a different tone, "I feel like I am. She does that to me. She leaches the life from me. I suppose she can't help it anymore than I can help the way I am, but I wonder how my father got me on her without dying of frostbite first. Sorry," he said, seeing her expression of surprise, "I don't mind my manners as I should."

"It's all right," she said absently, taking one of his hands in hers, responding to the pain in his voice and not what he'd said. "I don't mind. I've heard worse. Are you ill? I mean really sick, or is it just that she upset you?"

"Just?" he asked with a weary, tilted grin. "Lord, I wish there was a 'just' about it." His hand clasped hers. She noted it was cold, and held it tightly. "You say your father didn't care for you. But you cared for him, as he must have, in *some* way, for you, however ill advised or inept that care was. Because I've heard you quote him. That's good, no matter how bad he was,

because at least he never intentionally hurt you, did he?"

She shook her head. "No."

"My mama never cared that she did. Oh, blast," he said, wincing. "Listen to me. I *must* be sick. Here I am with a lovely woman inches away from me, and I'm blathering on like a schoolboy sent to bed early, whining about my parent. Forgive me again."

She leaned down to pull a pillow up behind his head. She heard him take in a breath and looked down at him. They were very close.

"Did you know," he asked with interest, his eyes on hers, "that you have the scent of heartsease in your hair? That's rare. I didn't know they could make perfume from them. You know, those pretty little flowers with tiny faces that smile up at you from the lawn. It's a fragile scent, so vague it only reminds you of spring, never insisting on it. Of course you know; what a foolish question." His eyes crinkled at the corners. "You probably have a bottle labeled 'heartsease' on your dressing table, just to break the hearts of men."

She shook her head, and slowly eased her hand from his. His words were lovely to hear, but they dismayed her. Or was it his tone? How could the tender tone of his voice soothe her even as it upset her?

He let her hand go. "Well, that's so," he said gently, using the hand she'd released to trace the edges of her cheek with his fingertips. "And did you know that you've the most damnably tempting mouth I've seen in many a day?"

But that she knew how to answer, though her voice didn't have the bite she'd normally have used. "You find many mouths tempting, sir," she said. "You're famous for it."

"So I am. So that makes me an expert, right? And I say yours is not only the most tempting, but the most impudent. I can resist beauty, but why couldn't you be dim?" he asked in mock despair.

She smiled, though she'd meant to step away.

He slowly ran a finger along the outline of her cheek, and she felt his touch down every seam in her body. Her eyes widened.

He smiled, put his hand at the back of her neck, raised his head as he drew hers down, and gently touched her mouth with his.

She felt her body tingle even as her mouth did. She closed her eyes and bent toward him. She felt the easy strength of his clasp; she'd never known such gentleness at a man's hands. His mouth was warm, soft velvet. She felt his lips part and the light tentative touch of his tongue. She opened her lips and tasted the dark sweetness of his mouth. Her hand went to his neck, and she felt his warm blood beating beneath her fingertips. His kiss set her own blood to humming, and she yearned and sighed into his mouth, drew closer still—and then suddenly remembered what a kiss led to.

All the sweet promise had only one end to it: sweating and pushing, grunting and shoving, and the pain of humiliation.

She pulled away, straightened her back, and stared down at him. "I don't do that," she said jerkily. "Please forget that. And don't do that again. I must leave."

"I'm sorry," he said, but she was gone and out the door.

Leland scowled, angry at himself Wrong of him, of course, to try for a seduction here and now. But he hadn't meant to. That was new. Her kiss had been so sweet. She'd ended it abruptly and run from him in fear. That was absurd. She wasn't a schoolroom miss or an ingénue. He never attempted them. She was a warm, ripe woman, and her obvious sympathy and understanding made him behave rashly. But not that rashly! What could he have done to her, after all? Especially here, in the earl's house. She should have known that; she'd been a married woman.

And yet she might have been right; who knew what he'd been trying to do? It was as much of a surprise to him as it had been to her. Her reaction hadn't been anger so much as fear. But he hadn't been attempting rape; surely she knew that. She must know there was nothing much in a kiss.

But there had been in this one. There'd been solace and understanding, desire—and terror, at the end, for her.

Leland lay back, frowning. Now, why should that be? He wanted to know as much as he wanted another kiss from her. *No,* he thought. There was nothing he wanted more than that.

Chapter 11

The earl paced his study. "So far as you know, then, Mrs. Tanner has no enemies?" he asked Helena.

"None," Helena answered.

"There haven't been any other visitors or incidents?"

"None," Helena said again, then added quietly. "If there were, you'd know of them, because Daisy hasn't gone many places without you."

He looked up at that, because of the flat tone of her voice. "You disapprove?"

She lowered her gaze. "It's not my place to approve or disapprove, my lord."

"But you do or don't. I've had to work for my supper in my time, and I know opinions are free to everyone, just not freely given to those we know can harm us. I wouldn't harm you whatever you said, you must know that."

"Yes," she said, looking at him directly. "But I don't know Mrs. Tanner or you well enough to make any judgments."

He studied her. She seemed to be a sensible woman. She was not young, yet not in her middle years, and always looked neat and calm. Her hair was worn plainly, drawn back prim as a nun's, but nothing could disguise the fact that it was a rich deep brown. Her face was sweet, and even in her modest gown, he could see she had a trim figure. She spoke well and behaved modestly, but he'd been in servitude once, and though he knew Daisy was a kind employer, he knew that no kind of service was as pleasant as being one's own master.

"Nicely said, though I don't believe it," he said. "But let it be. You might well disapprove of her spending so much time with me. I'm not sure I don't myself. She should be with lads her own age. I'm twice that. I feel it, most of the time. But not when I'm with her."

Helena looked down at her hands tightly clasped in her lap. If he said too much, he might later regret it and tell Daisy to turn her out. But he'd already said too much for her to hear, and so she didn't know what to say to him.

"My lord?" the butler said from the doorway. "Viscountess Haye wished to see you before she left."

"Send her in," the earl said.

The viscountess came in so quickly that Helena realized she must have been waiting in the hall. She ignored Helena and came right to the earl.

"I couldn't leave without thanking you again, my lord," she said with a hint of warmth. "My son is lucky in his choice of friends."

"You're welcome, my lady, but there's no need for thanks," the earl said.

The viscountess's smile was bitter. "But what am I saying? I meant, my *sons* are lucky."

Helena wished she were anywhere else. It was true that so far as the lady was concerned, she wasn't there, but even so, she didn't know what to do except pretend that she wasn't there, too. She stared at her slippers. Of course the world knew, by rumor and observation, that the viscountess was mother to the bastard half-Gypsy Daffyd. But it wasn't discussed in her presence.

"You've been kind to both of them," the viscountess went on. "*Kind?*" Her laughter was hollow. "Ridiculous word, say rather benevolent, and necessary."

The earl looked embarrassed. "It wasn't kindness. I like them both. In Daffyd's case, like a son. In Leland's, as a good friend."

"You've a positive knack for taking young persons under your wing," the viscountess said, smiling. "Daffyd, first. Then, when you returned to England, my son Haye. And now Mrs. Tanner.

You're very good with young people, my lord. You should be congratulated on your patience and charity."

Helena bit her lip. That was close to ridicule. Did the viscountess mean it that way? Was it because she suspected Daisy's plans for the earl? More interesting was the way the earl's face grew ruddy. Did he already return Daisy's feelings, or was he just embarrassed by praise? It mattered to Helena, though she hated the fact that it did.

"I'd like to show my gratitude, but I know you need for nothing," the viscountess said. "I also know you don't care for the social whirl, but Mrs. Tanner seems to appreciate it. So why not bring her to my home next Friday? I'm having a small party. Haye should be out of bed by then, so you'll have someone to talk to if you don't care to dance. I know it is late notice, but this way perhaps you'll agree before you think better of it. What say you? May I count on your presence?"

The earl laughed. "I'm not exactly a hermit. So, yes, thank you, I'd be delighted. I'll ask Mrs. Tanner as well."

"You will have the invitation in your hand within the hour. And so will she. Thank *you,* my lord," the viscountess said. "I look forward to it."

"I don't," the earl murmured after she'd swept from the room. He smiled at Helena. "I *am* a recluse, in point of fact. Or rather, I've become one.

I know that's not a good thing. I'm glad Daisy came to me. She saves me from myself."

But another woman could as well, Helena protested in her heart. Still, she only said, "Yes. She's a tonic, a true original, and a delight. Excuse me, my lord, but if you're done with me, may I rejoin her? It isn't the thing for her to be alone with the viscount in his bedchamber. He's bedridden, but not incapacitated, and who knows what his mother might think if she chose to go upstairs again for any reason."

The earl looked startled. "You're right!" he said. "I've done with questions. We should rejoin them straightaway."

But when they got back to the viscount's room, he was alone. Leland lay on his back, studying the ceiling.

"Where's Daisy?" the earl asked.

"I devoured her," Leland said in annoyance. "How the devil should I know? She left a few minutes ago, and I'm not permitted to follow."

"We must have just missed her," Helena said. "She's probably waiting for me downstairs."

Daisy was waiting in the front hall. Her face was a bit paler than usual. "Are you well?" the earl asked.

"Very," she said. "But it's time to go." She smiled at Helena. "I deserted the viscount when I realized that. I *am* learning proper behavior again; aren't you proud of me?"

Helena would have been if she hadn't seen the

distress beneath Daisy's words. The woman might have lived a life that would harden most people beyond recognition, but she was still a transparent liar.

"There's no way you won't be the belle of the ball," Helena said.

Daisy nodded glumly. There was no fault she could find with Madame Bertrand's latest effort. Her gown was yellow, with a low neck and long sleeves, and a pink sash beneath her breasts to show her figure to advantage. Her hair was done up with pink roses, and her maid had dusted a puff of rouge across her cheekbones. It might have been too much by day, but she'd glow in lamp and candlelight.

"I don't want to be sensational," Daisy said. "I only want to be able to enjoy myself."

"Why shouldn't you?" Helena asked.

Daisy hesitated. She'd been aching to talk to someone about her problem, but wasn't used to confiding in anyone, much less trusting them. It was true Helena was older, and better acquainted with Society, and yet Daisy wasn't sure she could share with her. It had been hard for Daisy since that morning she'd kissed Leland. She'd steeled herself, and had visited him again. They'd both pretended nothing had happened. But she could see the knowledge in his eyes, as well as the desire for more. She, too, felt the lure of him; it was intense and undeniable. It frightened her, and she hated to be afraid. She knew he wouldn't embarrass her in public. She was very worried about what might happen in private.

Daisy dismissed her maid and sat down on the edge of a chair. She picked a nonexistent thread from her skirt, smoothed it, and then without looking up, finally dared.

"What do you think of Viscount Haye?" she asked Helena. "I mean, really."

"It's not my place—"

"Bother!" Daisy said impatiently. "I asked, so it is."

"So it is, I suppose," Helena said. "Then I'll tell you. I think he's very attractive, though it's hard to know precisely why." She smiled. "He has the reputation of a rake, but he's so amusing that it seems to be something he invented to laugh at. In brief, I'd say he's charming and intelligent, and that for all his reputation, there's no real harm in him."

Daisy nodded. She pleated a bit of her skirt in her fingers. She had to ask more so that she'd know what to do next. The *ton* lived in a world alien to her, but not to Helena Masters. If she wanted to live in that world, she had to trust her companion. "He kissed me," she told Helena. "How do I go on with him after that?"

Helena frowned. So did Daisy. She knew she'd asked a question that a girl of sixteen might, not one a widow would.

"You mean socially?" Helena asked carefully.

"Aye, that," Daisy muttered. "And any other way."

"Did you protest? Or slap him? Or . . . "

"*I* kissed him back," Daisy said bitterly. "I can't blame him except it was like he'd thrown some sort of spell over me. I didn't protest, or slap him, but I did run away."

"Was it so distasteful?"

"Yes. No. I don't know," Daisy said. "Well, I do," she muttered to the floor. "It was nice, very nice. But I knew what comes after, so I got out of there fast as I could. There's nothing worse than what comes after, and I want no part of it. The question is: How do I prevent it in future without getting him angry? Because I do like to see him and talk to him, and I will, because he's Geoff's good friend."

She kept her eyes on the floor. The truth was, she couldn't forget that kiss. For a miracle, it had actually tempted her to try for more. She'd left him before *that* madness, and madness it would be. But she couldn't forget the feelings he had woken. She hadn't felt them in years, since before Tanner, in fact. They weren't desires she wanted, but she couldn't repress them. They made her squirm and ache, and even came to her in dreams she tried to forget when she woke.

"So what do I do?" she asked, scowling fiercely. She'd planned every step of her way back to England, and it was hard to find something that might block her goal here at the last.

"Do you intend to do it again?" Helena asked. "I mean, kiss him?"

"God, no!" Daisy said.

Helena remained silent a moment. Then she cleared her throat. "Stealing a kiss from a grown woman who seems to know what she's about isn't such a sin," she said. "Not even stealing two or three. Nor should it discourage your friendship with him if you make it clear it can't happen again. But what concerns me is the rest of what you said.

"Daisy, 'what comes after' isn't worse," she said slowly. "Well, I suppose it is if you're not married to the fellow and have no plans to be. You know what gossip is. But if it were done with discretion, no one would mind, or be surprised. You're a widow, you have more leeway, and the viscount is a single man. Of course, it would be wrong to have an *affaire* with him. Apart from the risk of bearing a child, which I assume he would be clever enough to make less possible, if you had an *affaire* and he left you, someone might find out. That wouldn't do wonders for your reputation. Actually, he'd be a brilliant match for you. He's intelligent, wealthy, has excellent address, and he doesn't have to answer to anyone. In fact, it would be quite a coup. But I don't say it could be done. He's defied matchmakers for years now."

Daisy's head snapped up. "I don't want to *marry* him!" she said in horror. "All I want to know is how to go on with him comfortably now after that kiss."

"You go on as you did before," Helena said. "He'll understand so long as you make it clear, by word or attitude, that you don't wish to have any more of it. But why do you say what comes after a kiss is so terrible?" she persisted. "It isn't, it's wonderful if you've the right man."

"Wonderful?" Daisy said in surprise. "No, thank you; *that* it is not. I suppose the viscount can't help it because that's the sort of man he is, a slave to his passions, and when he likes a woman all he can think of is having her. One of the best things about Geoff is that he likes me and yet doesn't expect that sort of thing. Maybe because he's older, maybe because he has such fine sensibilities, but he's above that."

Helena sat down quickly on a nearby chair. "Daisy!" she said breathlessly. "That's just not so. I'm sure it isn't. He's a man; the fact that he's older doesn't mean he's *dead.* Sensual pleasure is the right of any man of any age, and women, too. If the earl cared for a woman, naturally he'd want to have relations with her. I'm not saying he doesn't care for you, because clearly he does. But maybe because he has fine sensibilities he wouldn't steal a kiss unless he'd plans to marry you."

Daisy fiddled with the pleat she'd made in her skirt. "The truth of it is, Helena, that I don't like it." She looked up with sudden hope. "But you'll agree that an older man doesn't want to do it that often?"

Helena laughed in flustered surprise. "I don't know. I really don't. The best thing to do would be to ask him."

"*Talk* about it?" Daisy asked in shock.

"Why not? If the moment's right, of course. If you're seriously considering marrying him, you must discuss it. It's true Society may produce girls who have no idea of what to expect in the marriage bed. You do. The men you meet expect that. You're a woman grown, a widow to boot. The earl, or any grown man, will have certain expectations. It wouldn't be fair to enter into a marriage without discussing how you feel about the act of love with him first."

"*Act of love,*" Daisy muttered. "A pretty way of talking about a rude thing. It really is, you know. Like the way a person's entrails work: It's a thing of the body that polite people don't discuss, unless they use flowery or scientific speech. I came from a place where people said what they meant. They didn't say they had to find the 'withdrawing room' at the end of dinner, I can tell you that. And they didn't talk about 'the act of love,' neither. Instead they said f—" She paused. "I suppose I am too much of a lady—or you are—for me to go on, so I won't. But thank you. You've given me a lot to think about."

"Please feel free to talk about it with me any time," Helena said "But more important, please remember you can talk about it with anyone you think might one day be a lover."

"Little chance of that!" Daisy said.

Helena's expression was sympathetic. "Was it so bad then?"

"Then? Oh yes," Daisy said. She remembered Tanner's groping hands and insistent body, and shuddered. "I didn't like him, and so you can imagine how much I didn't like *that* with him." She gave Helena a clear-eyed look. "I'm not so stupid that I don't think it might be different for different people, or with different people. But honestly, I don't even like to think about it. Still, if and when Geoff asks me to marry him, I wouldn't lie to him."

She took a deep breath. "I'll cross that bridge when I come to it. In the meanwhile, thank you."

Helena nodded, but looked troubled.

Daisy went back to the dressing table and fiddled with a rose in her hair, pretending it had come loose. She thought about seeing Geoff tonight, and thought that, yes, fair was fair. It was a thing she should talk about with him someday. He was so kind and gentle, she thought she could.

She thought about seeing Leland Grant tonight, and shivered, but not in revulsion. He made her forget what she was afraid of. That was amazing, and dangerous. And yet . . . Daisy wondered. Sometimes in the past she'd thought about how it would be with someone she cared for. How would it be with someone who amused her? Just the fact that she was considering it could mean that she wouldn't always find the act hideous. Maybe there was something to it. All she knew of it, after all, she learned from Tanner's hands.

Daisy pushed Tanner from her mind. He was gone. And there were things here that she hadn't imagined, so why couldn't enjoyment in *that* be one of them, after all?

Helena said there was no harm in a kiss. Against all odds, Viscount Haye made Daisy wonder if there could be pleasure in one—or two.

Chapter 12

It was not a party. Leland smiled, the earl groaned, and Daisy gasped. The dowager viscountess Haye had invited them to what looked like a grand ball.

"Are you sure you feel well enough to go to attend?" Daisy asked again, as the carriage stopped.

"As I said, yes," Leland said in bored tones. "There's nothing left of my wound but the memory."

"Well, I think I have to go home and change," Daisy said nervously when she peered out the window to see the long line of carriages ahead of theirs, waiting to discharge their passengers at the front door to his mother's town house.

"I think you look not only proper, but wonderful," Helena said from her quiet corner of the coach.

Daisy shook her head. "No. I'll look downright shabby at a ball." She thought of the golden gown she'd never dared wear and breathed a silent sigh of relief. If they'd let her go back, she could get herself up in it and look like she belonged.

Leland laughed. "It's not a ball. It is, however, my mama's idea of a party. There's no dancing, unless someone gets drunk enough to bribe the fiddlers she has on hand to play a sprightlier tune. But they'd waste their money. There won't be room to pick up a coin if you drop it. It's just a fashionable *do,* with food and conversation, and it would never do to go to it dressed to the nines."

"Gads!" the earl exclaimed, looking at the torchlights outside and the windows inside the house ablaze with light. "It looks like an anthill that was set on fire."

"It will feel like one, too," Leland said. "We won't have to stay long but I think you ought to attend, my lord. *You'll* be the belle of the ball. Everyone in my mama's circle wants to see you; you've made yourself scarce to them. I can't blame you for that, but it makes it an excellent place to bring Daisy. They'll be so busy quizzing you, they won't have a chance to gape at her. She'll be eased into Society and plucked out again before her feet get too wet."

"Very well," the earl said, "If it's for Daisy, I'll do it."

He smiled, and so did Daisy. But Leland, watching them, did not.

"My lord, how kind of you to come to my little soirée," the viscountess said, as the earl bowed to her.

The babble of voices was so loud, Daisy could hardly hear what her hostess said. Still, when Geoff gestured to her, she inclined her head in a brief bow to the viscountess. She didn't like this kind of party any more than Geoff did, but while he knew he'd always be accepted here, she had to find out if she could be.

"Mrs. Tanner," the dowager said coolly. "How lovely you look this evening." She ignored Helena completely, and turned to speak to her son. "Haye," she said, "so you grace us with your presence, do you?"

He bowed. "As you see, Mama."

For a moment there was, in the middle of all that babble, a complete silence among the viscountess, her son, the earl, and Daisy. Then the dowager turned to greet another new arrival.

"It's done," Leland told Daisy as they moved away. "Now, all you have to do is make nonsensical conversation with anyone who speaks to you. Don't worry; no one will talk to you above a minute or two. The idea is to talk to as many people as possible, so you don't miss anything."

"Gads," the earl said.

Daisy looked around. There were masses of people everywhere: on the stairs, in chairs, and standing in groups that kept changing. The men dressed in black, blue, dun, and gray, with only an occasional glimpse of a red waistcoat to liven them up. She was surprised to see so few dandies, tulips of the *ton,* or Corinthians, because she'd expect those paragons of fashion to be at such a party. But most of the male guests were older men, and most were dressed conservatively.

She'd also expected to see gaggles of young women in white, as befit ladies in their first Seasons on the Town, and had wondered if there were any she could speak to since she wasn't that much older herself. But she saw only a few dispirited-looking young girls. There were many more women of a certain age, wearing gowns in every color of the rainbow. Many wore large plumes in their hair that bobbed up and down as they talked, as though they were weird birds of some sort, pecking at something on the ground. And how they talked!

It wasn't hot so much as airless, or loud so much as deafening.

Daisy nodded her greetings to everyone she was introduced to, but none of them seemed interested in her. It was the earl they'd come to see. He was immediately cornered by a pair of old neighbors who kept asking him questions about how he'd been keeping. Then an elderly couple greeted him and told him stories about their son, whom he'd evidently known in his youth. And then a trio of gentlemen, friends from his schooldays, wanted to know if he meant to stay on in London or if he'd visit with them in their country homes.

Daisy found herself standing apart, not knowing what to do. She tried to entertain herself. There was no way to see what the viscountess's home really looked like because of the crowd. She could only see that the ceilings were embossed, gilded, and high. If this was the *ton's* idea of a gala, then Daisy decided she'd prefer a tankard of sudsy beer with a few roistering friends on the beach, like in the bad old days in the colony.

Helena had been lost in the crowd; one moment Daisy had seen her, the next, she'd been swallowed up in the throng of guests. And so all Daisy could do was pretend to be interested as she stood and smiled until her jaw ached and her head swam.

"They've opened the doors to the terrace," Leland said as he appeared out of the crowd and came to her side. "Come along."

She hesitated.

"You look like you need the air," he said. "I realize you want to make a splash, but swooning at a party has been done, and it's *such* a cliché."

Daisy glowered, but put her hand on his arm

and let him lead her away. "Where's Helena?" she asked.

"Hired away by my mother. Carried off by Gypsies. I've no idea. She won't come to harm wherever she is. She might even be enjoying herself; do you begrudge it to her? Ah, here we are," he said without giving her time to answer.

She stopped before a long windowed door, dug in her heels, and glared at him.

"Why do you hesitate?" he asked. "No stigma need be attached to your stealing away with me, at least not here. It's as crowded in my mama's garden as it is indoors, but there's more air there."

She went with him.

The terrace was not as crowded as the salon. It was also not as bright; only a few torches lit the plain, square garden. But though there was enough room for a couple to speak privately, there were no deep shadows where anything illicit could be going on. The whole area was filled with partygoers.

He was right, Daisy thought as she stepped out; at least there was fresh air. She took a deep breath and felt a little better. "Do they really think this is having a good time?" she asked him quietly.

"Yes and no," he said, leaning on the low balustrade of the marble columns that marked off the terrace. "Yes, because if they hadn't been invited, they'd have been crushed. And no, because they *are* being crushed, and that means it was a party they'd have hated to miss. But most of them are too old for this.

"Mama's soirées usually have a broader cross-section of the *ton*," Leland murmured, as his eyes roamed over the guests. "It might mean that she fancies Geoff."

Daisy's head turned around so she could meet his eyes.

"Young women are harder for her to compete with," he said blandly. "You'll note there are few here, which means she wishes to compete. Mama is rich, titled, and however cold at heart, warm of body. Excessively so, to judge by her past record. She's been a widow for a long time. I believe she's bored with it now. *Affaires* of the heart are fine when you're young, but now I think she might prefer someone to sit around the fireside with. And Geoff is rich, titled, intelligent, and good-looking, for his age."

"For his age," Daisy repeated in a fierce whisper. "The man is not eighty. I don't know why you keep going on about his age."

"Don't you?" he asked mildly.

She was still.

His voice softened. "Daisy, my dear," he said quietly, "he isn't ancient but he is nearly twice your age. Why should that rankle? It's only truth. Those years have made him what he is, and he certainly isn't ashamed of them. Why should you be? Oh well, I might as well ask now as ever. What are your intentions?"

She stared at him.

"I know that's what a papa asks of his daughter's suitor, and Geoff's a man whose papa is long gone," Leland explained. "But I have a care for him. As do his sons. They like you; indeed, I do, too."

"Oh," she said, arching an eyebrow. "Such a care for him that you attempt to seduce his friend?"

"How else to find out her intentions?" He laughed. "Not so. I tried for my own reasons. Gloves off then, Daisy, because you and I are too intelligent to hint and feint and bluff, at least at something like this. I'm asking your intentions toward him. Are you merely a friend, or are you angling for more? You must know it's odd for a woman of your youth, beauty, and wealth to be making such a dead set at a fellow like Geoff. Or at least, to give him credit, because he is a remarkable man, for you to do so the minute your feet touched England's soil again. There are other suitable men, and you haven't even tried to meet one. Do you mean to marry him?"

She was as startled by his presumption as by how direct he was. She knew she could slap him and storm off. But she didn't want to create a scene. She darted a glance around. No one seemed to notice them, but if there was a quarrel, they would. She could laugh and say something cutting and witty. But she didn't feel very witty. Or she could pretend to blush and hide her face. That was paltry.

Instead, she could only stare.

His eyes never left hers, and his voice was so soft and confidential that she'd forgotten other partygoers surrounded them, until he'd shocked her. Again he seemed to have woven a net around her, becoming the only person in her immediate world. She had to respond in some way.

"I don't have to answer that," she said.

He shrugged. "No, you don't. But you don't deny it, so that's an answer in itself. So I'll ask another. Are your intentions honorable?"

Now she did laugh. "Yes, of course," she said. "Look, my lord, I come from prison, but I committed no crime. I lived among criminals for years, so I, of all people, know the penalties for mischief. But why would I want to make any? Have you thought of that? I just want to live in peace and tranquillity. That's my goal; those are my intentions."

He leaned back and looked at her with lazy amusement.

"And now I've a question for you," she said. "If Geoff's your good friend, then why are you making such a dead set at me yourself?"

He laughed. "If I knew Geoff was serious about you, my dear," he said softly, "I wouldn't go near you. But I don't know that. Do you?"

She shook her head. "No. But if he was, I'd like it, very much."

"I see. And why don't you think I'm your friend?"

"Because friends don't try to seduce friends."

He laughed again "I can't argue that," he said. "But what better way to make friends?"

Now she knew he was joking. She studied him. Again he dominated the scene and made her forget all others. But why? He was tall, fair, and not very handsome. For reasons she still didn't completely understand, he was also undeniably and utterly desirable. *There!* She'd thought it and wouldn't deny it. It was amazing that he made her feel such stirrings that she'd even *think* about such a thing.

But he was more than seductive. She believed he was, even with his less than honorable intentions toward her, an honorable man. She hadn't met many, but she knew one when she found one. He deserved an answer.

"Geoff was a gentleman to me when no one treated me like a person, much less a lady," she told him. "When I was sixteen I married a man I hated, because it was my father's wish. And, I admit, I was afraid of what would happen to me if I didn't. It was hell. Now I'm free, but I find I'm not. I can't be, without a husband. I don't want *affaires,* or amusements, or a life in the heights of Society. I just want to be left in peace. I want to be loved by a good, decent man and not plagued by others. That's it, that's all, but that's what I want. Now, can you see anything wrong with that?"

It was his turn to study her. Then he looked over her shoulder. "There," he said. "Look there, to your left. That woman in the yellow gown?"

She turned her head to see a brown-haired woman of middle years, with a thick body that showed too plainly in her thin, expensive silken gown. If she hadn't had such a disagreeable expression, she might have been somewhat attractive. But the expression seemed part of her general slumped, disconsolate pose.

"Lady Blodgett married at seventeen," he said softly. "It was a match made by her family, which is not uncommon. She's had four children in the seven years since. I know, as the world does, that she despises her husband, Lord Blodgett."

As Daisy tried to register the fact that the woman was near her own age, Leland went on, "And there, behind her. The lady in scarlet with the improbably red hair? Nothing like the glorious natural sunrise of your own. But do you see the redhead with so many plumes in her hair she looks like a demented macaw? She's the life of every soirée and a dashing and desperate flirt. She was married, at eighteen, by her family's decree, to a man more than twice her age. He's not her love, or anyone else's; he's a thoroughly nasty piece of work. But Lady Blodgett is the one that has affairs, not the chattering macaw. She only drinks her way through every social occasion."

He looked at her again. "I'm sorry, Daisy, but however terrible your circumstances, they weren't unique; you're not the only female ever forced into marriage with a lout. You were in prison, true. But theirs was the prison of convention. Yes, you faced privation. But theirs wasn't an easy path, either. Do you think it matters? Do you think if they'd a second chance, if their husbands keeled over tonight and set them free, that they'd be content with mere *peace* in the future? I doubt it. They'd look for joy. Life is to be lived while it can be, Daisy. Peace comes to all of us sooner or later, the eternal kind. Turmoil isn't all bad, and life can never be lived in peace until you find it for yourself, within yourself."

He stopped, and then surprised her by laughing out loud. "Oh Lord," he said, running a hand over his eyes. "Did you hear that? What claptrap. What right have I to recommend something I've never found?" His eyes were dark as the sky above them as he stared down at her. "But that's what I believe, Daisy. That's what I want to believe."

He shook his head. "And I never even mentioned the best reason for marrying a man of an appropriate age. What an oversight, especially from me! Pleasure in the marriage bed, my dear," he said, bending his head and whispering. "If it's good, it's worth twenty years of peace, any day or night."

She shivered at the feeling of his warm,

whispered breath on her ear. "Do you mean to discourage Geoff about me?"

He cocked his head to the side. "You disappoint me, Daisy; you cut me to the quick. No, I don't. I just wonder if you've thought it through. Because if you decide a decade from now, when Geoff may need you most, that you'd rather play in another bed than sleep in his, you might very well break his heart. I've seen that happen. I've no wish for Geoff to feel what my father did, though I'll allow that I like him much more than I did that sorry old man. My father doubtless deserved what he got, but sometimes I wonder if that didn't make him what he became.

"Mama cuckolded him with a Gypsy, to start, which is how I got my half brother, Daffyd. It didn't stop there. She became more discreet, as well as less fertile, but no more constant. Don't do that to Geoff, whatever you do, Daisy. Because *that,* I couldn't stand, or stand for."

"And all this is for Geoff?" she asked.

"Why no," he said, with a huge smile. "Of course not. It may have been at first, but now? I want you; of course you know that."

She stood a moment, staring at him, and then she sighed. "Well, keep wanting, if it makes you happy."

"The point is, I'd like to make you happy."

"Ha!" she said without humor. "Much luck with that. The best way to do that is to forget your desires. I don't share them, I don't like them, so you might as well cut line, and that's the truth."

"Them?" he asked.

"Don't play the fool, you know exactly what I mean!" she said angrily. "What you were talking about."

He looked puzzled.

"The marital act," she whispered.

He frowned in incomprehension.

"Coupling, having it off, swiving, f— *you know what I'm saying,"* she hissed.

"Oh," he said so blandly, she knew he'd understood right away and had been toying with her. "I see. So why do you want to marry Geoff? He's a vigorous man, and though he plays the doting papa with you, I assure you he is *not* a monk. There's a certain widow in Claridges Street who'd swear, happily, to that, too. She's not the only one. He prefers relationships to encounters, but that's not always possible."

Daisy stared.

"Poor Daisy," he said softly, his eyes caressing her. "You didn't know? If you think he'd be a safe harbor from demands of the flesh, I promise you that isn't so. If you love the man, you'll have to love him body *and* soul. Come, you're no fool. Your late husband was doubtless a beast; that doesn't mean all men are. So many women wouldn't be mad about lovemaking if that were true. *I'd* love to show you why."

"I'm sure you would!" she said, and scowled,

knowing that was a feeble retort. But she had to think about what he'd said as much as about how he made her feel just by being close, before she could come up with something clever. "I'd like to go in now," she said stiffly. "Geoff must be wondering where I am."

"Doubtless," he said calmly, and offered her his arm.

"Excuse me, my lord, but have you seen Mrs. Tanner?" Helena asked the earl breathlessly. "I've been looking everywhere for her."

He broke off the conversation he'd been having, said good-bye to the gentleman he'd been talking to, and took Helena aside. "Don't worry," he said softly. "She's with Haye."

"Not worry?" she gasped. "Being off somewhere with him could be fatal to her reputation!"

The earl laughed. "In the ordinary way, possibly. But not here. I saw them go outside to the garden. Don't worry, rackety he may be, but Leland knows I have her under my wing, and he wouldn't do anything to harm her in any way."

"But being seen alone with him would harm her," Helena insisted.

"He can't be alone with her, because half the party has been out that door in the past half hour, if only to breathe. It is deucedly hot in here. Would you care to come out with me, to find them?"

She shook her head. "Thank you, my lord, but I wouldn't presume. I'll just step out by myself."

"No," he said, taking her hand and putting it on his arm. "Come with me. There's no need for you to go alone." He smiled at her. She wore a neat blue gown with long sleeves, her hair was arranged primly, and the only ornament she wore was a golden locket at her throat. Still, if she hadn't been a companion, he thought, she'd have gotten a companion for herself by now. Helena Masters was a fine-looking woman, and a gentle-spoken, intelligent one, too.

"You take your duties seriously," he said, as they strolled toward the door to the terrace. "That's good but not necessary, here at least. Daisy may be young and inexperienced at social matters, but she's got a fine head on her shoulders."

She nodded. "But the viscount, while a friend of yours, is a man with a certain reputation, and after meeting him, I quite understand how he got it. That's all I worry about."

He stopped. "Never say Lee's got you entranced, too? The man has half the females in London ready to eat crumbs from his hand, but I thought you'd be able to resist him!"

Her eyes crinkled as she smiled, making her look much less severe, transforming her entirely, in fact, he thought. "No, no such luck," she said, laughing. "I haven't been enraptured in many a long year."

"Leland didn't beguile you?" he asked in mock

amazement. "Now, that is too bad. We have to find someone who does. Maybe I'll give it a try. What are you looking for in a gentleman?"

She saw that though he was joking, he was concerned. Her smile became sad. "I look for the impossible, my lord, because no man looks at me."

"Untrue!" he said. "Or if true, ridiculous. At least to me, if only because I've so recently come from a land that, for all its faults, recognizes a man or a woman for who they are rather than for what they're worth in pounds and shillings. You, Mrs. Masters, could name your price in rubies, were you to go to the colony at Botany Bay."

"Really? What do you suggest I steal to get there, then?" she asked.

He'd been smiling, but now his smile was arrested, and he looked at her as though he'd just seen something new in her.

She held her breath.

And then, as though called, he looked up.

Daisy and the viscount were coming back into the room. And then the earl appeared to forget everything except that Daisy was smiling at him.

While everyone else in the room turned to stare at Daisy, with sudden avid interest.

Chapter 13

Leland frowned at his naked knees. Folded up as he was in his bath, he couldn't help seeing them. He had a large tub, but he was larger than most men. His knees were unlovely, but not the source of his rage. He washed quickly, stood up, and took the towel his valet handed him. He stalked into his bedchamber. There were things he had to do this morning, and if he had to hoist people up out of their beds to do it, he would.

"Don't fuss," he told his valet. "This is fine, thank you."

He looked at himself in the glass and considered the result of his hurried toilette: one tall, thin man, dressed in correct morning clothes. His boots shone, his breeches were without a wrinkle, his neck cloth was pristine and tied just carelessly enough to make him the envy of every young blade in town. Much he cared this morning. But everything was as it should be. Except for the long face. He stared at himself in the glass. He looked like a murderer about to select a victim, and fast.

Good, he thought, and strode from the room.

His mother's butler stared at him.

"I'm not a frequent visitor," Leland said in clipped tones. "But surely, you know me. Kindly tell my mama that I wish to speak with her."

The butler took a step back. "Indeed, I know you, my lord, but we were not expecting company this morning. The household went to bed quite late last night, and your mama is still sleeping."

"Doubtless she didn't go to bed until dawn," Leland said. "It makes no matter. I wish to speak with her. *Now.*" When the butler hesitated, Leland added with acid sweetness, "Or would you prefer I wake her myself?"

"I shall bring word to her. If you would care to wait?" the butler asked, showing Leland the salon.

"I would not care to wait above five minutes. Tell her that," Leland said, and went into the room to pace.

It took a full fifteen minutes for the viscountess to come down the stair. Leland was astonished that it took so little time, and realized he must look even more murderous than he felt.

"Haye, what has happened?" his mother said from the doorway.

"I had thought you could tell me that," he said.

She wore a robe over her negligee; her hair was simply dressed, and though she looked well, the morning sunlight wasn't kind to her. It wasn't that she looked ancient, in fact she looked uncommonly young; her fair complexion was smooth even without powder. He supposed that was because she seldom laughed or scowled, and so her skin had remained relatively free of wrinkles. She took constant care of herself; he could still see the faint sheen of whatever cream she used on her skin. But her eyes showed her age: They were cold and too knowing. This morning, the effect of them staring out of her smooth face was unsettling.

"Sit down," she said. "And tell me your grievance. Because now I see it isn't an emergency, it's only that you're angry at something you wish to lay at my door. That's nothing new. But I don't know what crime it is this time. *Do* enlighten me."

He didn't sit, but only stood facing her. "Do you not?" he said. "Odd that you could forget so quickly. It was only last night."

Her cheeks showed a faint flush of pink, but she stared at him defiantly.

"You told everyone about Daisy Tanner while she was out of the room, did you?" he asked, though her reaction had given him his answer. "I only wonder what you told them."

"I?" she said.

"They might have guessed she had been a convict," he went on. "The earl never made a secret of his past, nor did any of his 'sons,' including my brother Daffyd. If your guests heard she was a friend of the earl's from Botany Bay, I imagine they could have supposed as much. But there had to be more to account for the sudden stir she made. We came in from the garden to find she was suddenly the center of attention. The party came to a dead halt, and she was gaped at. No one said a thing to her, but no one looked away. I fancy myself a brave fellow, but even I was taken aback. Obviously someone had said something appalling about her. I'm here to find out what it was.

"She was transported for her father's crimes," he said. "Anyone knowing that might have been shocked, but certainly not so much as they seemed to be last night. We had to get Daisy away before it broke her heart, but I need to know what you did so that I can undo it, swiftly."

"So it's you who has an interest there?" she asked, with what might have been a real smile. "Beware, Haye. If she's the earl's friend, he won't allow you to toy with her. Or you'll be caught. Have you remained single all these years so that you could find a convict bride?"

"*Ex* convict," he said, his dark blue stare as cold as her own. "Lovely footwork, madam, but we are not dancing. What did you tell them?"

She shrugged. "I mentioned she'd been a convict; I spoke of Botany Bay. I didn't know her crimes so I didn't detail them. I merely said she'd been a prisoner in the Antipodes, had married there and now was a widow. A wealthy one. Or so I surmised. Unless the earl has been paying her bills, in which case she was something else as well."

"Well, that makes sense," he said with quiet fury. "Sorrowful sense, but it accounts for why they were aghast. A gentleman doesn't invite his mistress to your soirées, is that it?"

"A *gentleman*," she said icily, "does not take his mistress to any gentlewoman's home. Indeed, he doesn't even invite them to his own. But, of course, you never understood that, did you?"

"That stung, did it?" he asked. "All those years of privation. Was it the fact that you were excluded from your lovers' homes that rankles, or that you couldn't have them at yours?"

She didn't reply.

"It hardly matters," he said. "So, all I have to do is tell your guests and the immediate world what she was in prison for to set matters right. And that she is wealthy enough and principled enough to pay her own way. That's simple. But why did you do it? You think Geoff's going to marry her? Who knows? He may. And why not?

She's bright, charming, and very unlike you in that she's highly moral, thoroughly prim, even prudish."

He strode to the door. "Then, good day, madam. I've work to do, or rather undo."

"Haye?" she said.

He stopped and looked at her.

"Do you really think he means to marry her?"

"I've no idea. Why? Did you think there was a chance he'd marry you? Unthink it, Mama. I believe you terrify him."

"Indeed," she said with a smile of bitter satisfaction. "I see. And what did *you* tell him about me?"

His smile was thin-lipped. "Nothing. That's the truth. What could I say, after all? I can only gossip about people I know. I never knew you, did I?"

He nodded, clapped on his hat, and left her house.

She sat in the salon for long moments, thinking, before she got up and left it herself.

"I don't want to go to any party," Daisy said plaintively. "You can say that you've explained things and eased my way, but I don't want to risk it. Why must I go? Does it mean that much to you, Geoff?" she asked the earl. "I thought you hated the social world."

"I don't hate it, I just . . . avoid it," he said. "I'm past the age for that nonsense. You're not."

They were in his study. He'd called her there to speak with her and asked Helena to wait outside. Daisy thought he'd have some wonderful surprise for her, and had been musing about whether he'd offer her a trip to his estate, or his hand in marriage. Instead, she found Leland there as well, now that he was up and about, he said, he'd spent the morning assuring that she could go back into Society and not be stared at.

"You're young and need diversion, and company," the earl said. "What sort of friends can you make if you're shunned by the polite world? They're not all poseurs and fops, you know."

"Exactly," Leland said sweetly. "Why, just look at me."

"Yes," the earl said seriously, causing Leland to look startled. "Well, face it, Lee, you're welcomed everywhere but you hardly ever go there."

Leland laughed. "That's the rhyme a caricaturist once put on a broadsheet about me," he told Daisy. "It may be true. I love the theater and music, and literature. Where should I find people to discuss such things with? In taverns? With the light ladies I am said to sometimes accompany? I go to parties and gentlemen's clubs as well as to sporting events because I need diverse friends."

"Just so," the earl agreed. "Daisy, you had friends in the Antipodes and I'll wager you miss them. But they wouldn't be suitable for you now. You need women of your position as well as of equal intelligence and wit."

Daisy sat still. "What *is* my position? Do you know? I don't."

"You will," Geoff said enigmatically. "So please reconsider. Especially after Lee has gone to so much effort to make you welcome. Yes, it's another party. And yes, many of the same people will be there. But Lee will have spoken to many of them, too, as will I. You can go without fear of being rejected, I promise."

"I'm not afraid of being rejected!" she said. "Well, I suppose I am. Who wouldn't be worried about being in a room full of people who dislike them? Well, maybe not the viscount," she added, and Leland smiled. "But the point is that I don't want them as my friends. I have you, Geoff."

Leland suddenly lost his smile and looked at her so intently that she lowered her gaze. "And the viscount, of course," she said quickly, "I have Daffyd and . . . Helena, and your other boys when they come to London again. I can talk to them. I never imagined myself flitting around Town from one party to another; that's not my way. I only need a few, good, close friends. I have them. Who needs more?"

"But I'm old enough to be your father, Daisy," the earl said slowly. "I'm hardly a friend, at least not in the context I meant." He looked down at some papers on his desk, and aimlessly moved them from one place to another. Then he looked up and turned the tables. "*Am* I your friend,

Daisy?" he asked softly. "Just what do you think I am to you?"

She darted a glance at Leland, but now his face bore only an expression of polite interest. Drat the man! she thought. She couldn't say anything to make Geoff consider a declaration with him in the room. "That's up to you, Geoff," she said.

He nodded. "So it is," he said. "Well, then, my dear," he said, looking at her with a peculiar expression, half amusement and half wonder. "Will you come with *me* to the party tomorrow night?"

She smiled. "Yes, of course, Geoff."

She looked at the viscount again. He was expressionless. But she rejoiced. She'd won! she thought with barely contained exhilaration. And it hadn't even taken that long. At least, not once she'd seen him again. All those years of dreaming about a kindly, tolerant husband were over. She'd traveled across a sea and halfway around the world to find safe harbor. Now all that was left was to go to the party, listen to Geoff's proposal—for surely he'd have a ring for her or some other family heirloom to seal the compact with by then—and her goal would be met.

She gazed at the earl with fond possession. He looked very well for a man of his years, she thought. He wasn't the sort to make any woman's heart beat faster, but she'd never wanted that. Still, he was fit. He wore tolerably fashionable clothes, which meant they were tight-fitting, and yet she couldn't see a bulging stomach. Though her father had been a similar age when she'd last seen him, Geoff was much more muscular than her father had ever been, and he certainly had more hair.

Then she glanced at Leland and saw rueful knowledge in his eyes. She remembered that he'd said Geoff also acted like younger men, as far as women were concerned. Which meant that he'd want to bed her.

The thought made the blood rush to her face, not in mounting desire, but with embarrassment. Kindly, charming, Geoff wanting her *that* way? The sudden vision she had of him, naked in bed with her, was appalling, repellent, beyond embarrassing. She didn't think of him that way.

In that moment, she could swear the viscount knew what she was thinking. He looked back at her with a deadly serious, sad expression, and nodded as though confirming her thoughts. She quickly turned her attention back to Geoff.

He, at least, was looking at her with warmth and approval, and obvious affection. He wasn't leering, but only smiling, and she realized that now he'd every right to think of her that way. Could she change the way she thought of him? Could she stroke his naked body? Could she relax in his arms as he mounted her? Would he make the same sounds, groaning as Tanner had while he was at it, carrying on like a pig at the trough? The thought was terrifying. Because then how could she ever think of him the same way again?

And unlike Tanner, would he expect her to enjoy it, as Leland had said women should? The viscount had turned her thinking so much, she no longer knew where she stood. She wondered if Geoff's kiss would shatter her defenses as Leland's had. She suddenly felt ill at the thought of sharing a warm, openmouthed kiss with Geoff. She shot to her feet.

"Well, thanks, Geoff," she said in a rush. "You've convinced me to go to the party. And thanks to you too, Viscount. So, should I wear the fantastic gold gown the modiste made for me, or is this less formal? What I mean is, what should I wear, do you think?"

"Whatever you wish. You'll look lovely in a sack, or even without one," Geoff said, laughing to show it was a jest.

He'd meant it as a joke and a compliment, she knew. But Leland didn't laugh, and neither did she. She was suddenly very sorry that he'd said it.

Daisy felt weary and apprehensive.

She hadn't been feeling well since the morning she'd met with Geoff and Leland. Now it was night, and she'd be seeing Geoff again, and maybe now he'd ask the question she'd come so many miles to hear. And for the first time in a long time, she didn't know what to do.

Every step of her life since the day she'd landed in Botany Bay, dazed and hurting in body and spirit, Tanner at her side, had been spent in daydreams and night fancies and dreams of escape.

She'd finally put those plans into action, and now she found herself wanting to escape again.

What would she say when Geoff asked her to marry him? She had to ask for more time. In the long night awake she'd just had, she'd decided to do that. But once he asked, she'd have to at least kiss him; that was only fair. She'd decided in the early hours of the morning that she'd do it, just to see what it was like.

And if it was unbearable?

Then she'd leave London, and go back to where she'd been born and raised, buy herself a cottage, and live alone, with chickens and geese and a dog. No one would bother her there; she wouldn't be ostracized by Society as she'd been in London, or threatened by greedy suitors as she'd been in Port Jackson. There were worse fates. One thing she knew. She'd never put herself into a prison again, whether it was made of laws or iron bars, or her conscience telling her to do her duty.

"I never thought blue would suit you, but that blue is vibrant, and you do look lovely," Helena said, as she gazed at Daisy in her new gown.

"It's the gold trim," Daisy said absently. "You look lovely, too. Red becomes you."

"It's too fast a color for a companion," Helena said. "I'll just go change."

"You won't," Daisy said. "I won't allow it. I'm a terrible employer, aren't I? Never mind. Wear it because you look good in it. Now, let's go downstairs; Geoff and the viscount are probably waiting. But one thing, Helena: If I meet that wall of eyes again, if people start whispering about me, I'm leaving. At once. Understood?"

"If they stare, it will be in wonder, because you're very attractive," Helena said. "If they whisper, it will be because you've been seen with the earl and the viscount, and gossips will be alerted. Because one is known for his flirts, and the other is never seen with a woman. They'll wonder which of them is the one you're involved with."

"Does going to a soirée with someone automatically mean you're involved with them?'

"With that pair of gentlemen?" Helena said. "Yes."

Well, so she was, or would be, or couldn't be, Daisy thought. She raised her head and went out the door. It was time to find out which of those fates hers would be.

But Geoff wasn't downstairs waiting for her. Only Leland, looking cool and self-possessed, and incredibly attractive in his severe black and white evening clothes.

"The earl had some last-minute business to take care of," Leland said. "He said he'd meet us there. So, ladies, I'm a very lucky man because I'm your sole escort tonight. Unless, of course, the idea appalls. Then I'll simply go hang myself in some convenient dark corner."

Helena laughed.

Daisy frowned. Did that mean Geoff had second thoughts? Maybe it meant he had to go somewhere to get that family heirloom so he could give it to her when she said yes. She frowned, wondering if that was what she would answer.

"Mrs. Tanner is obviously of two minds about it," she heard Leland say.

"No," she said, raising her head. "Thank you, we're grateful to you."

He bowed. "Thank you for that," he said. "Now, ladies, let's go dazzle them."

Daisy hesitated only at the last minute. They stood in the doorway, looking into a crowded ballroom, waiting for the butler to announce them. She held her breath.

"Don't worry," Leland said at her ear. "If they seem stiff when they look at you, it's only because they're afraid—of me. I can rake up old coals they'd rather not be roasted with. And so I told them. Courage."

Daisy nodded. When she heard her name announced, she stepped forward. She couldn't go more than two steps. Because she was swarmed.

"That's the only word I can use!" she told Leland an hour later, when he took her into the courtyard out back of the town house so she could breathe. "*Swarmed.* 'Oh, Mrs. Tanner, do you remember me?' " she quoted, laughing. "And, 'Dear Mrs. Tanner, how good to see you again!' when I don't remember ever seeing them in the first place. What did you threaten them with? What crime could they have committed that was so bad that they'd grovel—yes, *grovel* to get my attention? You'd have to beat me with chains to get me to do that, and I don't think I would even then!"

She subsided to giggles and sank down to sit on the wide marble lip of an ornamental fish-pond. "Oh, Lord! How could I have taken them seriously?" Her face grew grave. She looked up at him. "I know you threatened them. But I was a convicted criminal; surely they can't forget that."

Leland sat next to her. "They don't forget it, but they excuse it. Anyone would. Your crime was being a good daughter. Your punishment far exceeded the crime. It was a travesty of justice."

She shrugged. "Maybe. But people are hanged every day for less. I was lucky. I didn't stay in Newgate long, and I lived to get to Botany Bay. The only unlucky thing was having to marry Tanner."

"Geoff said he was a brute; Daffyd agreed," Leland said softly, conversationally, not wanting to break her mood when she was in such a confiding frame of mind. "What else? I know it's not my place to ask. But you could answer, if only because it might make you feel better, and I do want to know."

"Why?" she asked, turning her head to look at him, all traces of her hilarity gone.

"Because I like you," he said simply.

He sat so close to her, she could feel the warmth

of his hard thigh at her side through her thin gown. They were far enough away from the other guests to be alone, and yet not so far as to provoke a scandal. They could be seen, but only in silhouette. It was a cool, azure night; the moon was full and the sky free of clouds. The sounds of the party were in the background; the burbling of the fountain that fed the fishpond was the loudest thing they heard. It was curiously intimate, while being public. They could speak freely and not be overheard.

"Do you like me?" she asked. "Maybe you do. All right, I'll tell you. Why not? What did Tanner do? What he could, and that was a lot. He didn't like me much. But he didn't like anyone much. He did like having a woman and other men envying him for it. What else? I used to count up his virtues when I was feeling particularly blue, so I could get through another day.

"On the good side," she said, holding up one gloved hand and counting off on her fingers. "He wasn't a bad-looking man. I suppose it would have been worse if he looked disgusting. But he didn't. He was a little heavyset, to be sure, but men can carry extra weight. He was ginger-haired and had blue eyes. He wasn't a beau, but he wasn't ugly. That's a point in his favor, I suppose. He saved me from having to accommodate a lot of men; he told me that all the time. He did legally marry me, which I suppose he didn't have to do. And he became rich.

"On the bad side," she said, holding up her other hand. "He had a terrible temper, little learning, and no use for more. He had no talent for conversation, at least with women. He never read, though I think he could, and he didn't like to bathe. He cheated at cards, and hit people who couldn't hit back. When he drank he got meaner, and he drank a lot. He ate with his fingers, and spit wherever he chose. He couldn't have children; he hinted as much once when he was drunk and had the sobbing staggers—you know, when you drink so much you think everything's a misery? Lucky for me he forgot the next morning; he'd never forgive me knowing he couldn't father a brat. Although that might be one on the good side, I never decided. And I've run out of fingers."

She folded her hands in her lap and looked at them. "I hated him, pure and simple," she said in a harsh whisper. "The best day in our marriage was the day they came to tell me he was dead, gone over his horse's head and landed on his neck, breaking it. I cried. Because I was so glad. I lived in fear of him every minute of every hour of every year. I was his wife and his slave, and there was no way I could get even. So I celebrated when he died. Surely that's a sin."

Leland took one of her hands. "I'm sorry," he said.

"Only that?"

"What more can I say? I'm really sorry. You deserved better. You'll have it in future, if you remember that Tanner was an exceptionally bad man, and most men aren't remotely like him."

"So you think I can't be happy in future without a man?" she asked haughtily, snatching her hand from his.

"Don't you think that? Isn't that why you came back to England? Or would you prefer to live alone?"

"You *still* want to know if I'm trying to snare Geoff," she said angrily, bounding to her feet.

He rose slowly and caught her hand. "Do you still know?" he asked.

She stared up at him.

"Geoff's not your father, and he's not Tanner. He's a warmhearted, gentle man. Are you looking for that? If so, fine. But if you're not sure . . . Daisy," he said suddenly, "you should be sure. That's all I can say."

"But that's not all you *will* say," she said bitterly.

"Of course not," he said with a tilted smile. "You know me well. But why should it matter to you?"

She hesitated.

"Daisy Tanner," he said quietly, in a slow soft voice, his gaze locked on hers, "what I'd like to do now is take you in my arms and kiss you senseless. Not with violence, but with slow pleasure. I'd like to kiss you and hear you ask me to do it again. Not for my pride, but because I'd want to, again and again. I'd like to make love to you, with you knowing that you could stop it at any time you wished. I'd like to show you that you wouldn't want to.

"Unfortunately," he said in his normal dry, mocking tones, "we can be seen from the house, and if we were seen embracing it would be a scandal. Pray do *not* get a mote in your eye, or we'll find ourselves affianced. I don't want to force you to anything. But know this," he said in a softer voice, "you wouldn't run from me. *That,* I promise."

"You're very sure of yourself," she said with a shaky laugh.

"No, of you," he said. "You've bottled up too much for too long. You were meant for pleasure, and somehow, somewhere, you know it. Think of that when you think of your future, Daisy. That's all I ask. For your sake, and for the earl's."

"And yours," she said flatly.

"Of course," he said.

Chapter 14

Daisy didn't sleep well. Or rather, she thought bitterly when she woke, she slept too well in imaginary arms. She wondered how something that could feel so good in her dreams could make her shiver with fright when she woke and remembered it.

Pest of a man! she thought as she dressed. To intrude in her dreams the way he did in her life. What was he, after all? Take away that seductive voice, and all you'd have would be a tall, thin man with too many airs. No, she admitted, you'd also have those compelling blue eyes, that warm mouth, and that crooked smile. And that sudden wit, and slow drawl that made you think he'd never say anything important, until you found yourself helplessly laughing at the funny side of the truth he'd just shown you.

He also seemed to know things she'd rather not know about herself. And worst of all, just when everything was going right for a change, he'd come along and put a kink in her plans.

"You're not seeing the earl today?" Helena asked in surprise, when Daisy told her the plans for the day.

"No," Daisy said.

She turned her head to see how the short plumes on the side of her new hat curled against her cheek. "Isn't this dashing? Red feathers! I hope it doesn't rain. The hat cost a fortune. I could have had three whole peacocks for that price, and yet these look like dyed chicken feathers to me. Oh well, whatever they are, they look darling, especially with this new gown, don't they?"

She didn't mention that she'd decided to dress all in red the moment she saw the dashing woman the viscount had pointed out to her at the party in his mother's town house. She'd make him stare at *her*, this time, Daisy thought smugly. Her gown was crimson. It had long sleeves and a proper skirt; the neckline was no more low cut than was fashionable, but the color alone made her feel outrageous. She didn't want to be pawed. But she was woman enough to want to feel as though a man might long to touch her.

She turned from the looking glass. "I thought

I'd just spend the day shopping, getting things I need, maybe look at some of the town houses that are to let."

Helena stood staring at her.

Daisy shrugged. "I don't have to see Geoff every day, you know," she said. "Anyway, I think things have been moving at too fast a pace since I set foot in London. I came here, landed myself on poor Geoff, and haven't given him room to breathe since."

"I thought you wanted that," Helena said softly.

"I did. But now I need time to think things over, make decisions, and such. I think better when I'm doing something. I've no dinner to make or chores to do, so I hope walking and shopping will do it for me now."

Helena grew still. "Decisions to make? Has the earl asked for your hand?"

"No," Daisy said with a scowl. "He hasn't."

"Then why look at houses to let? Surely . . ." Helena took a deep breath. "Surely you know he will propose, or so it seems to me. So why look at houses to let unless you want to make a new home with him? But why? His town house is beautiful. Anyone would be happy there." She ducked her head. "I'm sorry, that's really not my business. Please excuse me for asking."

"No need to apologize," Daisy said, as she drew on her gloves. "My intentions weren't a secret. The truth is, I don't know what I thought

I knew, and I'm not sure of what I should say or do one way or the other. I'm at a standstill, Helena, and that's new to me. That's what comes from never having to decide anything important for so long. First my father did the thinking for me and then Tanner did. I think deciding's a thing you have to practice in order to be good at."

"I'd think it was simple," Helena persisted. "You obviously care for the earl. He obviously cares for you. Daisy. I know I presume, but I must. The earl's a wonderful man; anyone would be lucky to be the center of his attention. What's happened to change your mind?"

Leland Grant, Daisy wanted to say. *Things he said. Things he made me feel. The things he makes me feel even when I'm alone in my bed in the night. Things that used to frighten me, but now make me curious. Promises of pleasure in his eyes and at his hands and mouth that make me begin to feel things I thought were numbed forever, heart, soul, and body, of course body. He's wakened this suddenly bothersome body of mine. The way what he said is right, at least in that I'd have to be more than available, I'd have to be happy in Geoff's bed. It would only be fair. And I don't know I could be. I love Geoff, just not the thought of touching him and having him touch me.*

But she couldn't even say that aloud.

Daisy frowned and said instead, "It's a big step. I need time to think about it. So . . . Bother!" she exclaimed. She wrinkled her nose and blew a breath from the side of her mouth to set the red feathers by her cheek trembling. "It tickles. I don't need to fly; why do I need feathers? Oh well, it's on, and too much trouble to take off. Now, shall we go to buy a new hat that doesn't make me want to sneeze? Or should we buy some ribbons, or lace, slippers, hair pomade, violets, or melons?" She laughed. "See? There's too much choice in everything for me these days!"

"Is there anything you'd like to talk over?" Helena asked seriously. "I'm just a paid companion, and when you wed I'll be on my way to a new position. But I might be able to clear up a few matters for you. I was married, and happily, for ten years. I have two children I adore. I've been alone, unhappily for the most part, for five years. So I have experience in making choices. I'd be glad to listen to anything, help with anything you want to share with me."

"I know," Daisy said. "Thank you, but this is something I have to ask myself. Now. The Pantheon Bazaar for fripperies? The flower market for fun? Or do we go to a rental agent, so I can see what I could get for my money if I decide to go it alone? That might be interesting."

"Wherever you wish," Helena said stiffly.

"Oh, don't get formal with me!" Daisy cried in exasperation. "Listen. It makes sense. I *hated* being married. I do like Geoff. But I just don't know if I want a husband anymore. I mean, I always dreamed of having a decent man for a husband, a gentleman, someone who'd advise me and protect me and keep me safe, the way my father never did. That's what I thought when I stood on the shingle in Botany Bay all those years, staring out to sea, dreaming of the day I might be free. Now I am. And I have money. I have freedom to do whatever I choose. I never thought of that. So maybe I'd be best off if I just stayed Geoff's friend, and lived for myself. Yes, go ahead and stare. I know that's shocking. But that's what I'm thinking right now."

Helena shook her head. "I can't think of anything better than being married to a good, kind man who loves you."

"Well, I can!" Daisy snapped. "And that's trouble, isn't it? Or maybe it's just that I've got cold feet, here at the last. It's one thing to dream something, another when it actually starts going your way. I never made a choice for myself, not in all my life, not until my husband died. Now I can make decisions, and I don't want to make mistakes, because I'll have only myself to blame this time. It's easy to heap blame on someone else for your unhappiness. I know, I've done it most of my life, and rightly so. Now I have to bear that burden myself. I just don't know what to do. Time is what I need, and time I have. Come along, we can talk as we walk. I'm itching to be out, doing *something*."

She opened the door to see the hotel manager,

hand uplifted, poised to knock on it. It was hard to say which of them was more surprised. The manager was clearly more embarrassed. There was a stocky man in sober clothes, with a bright red vest, standing next to him; he stared at Daisy.

"Ah, Mrs. Tanner," the manager said, bowing. "Good morning. I was just coming to summon you. This is Mr. Robert Burrows, from Bow Street. He said he has business with you, and though I told him to wait below stairs," he continued with a sniff, "he insisted on coming with me."

"They hear the words 'Bow Street' and they flit," the man explained. "So it's best to collar them in their dens."

Daisy sniffed, too, and raised her nose in the air. "A Runner. I could smell him a mile away. Well, cully, what do you want with me?"

"Mrs. Daisy Tanner?" the Runner asked, his eyes narrowing as he looked at her. "I got a warrant for your arrest here," he said, tapping his vest pocket.

Daisy went totally still. "For what?"

"For the suspected murder of your husband, James Tanner," he said. "At His Majesty's penal colony at Botany Bay, in Port Jackson, that's what."

Daisy's face went ashen. Her legs grew weak; she put out a hand to lean against the door. Then she drew herself up.

"It isn't true," she said. "I didn't do it; it was an accident. I'm not going anywhere. Helena, send for Geoff. And the Viscount Haye; send for him, too. And, oh yes, my solicitor, the one I saw when I came to London. Ronald Arbus is his name; it's there in those papers on my desk. I'm not going anywhere," she snarled at the Runner. "I have money, and so I guess I have enemies, but they're not getting it or me. I'm staying right here."

"You don't have to go to Bow Street," the earl said as he paced. "I've friends in high places. I gave my word as your bond. You will stay in London, won't you?" he asked, looking up at Daisy.

She nodded. They were in his town house. She sat in his study and felt as though she were already in a witness chair. Her hands were clenched to fists in her lap. Geoff was pacing; Leland stood by a window and watched her, unblinking. Helena sat nearby, looking as though she might break into tears at any moment.

"I won't run," Daisy said. "Because I didn't do anything."

"Oh well, that," the earl said. "Of course."

"I know everyone says that they're not guilty," Daisy said angrily. "But I mean it. Tanner went riding, well, racing is what he was doing, to win a wager with a mate of his. He came back dead as the door they carried him in on. His horse shied and bucked. Everyone said so. I was home, making dinner for him, where he expected me to be every day. So who says I did it? Or anything?"

"A complaint has been laid against you," the earl said. "An accusation. They say it was an accident, but claim that you were complicit in it."

"What?" Daisy exclaimed. "They think I ran to where he was, stood by the side of the road, and waved my hands at his horse?"

"No," Leland finally said. "They claim you put a burr under the saddle."

"Well, it took them long enough to say it!" Daisy said. "Now, when there's no way anyone can look to see. Why would I do that? A burr under the saddle? That's rich, that is. If I wanted to be rid of Tanner—and I did—I'd have done it where I could watch to make sure it was done right. I thought about it, many times. Lord! Setting a burr under his saddle? What good would it do if he fell off his horse and only broke something? He'd give me the devil of a time when he so much as got a bellyache; if he had a broken leg, it would pain me more than him. He'd break my head if he even thought I'd done such a thing. It's a lie. And they can't prove it."

"Possibly not," Geoff said. "But they can pay someone to swear to it, and that's what worries me. Well, you know the type of people we lived among in Port Jackson, Daisy."

"I do," she said. "And I know they weren't all

bad. No one wants to get the name of a rat, neither, Geoff. You know that!"

"Possibly," he said. "But there's more. Everyone knew you hated Tanner; you never made a secret of it. That gets them a foot in the door."

"Possibly?" Daisy echoed, seizing on the first thing he'd said. "Oh, Geoff. I didn't break Tanner's neck for him, but you saying that? You fair break my heart, you do."

He came to her and took her hand. "I don't think you did anything, Daisy. I'm just saying the road ahead may be rocky."

She slowly withdrew her hand and raised her head. She glanced over at Leland, and caught her breath on a stifled sob. "My life's been rocky. I'm used to that. I didn't do Tanner in, though I'll never deny I wished I could. So does that mean they can put me in prison again? Or send me back to Botany Bay?"

She sat straight in her chair, clearly afraid, looking desperate but proud, like a queen on her way to the tumbrels. Or so Leland thought. Her flaming hair and outrageously red gown accentuated the fact that her complexion was too white, and her eyes too bright. She was crestfallen at the moment, but there was something unquenchable about her fire. She was all spirit and rage, and he thought, yes, she could kill a man if she had to, but not by such a craven scheme as putting a burr under his saddle. She would, he thought, warn the fellow first and then, if she had to, yes, she might well put a bullet through him or cut out his heart. But only if she or someone she loved was in danger, and she had no other way to stop it.

"So who is my accuser?" Daisy asked.

"Bow Street will not divulge the name," Leland said. "Yes, I know, I asked, and so did the earl, but that they're adamant about."

"Because they're afraid I'd kill the fellow!" Daisy said with a sniff. "Well, I wouldn't, you know. *Him*, I'd try to maim."

Leland laughed.

"I would," she said, looking at him. "Of all the low tricks! No one, not anyone in all of Port Jackson, ever said a thing like that. And I had those who didn't like me. Well, no one's perfect, and I'm certainly not. I didn't like Morrison, our butcher, for example. I hated him because he charged too much, and put his hands on rumps and breasts that were no part of his business or his merchandise, and so I told him, and everyone, you can be sure.

"And there was Mrs. Coleman," she said. "Now, there was a criminal! She poisoned two husbands and never denied it. Not because they were cruel, though they might have been, but for their money. She only got free because she married a guard. I wouldn't ever take tea with that one, and so I said."

She stopped and looked down. "I said things too freely, I suppose. Not about those two, believe me! But about others, yes, I might have done. I was unhappy, and unhappy people try to make others feel the same way. I should have been more charitable. That doesn't make me a murderess!" she said, looking up at their faces.

They looked at each other, and they didn't smile.

She swallowed hard. "I know more about the law than most females, from being exposed to it so young and so often. But doesn't my accuser have to face me in court?"

"So he would," the earl said. "But we don't believe it will ever come to that."

"Why not?" Daisy asked. She frowned as the men exchanged looks again. Leland, looking more tense and sober than she'd ever seen him; Geoff, growing a little red around the ears.

"I'll tell you later," the earl said evasively. "If it even comes to that."

"For now," Leland said abruptly, "we need you to relax, settle down, and make a list of anyone you think might mean you harm. *Anyone,*" he said. "First, from the days before your father was arrested. Someone had to inform on him. We'll search the old records, but we'd like to know who you think that might have been. Include anyone you may have met in Newgate prison who might bear a grudge, and anyone similarly bent that you can remember from the ship that brought you to Botany Bay. We'd also like a list of those you knew from then on, of course. That will give us something to work with."

"We need to know who did this to you," the earl said.

Daisy's eyes widened. "Will they be able to put me in Newgate again?" she asked again. She frowned to hear her voice shake.

"No," Leland said. "Not while I live."

"Nor I," the earl agreed.

She nodded, relieved. Then she raised her head. "You know, actually, I don't think my accuser is anyone we know from those bad days, Geoff. Because, say I was put in jail: Even if I were transported again, who'd profit? What good would it do them? They couldn't get my money. So why bother? Convicts don't like courts, do they, Geoff?" she asked, like a child in the night wanting to be told there was nothing in her darkened wardrobe but imagination. "Don't you remember?"

"Yes," he said. "But they could easily pay someone else to broach the suit for them."

"I see," she said, thinking hard. "It could even be someone who never did anything bad, someone who just didn't want me getting too close to you, Geoff. Or you, my lord," she said, looking straight at Leland.

The earl stared at her. Leland put his head to side as he considered her.

"Well, you two foisted me off on Society," she said. "There are high sticklers who could be mighty mad that you introduced a common convict to the cream of the *ton.* They mightn't like having to rub elbows with such as me, whether I was guilty or not. Accusing me of a murder is just the kind of sneaking, rotten, rancid thing a person like that would do."

"So it would be," the earl said, exchanging a look with Leland.

"So it *might* be," Leland said sharply. He seemed, for the first time since she'd known him, agitated, all his customary lazy good humor vanished. "It's all conjecture. I must get some real investigation started. So I have to leave now. There are people to speak to, and more to be threatened. Mrs. Masters?" he said through tightened lips. "If I might see you outside for a moment?"

Helena looked surprised.

"Not to worry," Leland assured her, more gently. "No one suspects you of anything. I just need to speak with you, alone."

Helena's expression cleared. "Of course, my lord," she said quietly. "I'll be just outside, Daisy," she said, and went to the door.

Leland followed.

Daisy found herself alone, with Geoff. Then, and only then, did she suddenly understand the unspoken conversation he'd had with the viscount, as clearly as if she had heard it.

"Oh, by all that's holy," she muttered, putting her hand to her forehead. "Now I've done it. I've gone and forced your hand, haven't I?"

"No, Daisy," the earl said, as he came to stand before her. "You've gone and made me realize that I should ask for your hand, and not dilly-dally anymore."

"That's what I meant," she said miserably.

Chapter 15

"No one can touch you if you're my wife," the earl told Daisy. "There'd be no more talk of murders and such nonsense."

He hesitated. "I promise you won't be prosecuted for Tanner's death, but . . . I'd like to know. Just between the two of us, and I'll never speak it again. You had just cause, and I couldn't blame you, and wouldn't. But . . . you didn't have a hand in it, did you?"

"Oh, Geoff," she said sadly.

"I'm sorry I asked, but I had to," he said, his face becoming ruddy. "But think on, if you'd been me, you would have done it, too."

"Likely," she said. She looked around the room and sighed. The bookcases were filled with heavy, beautifully covered tomes. She didn't doubt he'd read them all. It was the room of a rich and educated man. Geoff was proposing marriage to her, but for the first time since she'd met him, that prospect had never seemed farther away.

"So," he said, smiling again. "Give me your answer and I'll arrange all the details. My dear Daisy, will you marry me? I confess that I mightn't have had the audacity to ask a woman half my age for her hand, but it's clear now that you need me. We'll deal very well together, I think, and you'll never have to worry again."

He hit his forehead with his hand. "Ridiculous proposal! Where's the romance. Where's the drama? I ought to have brought flowers, or jewelry. But I never thought I'd actually ask. I've been thinking about this for some days now. Only a crisis like this could have forced me into it, though, and I admit, I've never been happier that it did. It seems the right thing to do for both of us. I may be too old, but not if you don't think I am. We might even be able to start a new family. That *will* be odd—having a child my grandchildren's age. But we won't be the first or last to do something like that. I'm old"—he chuckled—"but not incapable. And never fear! You know my boys, Christian, Amyas, and Daffyd. And they know you. They won't mind; in fact, they'll be glad, I think."

He put an arm around her waist, the other

went to the back of her neck, and he started to draw near. He was tentative and gentle. He smelled of good shaving soap. But as he neared she could see how weathered his skin was, and that he had a few freckled blotches on his forehead. He had fine eyes, but there were lines around them, as well as those furrows that ran down from the sides of his nose to the sides of his mouth. She saw he was looking at her lips, and his own parted. She closed her eyes. He touched her mouth gently with his.

His mouth was warm and dry, and felt so terribly wrong, she wanted to weep. Her stomach seemed to do a little flip. She shuddered and pulled away.

He dropped his arms and drew back, looking at her with concern.

Daisy looked into his face. It was a dear face to her. So she had to place her words as carefully as she could. "Geoff," she said softly. "No. It won't do. I like you very much. The truth is, I came to England with just this in mind. I guess you knew that; everybody did. But do you know why? It's because you made such an impression on me when I met you. Remember? You were a prisoner, dressed like the others, but you stood out. Everyone listened to what you said. You did the books for the governor! Even Tanner didn't have a bad thing to say against you. Then you were free, but you were still nice to me. Some days, when I was feeling especially beaten down and trapped, I'd see you, and you always had a smile and a comforting word for me. You were such a gentleman, you made me start dreaming of coming back home one day and meeting a world full of men like you.

"Now here I am, and you're still a gentleman. And you're asking what I wanted to hear. But now I know it's not right. It couldn't be, though you *would* be the one to ask in order to set me free again. Geoff, it wasn't a romantic proposal because it couldn't be. We're not in love. I like you very much but I don't like to think of being in bed with you, or with any man. Thing is, I don't know if I ever can."

His expression was instantly one of deep concern.

She nodded. "See, when you were the pattern card of my dreams, that seemed fine, because I thought you wouldn't care." She paused; there was no way she could tell him that had been because of how old he was. "But now I know that wouldn't be fair to the real man I'm talking to," she said instead. "So thanks, Geoff, but marriage between us wouldn't be right."

"Because I'm so old?" he asked.

Trust him to come right out with it. She thought about her answer. "No," she finally said in all truth. "Actually, because you're not as old as I thought you'd be."

"Ah!" he said. "I think I see." He stepped back. He didn't seem crushed, or relieved.

She suddenly wondered if this proposal was just Geoff doing what he thought was the right thing. It would be very like him.

"So, what are you going to do?" he asked.

"Fight," she said, with a shrug. "I didn't kill Tanner. They can't prove anything because there's nothing to prove. I'll stay on here in England and make a nice, quiet life for myself. Maybe I'll look for a ninety-year-old man," she added, on a laugh.

"You would tempt him, too," the earl said. "But I'm not taking back my proposal. That may be the only way you can really be safe now. They would not deport the wife of an earl with so little evidence. They'd be reluctant to even lay charges, especially about something that happened in another time and place. As it is, they might not be able to do more than frighten you, which, poor girl, they've done too well. But remember, there are enough corrupt souls back in the colony who'd lie for nothing, not to mention a sum of money. It would only take one or two to swear to your misdeeds to make enough of a case to have you brought to trial, here, or as I think they'd prefer, there. You might never be convicted, but it's a long journey there and back again, as you know. Someone would like to make you vulnerable again."

"For my money," she breathed.

"Yes, I think so. You're beautiful, but few men go to such trouble for beauty as they will for money."

She laughed. "Too true! But I can't go wrecking your life for my neck, can I? That's just the kind of thing my father would do. I aim to be different. Can't you be my friend and put in a word for me here, even if we don't marry?"

She stood in sunlight, and he couldn't say whether it was that, or the very fact of her presence, that made the rest of his study look dark. She was at that moment so lovely, so fragile and helpless-looking, that he wished he could say or do anything to make her agree to marry him. It shocked him. He'd only asked her because he'd thought she needed him. Now, for the first time, he realized that he wanted something as bright and beautiful as she was in his life. He'd only looked forward to his grandchildren before. Now he realized he himself had a life left to live.

"Of course I can, and I'll remain your friend," he told her. "Please remember, I'd never do anything to harm you or frighten you." He coughed, and his face became ruddy again. "If you didn't want to have marital relations, I could wait until you did. That wouldn't be a tragedy. I'm a grown man and not a slave to my appetites. Who knows? With time and with confidence, and confidence in me as well, it might be a thing you could come to—if not want, precisely—then accept. And after that, in time, you could come to actually enjoy it. It's truth, believe it or not."

He put up a hand. "I know, it sounds impossible now, but think about it. Don't worry that I'll keep asking you to marry me, either, because I won't. But should you change your mind, I'm here. I always will be, for you. Now, in the meanwhile," he said more briskly, "stay close. We can be friends, if not lovers, so don't be embarrassed or shy with me. Let's pretend I didn't offer what I did, while remembering what it was I offered."

He laughed so that she could. "And don't go on any long trips, or with any strangers," he warned her. "Send to me if anything unusual happens. We'll keep investigating."

"*We?*" she asked. "Oh! You and the viscount. And that's what you two were wigwagging your eyebrows about, right? He knew you were going to ask me to marry you, in order to protect me?"

"Let's say he knew, and leave it at that," the earl said wryly. "He'll be surprised at the outcome. It won't be my manly attributes he'll think you didn't appreciate, but he'll be shocked that you turned down my offer. I *am* one of the wealthiest men in England now, and he, I'm afraid, is too cynical. This may actually help set him straight and show him all women aren't interested only in a fellow's money and titles. But yes, we'll be working together on your problem. If my boys were here, they'd do the same. It might be that we can stop it here and now."

"I hope so!" she said, and turned to leave.

"And remember," he added, "my offer stands."

She looked back at him. "It stands even though

I won't lie down for you?" she asked with an attempt at humor.

"Even though," he said. "I'm not Tanner. I could never be. You have to learn to stop thinking of him and the things he did. Give it time."

"I know," she said. "Still, it's not a matter of thinking anymore, it's part of me. But Geoff? You are a true friend."

He bowed. "I will always be one. Depend on it."

"I'll remember," she promised.

"And you'll continue to see London with me?" he asked. "We've tickets for the theater tomorrow night."

"I look forward to it," she said.

He opened the door for her, and she stepped out, feeling terrible and wickedly ungrateful and relieved, all at once.

Helena was standing in the hallway, talking to Leland. They both looked up. Daisy's gaze flew to Leland. His blue gaze locked on hers, sober and cold. His face was unsmiling, his long body, tensed. She didn't know what expression she wore, but she knew she wasn't smiling. Neither was Geoff. Leland looked puzzled. Helena, surprised.

"We're leaving now," she told Helena. "Good day," she said to Leland, and then, quickly as she could, she stepped out into the sunshine again, and breathed deep.

"You've a guest waiting in the lobby," Helena said.

Daisy was sitting curled up in the window seat, in her dressing gown, looking down, watching London wake up to a new day. "You know I can't ask anyone to come up until I know who it is," she said.

"It's Viscount Haye."

Daisy frowned. "Here? Now? This early? That's peculiar. Unless he's on his way home from a party. That makes more sense. Did he send a message?"

Helena looked at the card in her hand. "He asks to speak with you."

"Then it's probably an impostor," Daisy said, turning back to the window again. "He never asks, he orders. Did you know how right you were? No lady walks out at this hour. There's not one in the street. There are lots of maids and vendors, nannies and nursemaids and such, and ladies riding down to the equestrian paths in the park, but not one lady on foot. You said most don't rise until noon, and I thought you were joking. But there's not one in sight, and it looks like a glorious day. Sheep, that's what the ladies of London are. I'm glad I'm not one of them." *Or ever going to be one,* she thought, and fell still.

"This is the viscount's card," Helena said. "And the manager has been warned and wouldn't disturb you if he thought it was an impostor. I think you ought to go down and see what he wants."

Daisy shrugged. "I'll have to get dressed."

"He says that he expects to see you in ten minutes."

Daisy sat upright. "Now *that* sounds like him." She went quickly to her wardrobe. "I'll just drop a gown over my head. What shall I wear? The rose or the new yellow sprigged muslin?"

Daisy was wearing a new yellow gown as she went down the stairs ten minutes later. The gossamer skirts floated and drifted behind her, making her feel young and light. She'd wanted to wait and be late, just to show him she could be. But she decided against it. She was bursting with curiosity.

Leland didn't look as though he'd come from an all-night party. He was dressed in correct morning clothes. He looked elegant and amused, as ever. His hair was still damp from morning ablutions; his face was freshly shaven, his eyes bright and clear. He was wide-awake in every way.

"Good morning," he said, bowing to Daisy and Helena. He eyed Daisy's gown with approval. "Very nice, indeed," he murmured. "Despite the cliché, I must say that you look fresh as your namesake. It's good to see you haven't adopted Town hours. I wanted to speak with you without multitudes hovering nearby. That let out most of my usual haunts: soirées, musicales and parties, and the theater. But we can go for a stroll in the fresh morning air. Will you come for a walk with me?

"Helena," he said, "I know your devotion to duty and it is commendable. But if you don't mind, I'd rather you didn't follow *too* closely. I need some privacy with Daisy. There are things of a delicate nature I wish to say."

Lud! Daisy thought; he was going to give her hell for turning Geoff down. Well, she could face it, in fact, welcomed it, because she felt bad about it herself.

"If that meets with her approval," Helena said primly.

"It's fine with me," Daisy said. "I like the morning. I know you're probably used to seeing it the other way 'round, my lord, from the night as it turns into day. But I always liked morning best. You get to breathe the air before everyone else gets to it."

"When I'm in the countryside I rise when I'd be going to bed in London," he said, taking her hand and placing it on his sleeve. "There's really not much else to do at night in the country," he added, "unless you have company."

She laughed out loud. "Now *that* sounds like you. I was beginning to wonder if someone was posing as you."

"So pleased to have relieved your mind," he said as they went out to the street. "Believe it or not, it was an inadvertent double entendre. But a good one," he mused. "I must remember it."

They walked on toward the park, Helena a discreet few paces behind them.

"As I thought," he said when they went through the park gates. "No one who knows anyone is out this early. Oh, some rugged young men and women are doubtless galloping hither and yon. But they use the equestrian gates, and go deep into the park. We're just going to promenade on its perimeters. Helena, would you like to feed the ducks? They look ravenous. Or maybe you'd prefer to rest on that bench over there? I'll just stroll on 'round the lake with Daisy. Nothing dreadful will transpire. Even *I* can't think of a way to disgrace or dishonor her here."

Helena smiled. "I'd love to sit and enjoy the morning sunlight, my lord. As it happens, I've a book with me. Take your time."

"I always do," he said with a lazy smile.

"How do you make even the most innocent statement sound so immoral?" Daisy asked him as they walked on.

"It's a gift," he said. "But that wasn't an innocent statement."

She laughed. It was pleasant strolling the path with him; his company wasn't so unnerving in the day as it was by moonlight and lamplight. He was still a strong presence and a fascinating male, but she felt less threatened in such mundane surroundings. There were nannies and prams, toddlers, old folks, and many dogs everywhere. She could see a milkmaid in the distance, hurrying to where the cows grazed on the meadow. The trees were in full leaf; the day was mild, Daisy felt relaxed and happy for the first time in a long time. Which was odd, because she knew he'd soon drop his calm façade and read her the riot act.

"You turned the earl down," he finally said.

She nodded, and watched her slippers as they walked on. "I listened to your advice, after all. It was best for him. He's a very nice man. I'd have made a bad wife. You were right."

"I never said you'd make a bad wife. I just said you wouldn't be the right one for him."

"Six of one, half dozen of the other," she said. "I'll leave London when this business of accusing me of all sorts of mischief about Tanner is over. I think I'd like a quiet life, after all."

"Quieter than one spent with a scholarly man twice your age?"

That made her look up. He was serious. She looked down again. "He's not dead. I realized that old doesn't mean incapable. I just don't want . . . a capable husband."

"Because of your experiences with your late husband? I can understand that, certainly. Did you know," he said idly, "that I was savaged by one of my father's hunting dogs when I was a tot? It's true. I got between him and his prey. He didn't kill me, after all, and looked very shamed when they pulled him off me. He was a valuable hound, and lived to a ripe old age. I almost didn't. Yet I bear no scars, because my nurse was a wonder with a needle; she could mend sheets so you'd never know they'd been torn, and, it turned out, earlobes and scalp lesions with the same deft hand.

"Well," he said, rubbing the back of his head, "I may have scars at that, it's just that I can't see them. If I lose my hair, perhaps I will. My point," he went on, "is that though I had parents who didn't care, my nurse did. Do you know what she put into my bed to cheer me as I lay convalescing? A puppy. Imagine that. I learned, early on, that experience can teach you some things, but it's far better to keep learning new things."

"Geoff isn't a puppy," she said in annoyance. "And it isn't a thing I can think about and banish."

"Neither were my wounds," he said. They'd stopped walking, and stood in a quiet shaded spot, beneath a huge oak.

She watched him suspiciously. They were, she realized, now out of sight of most people in the park.

"But the feel of that puppy!" he said, smiling. "Lord, I can still remember. She was fat and smooth-coated; she felt like my mother's seal cape, only of course she was warmer. Her tongue was warm, too, and her teeth prickled when she nibbled at my fingers. My attacker had been all fangs and claws. The puppy was nothing like that. I hesitate to ruin my manly reputation, but I still shudder when a dog bares its teeth. The difference is that I also quite like dogs of any size or shape, purebred or mongrel. Speaking of which," he went on casually, "your husband was doubtless a cur. Most men are not. I certainly am not. Neither is Geoff, but he was so devastated by your refusal, he confessed he wouldn't know how to court you now. I do. I could. Would you care to marry me?"

She stared.

"I would make a most unexceptional husband," he said serenely. "Once I was wed, I'd give up the chase. That, I promise. I'd never do to any other person what my unfaithful mama did to my father and brothers, and me. There are other advantages. I'd be able to help you dress, because among my few talents is a fine sense of fashion. I possess a melodic tenor, too; I like to ride, spar and fence, and discuss current affairs, in all senses of the words. Which means I'd have interests to take me from the house so I wouldn't hang at your elbow all the time.

"My estate in the north is historic; it's actually quite magnificent," he said. "But I don't go there often, because that's where my mother lives. I prefer my little country home in the West Country. I'd want to remove to London for the Season, though. I love the theater, and am thinking of going into politics. I've always imagined dabbling in politics is even more delicious than gossiping. After all, just think of all the lives you can actually change by discussing them. And," he concluded, "I'm very rich. So, what say you? If you were married to me, no one could or would dare prosecute you for anything. Unless, of course," he said thoughtfully, "you decide to heave a bomb at our prince after shouting some stirring republican slogan at him, or stabbed him repeatedly, in public."

"Are you mad?" she gasped.

"Almost certainly," he said. "But benignly so."

"Why in God's name would you want to marry me?"

"I collect originals," he said.

"I'm a convict—or was," she blurted. "I'm well-born but not titled. And I'm wealthy, but not rich."

He smiled. "You also need some lessons in basic English. You probably meant to say it the other way around: rich but not wealthy. It hardly matters. I have enough money to last me and you, and our heirs, all their lives."

"I won't be giving you heirs," she said angrily. "Don't you understand? I don't *like* the process."

His smile faded. Something else, something both tender and determined, lit his eyes. He ran one kid-gloved finger down the side of her cheek. "Your lips told me otherwise the other day. You don't like what you know. I can show you what you don't. I can show you so well, you'll be amazed at how you felt before." His eyes never left hers.

She again felt that he'd shrunk the world to just the two of them.

"It will be slow going," he said, his finger slowly traveling down her cheek to her lips. "And only going forward when you agree, but it will, and you will. I think, deep down, Daisy, that you already know that."

He lowered his head to touch her lips with his. She didn't move. Again, she felt the shock of his mouth on hers through her body. His lips touched hers for only a moment, but as they did, she felt a thrilling current of sensation.

He drew back, his eyes dark with some emotion that his expression didn't show.

"I might not be able to give you an heir, even . . . if I wanted to," she stammered. "I didn't before. Tanner confessed it might be his fault, but how do you know it wasn't mine?"

"I don't," he said softly. "But I haven't fathered any babes, either. Of course, I've been careful, but one wonders if it was my prudence or my lack of ability. At any event, *I* sometimes wonder. So, we start even. If we can't produce a child, we'll at least have a flock of nieces and nephews. And we can take in as many fosterlings as you wish."

"But Geoff . . . " she began to say.

He shrugged. "He knows how I feel, and though he'd rather you accept him, he's given me his permission. Now, all I need is yours."

"But why?" she demanded.

"Because he cares for you."

"I mean," she said with reluctant amusement

at his deliberate misunderstanding, "why are you asking me?"

"Because," he said, smiling with infinite tenderness, "I like you, as well as want you. And you like me. In spite of how you think you feel, and what you say, your breath, your eyes, your skin tell me so. And you're lovely," he went on softly. "You're clever and strong, too. You're like no other woman I've met. And you need me, Daisy. You've no idea of how much I need that. *I* didn't, certainly. There are other reasons even I don't know yet, but my pulse, and *my* skin, and my heart do, and they never lie."

He bowed his head and kissed her again, gently. She thought she'd stop him, but she didn't try. Instead, she leaned toward him, without thought of anything but recapturing the sensations he brought to her. His mouth was warm and soft; he touched the margin of her lips with his tongue and without realizing it, she opened her lips and breathed in the thrilling taste of him. It made her want more. He put one large hand on her waist and drew her closer. He deepened the kiss, one large hand on her back, the other stroking her cheek, her neck, her breast . . . And then to her surprise and guilty dismay, he stopped.

"Think about it," he said, touching a finger to her chin. "Geoff's offer still stands. Mine is in your pocket as well. Think long, and deep, Daisy, and let me know tomorrow."

"Tomorrow?"

"Yes. Because you do have enemies, and we have to end this nonsense that threatens you. And also because with all my oddities, I won't be anyone's second choice, or last resort. Now," he said with perfect calm, only belied by the blue fire in his eyes, "shall we get back to Helena? The poor lady will begin to worry, and we can't have that."

Daisy stood and looked at him, her hand to her lips, still tingling from his kiss. "You're serious?"

"Oh, very," he said. "The point now is, are you?"

Chapter 16

He was quite mad, barking mad; that was all there was to it.

Leland sat back in the deep chair beside his glowing hearth and pondered. The household was asleep. He had too much to think about to close his eyes. He stared into the heart of the fire without seeing it. What to do next? Offer himself up to the authorities and be clapped in Bedlam? Or actually go on with it? No saying if she'd accept him. But if she did?

What had he been thinking of?

Her eyes, her breasts, her lips, her laughter, and her unquenchable spirit, that was what. But why?

Women had been thrown at his head since he'd

been a youth, newly come into the title. Which was why they had been, of course. He never deceived himself. He'd been gangly and awkward with his new growth, his voice still cracked, he'd tripped over things and stammered when he spoke to a female. He'd been an unlicked cub with no mama bear to show him how to go on, but oh! how the matrons had wanted him to marry their daughters. Their daughters, he'd realized, had more sense.

In the months before his father had died so suddenly, being a mere heir hadn't been enough to ensure his popularity with the ladies. He'd been to enough social occasions to see how the lovely young things offered that Season reacted to him. They'd huddled together when they saw him approach, and he'd heard their giggles when they'd looked at him.

That was why he'd adopted his pose of a fop, a cynic, a care-for-nothing but fashion and fripperies. He'd cultivated an acid wit and slashing tongue. After all, it was impossible to hurt the feelings of someone who didn't appear to have any, and who, if push came to shove, could insult you worse than you had him.

Yet when he'd inherited the title, the eligible females nevertheless threw themselves at him. The good part of it was that because he was so amusing, ineligible females did the same. They helped him discover the sensual side of himself; he found he purely loved sex and also loved giving pleasure. In that, at least, for a wonder, he was never awkward or clumsy. Maybe because it came so naturally to him. He genuinely liked women, and was delighted that he could make them like him for more than his title and funds.

But the mask he wore in public was impossible to remove in private, because he came to realize that his paramours didn't want him to. It became part of him, which was not to say it was necessarily a bad part. He enjoyed amusing people. He'd hoped someday to meet someone who could laugh with him, as well as at him, if she got angry enough. But he'd thought she'd be wellborn, virginal and docile. Someone lovely, but not outrageously so; someone clever, but not aggressively so. Someone who'd faint with joy at the thought of his asking for her hand, and obediently give up her body with it, on demand.

Instead, he'd hung his heart on the whims of a female with an angelic face and a devil of a body, a criminal past; a widow who feared men and who wasn't sure if she wanted so much as his hand, even in marriage. But she also possessed a spirit as fiery as her hair, and a code of honor that could shame a parson.

Was he mad?

He hardly knew her—but no. He smiled to himself. He knew her better than most of the women matchmakers had thrown at his head all these past years. He knew her better than any of the young things he'd danced with at Almack's and partnered at too many social events. He knew her *far* better than most of the women he'd bedded, even those he'd stayed with as long as a month. He didn't know if he'd know a female better if he stayed with her longer; he never had.

Daisy, he thought, he could stay with forever. He liked her conversation; he admired her courage. He could amuse her, but she could make him laugh, too. And most important, he felt at home with her. He didn't know why, but he did.

He'd started seeing her because he'd worried about her using her wiles on Geoff. Which was why, he suspected, he'd forgotten to guard his own heart. Impossible to be on guard against a woman who spoke her mind, didn't try to impress him, though she did, and seemed always to tell the truth. He pitied her past and found himself wanting to ensure her future, with him. He admitted it might very well be that her past was what drew him to her, because she hadn't been cosseted and pampered, and didn't expect even the smallest courtesies from him.

But it certainly wasn't pity motivating him now. He recognized a kindred spirit, and he admitted his lust. His need for her was, however, more than that. He simply liked being with her, and looked forward to it every day.

Still, he didn't know her well enough to marry. He wondered if he ever would. That charmed him.

His mother would have a fit. That delighted him.

If Daisy became his wife, he knew he'd have a confidante, an honest friend, and a partner. Convincing her to be his partner in bed, however, would take time and effort. He could hardly wait.

But would she accept him?

He'd gambled. If he lost, Leland thought, laying his head back, closing his eyes, he wondered if it was likely he'd lose more than he now knew.

A viscount or an earl?

A thoroughly kind and fantastically rich older gentleman, or a thoroughly shocking, fascinating younger one? Also rich, of course.

Oh, poor me, what a terrible decision to have to make, Daisy thought. She chuckled, and hastily stopped when she heard herself. She didn't want to wake her maid or Helena. The hotel suite remained silent; the streets outside were still. Daisy wished it were morning, but there were hours yet to go. She was restless and anxious, but if she got up, she'd wake them, and there were things she wasn't ready to talk about yet.

She lay on her back and studied the patterns the moonlight made on the high ceiling above her. The truth was that she didn't want to marry anyone.

She scowled. She hated it when she lied to

herself. There was no question that Leland had stirred things in her that she hadn't known existed . . . She frowned, fiercely. Of course she'd known; she'd just denied those feelings for so long that they'd begun to wither. Even when Tanner had been alive, there'd been times when she'd responded to another man's smile, or walk, or appearance. She'd always hastily buried such thoughts, lest Tanner guess and beat her black and blue.

But Leland wasn't Tanner. And neither was Geoff.

What if she married Geoff, and found herself longing for what he couldn't give her? Because as much as she cared for him, and she did, she felt exactly no desire for him. In fact, his kiss had embarrassed and shamed her. So, then, marriage to Geoff was out.

And so, then, marriage to Leland Grant, Viscount Haye? She sucked in a breath and blew it out. Well, not only did he tempt her, the truth was, she liked him. In spite of his airs and his acid comments, or maybe because of them. He made her feel awake, and every hour she was with him seemed important. But oh, that mother of his! What an icy article she was. Now, there was a female whose eyes showed she could consider blue murder! Still, he was a grown man, and his mother seemed to make him either rueful or sad but nothing more. He even said her exploits were what made him vow he'd be faithful to his wife. But could he be? He was said to love the ladies. He didn't deny it.

That made her worry, too. She was drawn to him, but could she really ever fully respond to him? Fine thing that would be! A man like that married to a woman who could never give him what he wanted—even if she found herself wanting to try. And the truth was that she did want to.

So what about a tryst? A tryout? A test. Just one night . . .

Daisy sat up and locked her arms around her knees, laid her cheek on her knees, and thought.

She had to concentrate on the issue. The thing was that someone was after her, accusing her of murder. To imagine that she'd had a hand in killing Tanner! She'd love to have done it, to be sure. But she didn't have the means, the opportunity, the courage, or to come right on down to it, the sort of soul that *could* have done it. Now, if he'd died of a blow to the head, that would have made sense. She'd always thought that one day she'd just lose all control, seize up a flatiron, or a fireplace poker, or a . . . but she'd never done it.

Still, it made perfect sense to accuse her. Anyone back in the colony would have known how Tanner bullied her and how she despised him. So it could be someone who had hated her back then. There were a lot of hate-filled people there. It might be a friend of Tanner's bent on mischief, or just someone who envied her newfound wealth and liberty. It might even be someone here in England who wanted her out of the way.

Daisy frowned. She hated herself for thinking it, but she'd seen the glances Helena cast at Geoff. Geoff hadn't. It was as though he didn't realize Helena was there. It was sad, and it was futile, but could Helena think that Geoff would notice her if her employer were gone?

Daisy didn't want to think about it.

But she wasn't sure of anyone now. She sighed. It didn't matter. Someone had laid information against her. True or false, she knew enough about the law to know that a woman never did well in the prisoner's dock, and one who'd been a convict wouldn't get a fair chance in court. But she also knew that if you had friends in high places, the law didn't apply to you. She needed a man of wealth and power to protect her with more than his cooperation. She needed his name.

But she didn't want to prostitute herself, be a liar or a cheat. And she'd vowed she'd never be a prisoner again: not any man's or any state's. Still, if she had to marry, then was it too much to ask that she find not only peace, but pleasure in her future?

Could she?

Or should she just pack up her things and disappear into the countryside? She could give herself a new name and live out her days alone. And never have a baby to call her own. Well, she mightn't be able to anyway. Daisy sighed again. It wouldn't matter to Geoff, she supposed. He had his heir. Leland had said he didn't care, though.

But was that fair? She had to decide soon.

Daisy didn't sleep that night.

Chapter 17

"I've got the special license," the earl said, patting his pocket. "Everything's been signed and stamped, and is ready to use."

Leland nodded, then kept moving his head one way and another as he stared into his mirror. "Not too high," he finally murmured, "not too formal, but certainly not so casual. This will not work," he told his valet, who was hovering behind him. He stripped off his neck cloth. "Bring another, please. The trick will be to get the fall just right," he told Geoff.

"You will, you will," the earl said absently, still patting his pocket. "Have you the ring?"

"Of course," Leland said, as he lowered his chin into the crisp, clean white folds of the neck cloth his valet had just handed him. "Ah. Perfect! Thank you. Have you my bags packed?" he asked the valet.

"I'll just make sure all is in order," the man said, bowed, and left his master and the earl alone in Leland's bedchamber.

"Are your bags packed?" Leland asked the earl.

"It's all done," he said. "I'm not so fastidious as you."

Leland cast a critical eye over him. "Obviously. That waistcoat will do for the coach ride, but you can't mean to wear it in the chapel."

"No one will notice," the earl said impatiently. "I'm not posing for a painting. It's a marriage ceremony, over before you know it. It's not as though there will be throngs of invited guests. Just a few people we both know. Anyhow, I've been through it before. Trust me, nothing is noticed but the bride."

"*I'll* notice," Leland said.

"Damn it, Lee, but a sorry, hurried, hole-in-the-wall sort of ceremony it will be, too," Geoff said, ignoring the comment about his clothes. "I know it's necessary, but I can't help but wonder. Are we doing the right thing, after all?"

"No, of course we're not. We ought to have the ceremony in Newgate, with the bride carrying her chains instead of a bouquet, and the jailers as bridesmaids, blotting tears from their cheeks with their truncheons. How novel. It might start a new style," Leland said caustically. Then he sighed.

"Don't you think I've been over this in my mind for a week now?" he asked in a softer voice. "It isn't the right thing, but it's the only thing. Whoever laid information against her is adamant. Someone has either paid a great deal of money to the right people in high places, or else he or she lives in them. As it is, now there's enough reason for Bow Street to keep her in prison 'pending investigation.'

"They can't prove anything but they don't want her getting away until they do," he went on. "It would be a hideous experience for most young women even if it were only for a few hours. But once they have Daisy, it could be for longer. They might say they have to bring witnesses or evidence or whatnot from the Antipodes. You of all people must know what that could do to Daisy, even if we paid to have her kept in the best apartments at the place."

The earl nodded, but didn't look happy.

"I know it's a scrambling sort of affair, and I know she deserves better," Leland said. "But there's nothing better to be done for her right now. Once she has that ring on her finger, and a new name to go with it, she'll be untouchable. Or at least she will be unless there's much more compelling evidence than simply one person's word against another's. We haven't found out who that person is yet, either." He frowned, and turned to meet the earl's eyes. The earl looked away.

"You don't think she did it, do you?" Leland asked incredulously.

The earl shook his head. "No. I admit I pondered it. But no, I don't think she did."

"Nor do I. And once she's titled, with wealth and position behind her, her accuser will have to slack off. She'll be free."

"But married," the earl said.

"Well, yes, that's the point," Leland said.

He turned back to the looking glass and brushed a tiny speck from his jacket. It was a sober blue jacket, worn over a light blue waistcoat, and it looked simple but elegant with his slate gray breeches and black half boots. His hair was brushed back; he had a single sapphire pin his neck cloth, and a single gold signet ring on his right hand.

The earl, reflected in the mirror behind him, wore a dark blue jacket, blue waistcoat, black breeches, and a troubled expression.

"You look like you're going to a funeral, not a wedding," Leland remarked over his shoulder. "Having a change of heart? If you want to change your mind along with it, do so now. Once we get into the coach and head into the countryside, it will be much too late. Riding away with the pair of us for an overnight trip will certainly ruin her even if the charges against her don't. And remember, the slightest hint of a loss of resolve on either of our parts will send Daisy running on her own. You saw her face when she agreed to this. It's not what she wants, either."

"Do you think she'll come to wanting it," the earl asked nervously. "Or at least reconcile herself to this marriage, in the days to come?"

Leland turned away from the mirror. His expression was sober. "I do, so much so that I'll lay a wager on it, if you like. Daisy wouldn't agree under *any* circumstances if it went against her deepest desires, and you know it. She's a very opinionated creature," he said with a small smile. "In fact, I think this is the best thing for her, however she came to it. I also think that one day she'll thank that nameless informer. Because instead of ruining her, this will make her happier than she's been in years. At least, so I earnestly hope."

"Yes, so do I, of course," the earl said. "I just wanted to be sure you're totally in agreement."

"Oh no," Leland said. "It's merely a whim on my part. Every so often I just feel the need to cancel all my engagements, throw my clothes in a basket, get into my coach, and leave London in the middle of the night, to ride off into the west. I'm funny that way, I get these mad impulses . . . "

"Don't jest, Lee!" the earl said sharply. "It's not just inconvenience for her; it will change her life forever. *I*, at least, worry about that. I love the girl and don't want to see her make a bad choice in order to avoid what might or might not be a worse fate."

Leland stood still and lifted his chin so it seemed as if he were looking down his long nose at the earl. "Firstly," he said frostily, "she is not a girl. She's a woman. Once married and now widowed, in fact. Secondly, *I* at least don't happen to think it's a bad choice for any reason. And thirdly, if you have so many doubts, then I don't think you should be part of this in any way. If you leave now, that likely *will* break her heart. But if you do go on with this, I'll ape the ceremony and ask you to speak now, or forever hold your peace. Well?"

The earl sighed and held out both hands in a gesture of surrender. "I have spoken; I won't do so again. I have doubts, but you know my reasons. However, I agree. This is for the best. I can think of no other solution. It would be better if she'd come to the decision of her own free will instead of having to accept in order to preserve her freedom. But good things can come from necessity as well as from free choice. It's the right thing, it's only that I tend to worry. I raised a child, you see, and took on two others, so I'm in the habit of it."

"Don't," Leland said gently. "It will be for the best, my lord, you'll see. So," he said, squaring his shoulders. "The Runner has been sent on a false trail, we're in readiness, and it's dark as it will get tonight. Shall we get on with it?"

* * *

Daisy hesitated.

"Afraid of making a misstep?" Leland asked, at her side. "Don't worry, I'm here, it won't happen."

"But it's like stepping into the dark," she said.

"The coachman can't light his lamps," he whispered. "We don't want to be seen. It's best that whatever enemy you have is unaware of this step you're taking. But take my arm, I won't let you fall."

The carriage had come around back of her hotel, to the servants' entrance, near the stables. There were lanterns burning on either side of the rear door, and some by the stables, but they didn't illuminate the scene. Daisy leaned on the viscount's arm, and then with him to guide her, she ducked into the coach.

"Good evening, Daisy," Geoff said from the darkness of the interior. "And a good evening to you, too, Mrs. Masters," he said as Helena stepped in behind Daisy. "I'm sorry that we have to meet in such a clandestine manner, but we don't want to be observed. Good," he told Leland, who followed Helena into the coach. "Now we can leave; we have a long way yet to go."

The coach rattled down the side alley, over the rough cobbles, and then turned into the high street.

"It sounds like thunder," Daisy said nervously. "Anyone can hear it."

"The hotel gets deliveries at night," Leland

said. "They'll take no notice. Anyway, the coins I left with the staff will muffle the noise. Just sit back. Sleep if you wish."

"Sleep?" she asked incredulously.

"Yes," he said. "No one expects scintillating conversation now. Sit back, close your eyes, and when you wake, we'll be there."

"I couldn't sleep!" she declared. "What sort of a person do you think I am? I'm sneaking out of London to escape the Runners, off to marry a man in order to save my neck, and you say 'sleep'?"

"Doze, then," Leland said calmly.

"Well, you may sleep if you wish," she said heatedly. "But I could not, not for anything."

"Very well, fight then," he said equitably, lay back against the leather squabs, and closed his eyes.

Daisy could see him do it. It was a soft, late spring evening. Even though it was full dark, fair skies and a half moon made it bright enough to see, once her eyes had adjusted to the dark. "We should have left on a cloudy night," she said moodily.

"And risk getting our wheels mired if it started to rain? I think not," Leland said, without opening an eye.

"The farther we go, the easier it will be," the earl told her. "The coachman is taking a side route for a while, and there's a footman on back of the carriage to see if we're being followed.

There's our other coach, following slowly, with your maid and our valets. So you may rest easy, Daisy. We're here to watch over you. And you're doing the right thing."

"I wish I was sure of that," she said. "Oh, I'm not complaining. I know what I must do, and believe me, I'm grateful for your sacrifice and cooperation. But when I think of the future . . . "

"So don't," Leland said lazily. "Such a lot of trouble anticipating trouble. Just live for the moment and let the next ones fall into place. You're getting married. You're ensuring your freedom."

"I have come to see that is a contradiction in terms," she said coldly.

"Daisy!" Helena gasped. "Excuse me, but I must tell you that's rude. Think of your groom, and how he must feel. He's doing a brave and noble thing."

"Yes," Daisy said, abashed. "I'm sorry. That was rude. I am fully aware of the honor being done me."

"Now *that* sounds worse," Leland commented, opening an eye.

"Well, I meant it," she said angrily.

"My dear, we know it," the earl said. "Stop teasing her, Lee."

"Oh yes," Leland said. "I beg your pardon. I ought to let her sit and stew and worry, instead of lacing into me, which, by the way, seems to elevate her mood considerably."

The earl turned in outrage to stare at Leland,

but before he could say anything, he heard a giggle.

"Too right," Daisy said, her voice filled with laughter. "I've a terrible temper. I suppose I use it too much these days, but you've no idea of what a luxury that is! It's so nice to quarrel without being afraid of being slapped. Forgive me, I didn't mean to snap your head off."

"Quite all right," Leland said graciously.

"But marriage is a big step," she said, "especially being married in such a hurry. Although, mind, I'm grateful, I really am. So, I'm nervous. But I'd be a sight more so if I thought Bow Street was going to clap me in jail. They can't now, right?"

"They can't and won't," Geoff reassured her. "I've spoken to many people in power, as has Lee, and even if Bow Street were to stop us now, they couldn't put you in jail, not right away. And once you're married, they likely never can. We have some influence, you know. You won't be an obscure ex-convict anymore, but a woman married to a gentleman of standing, with friends in the right places. Someone wants to make trouble for you. We'll find out who it is and they'll be in for a surprise. It's a crime to give false witness. Don't worry. We're here, so are you, and so you will remain. I promise that."

"Thank you," Daisy said softly.

But nevertheless, the earl sat on the edge of his seat until the coach had left London and was rolling along the road west.

No one spoke for a while. Daisy could see Leland, across from her; his eyes were closed again, his hands folded in his lap, his long body relaxed. In time, Helena closed her eyes, and by her deep and even breathing, Daisy could tell she was sleeping, too. The earl also finally closed his eyes, and Daisy soon heard him accompanying Helena with light, regular snores.

She felt like the only person awake in the world. She stared into the darkness outside the coach. The coachman had stopped to light the lamps once they'd left Town, and now she could see their bright, intermittent flare.

"Any last requests, any last wishes?" a soft low voice asked.

Daisy sat up. The viscount was awake and watching her; she could see the lamplight reflected in his eyes.

"I'd like a beefsteak, that's what all the lags ask for before they're marched to the sheriff's picture frame. And a trifle, I think, a big one, made with sherry," she said whimsically. She was nervous, and it felt good to jest.

"I didn't mean for your last meal," he said appreciatively, with laughter in his voice. "But you'll have it, if you want. Only I believe it will have to be at your wedding breakfast, because the thing must be done as soon as the sun rises. Do you really think of it as an ending?" he asked suddenly, in a soft, sober voice.

"Oh, I don't know," she said on a gusty sigh. "I

don't know anything anymore. I was so full of plans when I set sail for England, I didn't look to the left or right. Now I have to act, and fast. How can I say if it's wrong or right?"

"Excellent meter," he said. "You should think of composing poetry. Don't worry. I know that's easy to say, but your new husband, whatever his sins, will be nothing like your old one. *That,* I can assure you."

"I know. Still, I've been my own boss since Tanner died, and it will be hard for me to buckle under to someone else's rule again."

"Your husband won't be a ruler," Leland said. "At least, he shouldn't be. There's no fun for a fair man in that. And whatever else he may be, you must admit he is a fair man. Or at least, I hope you know that."

"I do," she said softly.

"Good, nicely put, keep rehearsing that line. And be easy. It won't be an ending if you look at it as a beginning. I hear that husbands have done just that sort of rationalizing since the beginning of time."

She smiled. "All right," she said.

"Good, now sleep," he whispered. "We don't want to wake the beautiful dreamers, and you make me laugh, which would certainly do it. And most important, you have to be a wide-awake bride when the dawn comes. I think any vicar would be wary if a bride stumbled into his church all bleary-eyed and yawning. Drugs, not love, would be suspected. After all, look at the pair accompanying you, the earl and myself. One fellow who keeps saying he looks old enough to be your father, and the other, a beanpole of a figure, not like any Romeo outside of satirical broadsheets. And with your companion looking so nervous? No, special license or not, with such a weird wedding party in tow, and the bride half asleep on her feet, an honorable vicar would never marry you."

She smiled again, and yawned, because he'd mentioned it. Then she closed her eyes. And so she slept until the long journey was over.

Leland stayed awake, watching her, and thinking hard.

Daisy opened her eyes to a soft, rosy dawn. And to the sight of Leland's dark blue gaze fixed on her.

"We're almost there," he said. "Ready or not."

"I'm ready," Daisy said, sitting up and rubbing her eyes. "I just need to wash up first."

"Of course the child must have time to change," the earl said. "We'll go to the inn in town first, and then to the chapel. That way, Daisy, you'll enter your new home the mistress of it."

"I shouldn't worry about that," Leland remarked lazily. "No doubt the servants will use the time to whip themselves into a frenzy making sure the house is in perfect order."

"Very well," she said, taking a deep breath,

almost as nervous about taking on the duties of a mistress of a huge estate as she was about taking on a husband. "I just need a few minutes. I'd like to change my gown. You're supposed to be married in your best, and I've brought mine with me."

That was why the groom caught his breath that morning, when his bride finally came to meet him at the church.

Daisy smiled. Much that had been done was out of her control. How she looked at her wedding was the one thing she'd planned, since the day she'd realized she had to be married.

She'd had her hair done up high, so the weight of it could be caught in long curls that fell to her shoulders, and left her neck exposed. That wasn't all that was exposed. She wore her best gown, her fabulous gold gown, the one she'd wanted to save for a ball.

"Are you sure you want to wear this today?" Helena had asked as Daisy's maid helped drop it over her mistress's head. But when the gown fell into place, Helena sighed. "Of course," she said.

The gown had been fit to her body by a master's hand, but Daisy's lush body needed no artificial enhancement. The gown didn't flatter her so much as display her. Her high breasts, slender waist, lithe hips, and pert derriere did the rest. Most brides wore their best on their wedding day, but few wore a gown made by an expert modiste for wearing at a grand ball, and yet it was perfect for Daisy today, and she knew it. She wasn't a blushing bride or a frightened virgin. She was a woman grown doing what she believed was best for her, and she wanted her groom to know she could have done even better, if she'd chosen to.

She met Geoff in the vestry of the old chapel, and smiled when she saw his expression. He took her hand in his, and speechlessly, never taking his eyes off her, led her slowly down the aisle. The gold cloth caught the sunlight and reflected it back so that it made Daisy glow as though she were still surrounded by the sunshine she'd left behind as she'd entered the ancient church. The flowing train of pink tulle that drifted in her wake lent color to her pale face. With her red-gold hair and the gold and pink gown, she outshone all the antique stained glass windows above her.

But when she saw her groom's face, where he stood at the altar, waiting for her, her smile outshone it all.

"You honor me," Leland said, as he took her hand.

Chapter 18

All the while the vicar was talking, reciting text and explaining vows, Daisy kept reminding herself she was doing this because she had no choice, and wondering, even as she did, if there'd be some flash of divine retribution. Because she suddenly wondered if she was telling herself a lie.

She wasn't unhappy. She didn't feel trapped, or even frightened. Not now, not anymore. Instead, here at the altar, at the last moments of her independence, whenever she dared a glance at Leland, she definitely felt a thrill of . . . pride? Or joy? Or was it simply wonder because here she was, actually marrying a man she admired and maybe secretly desired? That last was cause for alarm. But she couldn't feel even that now.

Still, she did shiver. It wasn't because of the thin material of her gown, or the fact that the ancient stones around her never let go of the cold, even in summer. It was because he'd been right. Her very *skin* was reacting to him, telling her he was beside her.

Leland Grant, Viscount Haye, stood at her elbow, correct and sober. He was so tall and stood so straight, she couldn't see his expression without craning her neck. And here she was, parroting words that would soon make him her master. But she couldn't summon up a twinge of fear. For all that he was, and that included his reputation, she never for a moment thought he'd ever hurt her in any way. She was so stunned by this revelation that she almost missed her turn at making vows.

He turned his head and looked at her, and she saw a hint of alarm in his cobalt eyes. So she flashed a smile of apology and said yes, she would, and knew in that instant that she would and maybe could make something of this marriage. In time, of course. She'd every reason to hope he'd give her that time.

He bent his head and touched her lips with his when the vicar announced they were man and wife. Then he smiled at her. "Well, there we are," he said. "Good morning, my lady Haye, and well done. Welcome to my life."

"Congratulations!" the earl said, shaking Leland's hand.

Geoff took Daisy's hand in both of his. Though his smile was tinged with sadness, it wasn't forced. "Yes, and very well done," he told her.

"Congratulations, my lord," Helena told Leland. "I'm so happy for you," she told Daisy, though her smile was wobbly, and she'd tears in her eyes.

They took the congratulations of an elderly couple Leland called his neighbors, the vicar's wife, and a handful of other well-dressed local people he'd summoned to see his wedding.

"I'm sorry my boys couldn't be here," Geoff said. "But none of them could come so far on such short notice. I've sent word, and I'll wager they'll be here as soon as they may, though. You are staying on here for a while? Or are you taking a honeymoon trip?"

"I hadn't thought of that," Leland said. "What would you like, my dear?" he asked Daisy.

She flushed at the new, intimate way his "my dear" sounded to her now. She shook her head. "I'm not really anxious to travel," she admitted. "My last voyage was so long, I don't know if I could face another boat yet."

"So we'll stay on here a while, then see what you would like," Leland said.

She nodded, gratefully.

"And of course, I'll give a party for you when

you come back to town. I'll invite the immediate world," the earl said. "It will be the event of the Season."

"So it will, and thank you," Leland said. "It will be good for Daisy to be introduced to polite Society, and I emphasize the 'polite.' I fear I don't have enough respectable friends to fill a teacup, but everyone in London will thunder to your door if you invite them, my lord."

"As if you don't know everyone in Society," the earl scoffed.

"Alas, I do. But you know the worthy ones, who may not yearn to be premiere members of 'Society,' " Leland said. "It's easy to find people to drink, gamble, and carouse with. It's harder to find any to socialize with *and* enjoy it. There must be some decent folk who would spend time with us, although I allow that I, at least, will have to win them over. I'm confident that in time my commendable behavior will lull them, and my lady will enchant them, but you must introduce us to them. You can be our guide in that. I want Daisy to know the best people. Those are the ones who doubtless know *of* me, but I doubt they know me."

"I'll see what I can do." The earl laughed.

Then he and the other guests stood and smiled at one another, and shuffled their feet. It was an uncomfortable moment. For the first time this glorious May morning, Daisy had the time to take in her surroundings. There was a basket of flowers at the altar, and sunlight streamed in the high windows. But the old church, small as it was, was almost empty. Their little wedding party looked pathetic, the scrambled haste of the affair now seemed obvious.

It seemed to occur to the bridegroom, too.

"I suggest we all repair to the inn," Leland told them. "It's just down the road. They'll serve a lovely breakfast, the landlord promised his finest victuals, and you all are to be my guests. I'd invite you back to my home, but my staff is still preparing it for us."

A peculiar strained silence met his words, and those few assembled tried to avoid his eye. Daisy wondered why.

Leland's smile was wry. "An awkward moment, to be sure," he told her. "The problem is that my home here has long been known as an oasis to those of my friends or acquaintances who found themselves at loose ends . . . "

He looked at Geoff, and his smile grew wider. "Unfortunate choice of words, even if it is also most unfortunately apt. Let us not mention their ends, shall we? Though that's all they seem to think about when they're here. You see," he told Daisy, "my home has been an open house to those on the rackety fringe of the *ton*, those who seek privacy and comfort while they escape their creditors, or in some cases, their husbands or wives. That's all going to be changed now, along with the sheets. Doubtless my staff is even now airing the beds, after turfing out those who were in them. This may take some time. I don't know who might still be there, if anyone, but I won't take you home with me until I'm assured they're not."

"What a thing to tell your new wife!" the earl exclaimed.

Daisy was only thinking how odd it was to go to a place called home that she didn't know, with a man she hardly knew. Then she remembered that she'd done it before, in far worse fashion. She repressed an involuntary shudder at the memory, and waited for her new husband to speak again.

"Worse if I didn't tell her, I think," Leland said. "Now, who's for a wedding breakfast, and a toast to the future?"

They piled out of the church and into the sunshine, and Daisy let out a long breath. She felt relieved, almost merry, until she stepped down through the churchyard and saw the sunlight glinting on her wedding dress. She felt, for the first time, a little foolish.

"What's the matter?" Leland asked.

"My gown seemed so magnificent in the box and in madame's shop," she explained, holding out a pleat of her golden skirt, "but here, in the daylight, it looks less so. The truth is that it looks almost tawdry."

"It *is* magnificent; you look magnificent in it," he said. "Although I'll grant it's not the thing if you were going berry picking. So of course it looks a bit out of place in a country churchyard. Don't fret; we'll soon be at the inn, where it will resume its grandeur."

He took her hand and led her to the waiting carriage that would carry them into the small village they'd passed on the way.

The local inn was as crowded as the church hadn't been. Since it was smaller, it seemed even more so. But all the villagers seemed to have heard about the wedding and that the bride and groom were going to breakfast there, and had come to look for themselves. The couple were showered with greetings and congratulations the moment they stepped in the door.

"I wish I'd known they cared," Leland whispered to Daisy, "I'd have invited them all to the church."

She wondered if it was the marriage they were applauding, or the free drinks for all that Leland immediately called for. He bent his head to her ear again. "It's not just the free pints and idle curiosity. They rejoice because they feel proprietary about me. I see now that they were less than pleased when my home was a playground for the rich and unscrupulous, because our marriage seems to have honestly thrilled them. As they don't know you, or me, I suppose it's because it can't have been pleasant for them before, having their village known as the town at the foot of the sinful lord's pleasure palace. I wish I'd known. Believe it or not, I feel guilty about it now."

She wouldn't have guessed from his manner. He wasn't apologetic. But he was courteous and charming. Not a sly or salacious comment passed his lips. The tall, elegant gentleman didn't seem to be the toast of the *ton* or a wicked gossip, not here in his home village.

She didn't feel odd about her extravagant gown anymore, either. It was so dim in the inn that the gown glowed, rather than shouted, and there wasn't room for the long tulle train to trail after her. The women in the inn seemed to genuinely admire it, and she turned for their inspection so many times that she got dizzy, which made her, and them, laugh. She could only hope they'd keep laughing merrily and not in derision when they heard her whole story. Because she didn't doubt they would. She'd lived most of her life in a small village and knew how news traveled.

The landlord brought out platters of cold ham and warm pasties; sliced beef and cooked eggs; loaves of bread; plates of toast, jams, and cakes. Ale flowed and toasts were made as Leland invited all to share his wedding breakfast. He and his bride were too busy talking to people to have any of it themselves.

They were chatting with a farmer and his wife when Leland looked up over the heads of the crowd, and his face lit with real pleasure.

"Daffy, you dog!" he exclaimed. "You've come, after all!"

Daffyd grinned broadly and came through the

crowd to take his half brother's hand. "I missed the ceremony because my horse threw a shoe, but I'd have walked the rest of the way if I'd had to. Meg couldn't come, of course; she's still awaiting our new arrival. But I couldn't miss this, even if it means I can only congratulate you for an hour before I tear back home again. I represent the family," he told Daisy. "Amyas is too far off for a brief visit. And we know you don't want guests on your honeymoon. He and Christian wrote to say they'll come with their families as soon as your honeymoon's over. We all hope that will be never."

He laughed and batted Leland's shoulder. "Just joking. We're all planning to see you later this summer even if you're throwing dishes at each other by then.

"Daisy," he said, turning to her, his expression showing he spoke with all sincerity, "my warmest greetings and best wishes. I don't know what he said to convince you to marry him, but I'm glad of it and happy for the two of you. Ho, Geoff!" he called as he saw the earl coming toward them, "Want to come back home with me after the celebration? Meg and I would be honored if you were with us when your grandchild arrives."

"You don't need me underfoot," the earl said. "I can't now anyway. I've promises to keep. And you really don't need anyone to help you pace. But I'll come to see you soon."

"As soon as you may, I hope you will,"

Daffyd said, then craned his neck to survey the crowd. "Where's our sainted mama?" he asked Leland.

Leland shrugged a shoulder. "Who knows? Not I."

"She refused your invitation?" the earl asked, his eyes widening.

Daisy's eyes widened, too. For the first time in her whole tumultuous journey to wedlock, she thought about her groom's mother, and realized that the icy lady wasn't there.

"No, she couldn't attend," Leland said. "Because she wasn't, in the strictest sense of the word, invited."

Daisy put her hand to her mouth and bit back whatever exclamation she'd have made. This was dreadful. Why had he married her if he'd known his mother would hate her?

"I sent her a note telling her of my intentions," Leland went on lazily. "As she sent none back to ask for more details, I didn't feel I had to provide them. Of course, I only sent the note yesterday. No matter. There's time enough for her to welcome Daisy to the family."

A silence fell over all three men.

Daisy swallowed hard, and said carefully, "So she didn't avoid the wedding, so much as not know about it in time?"

"Precisely," Leland said.

A look of comprehension dawned on his half brother's face. "Well done," he murmured.

"Masterful," the earl agreed.

Daisy didn't pretend she didn't follow. "Oh, I see," she said bleakly. "She couldn't insult me by not coming if she didn't know she could."

"No," Leland said. "Actually, my dear, it had little to do with you. Does that hurt your feelings? Don't let it. Ever selfish, it was *my* feelings I was considering. She'll see us in London at the earl's party, and believe me, that will suit her better. She never took much interest in my affairs; I'd no reason to suspect she'd want to now."

Daisy kept looking up into his eyes.

Leland touched her cheek. "Please don't be offended. She won't be, I promise you. She'll only be chagrined at having missed a party. It's all she ever cares about, anyway. So if we tell her it was only for the local gentry, she'll be appeased."

"She won't be happy with me," Daisy declared, her eyes still searching his.

"She wouldn't be happy with any female I married," Leland said gently. "She won't like being displaced and made to look like the dowager. But don't worry. She tends to ignore those things that distress her, and she'll never interfere with our lives. We won't be living at Haye Hall so we'll scarcely ever see each other. Still, family is family. If my younger brother weren't off on the Continent on his grand tour broadening his mind and doubtless pleasing his body even more, he'd have been here. I'd have seen to it."

Daisy drew in her breath. She felt ashamed of

herself. She'd forgotten all about his younger brother, whom she'd never met. Her only excuse was that Leland never mentioned him.

"We aren't close, but we aren't estranged either," Leland explained, to show he understood her confusion "We've just got little in common and less interest in finding what that little might be. Still, when he eventually does decide to return to England, you'll meet him, I promise."

"God!" Daffyd said, swatting his own forehead. *"Martin!* I'd forgotten all about him. Her youngest, got off your father. He was born years after me. I suppose he's as related to me as you are, but I only met him once and haven't thought of him since!"

"No more should you," Leland said calmly. "He seldom thinks of us. We embarrass him, I think. But to be charitable, and disregarding our notoriety, it may just be that he's at that stage of life when all his relatives do that. Likely he'll outgrow that in a few more decades."

They laughed, and the uncomfortable moment passed. Another came soon enough.

"Daisy? Rather, I suppose I should say, Lady Haye?" a soft voice asked.

Helena twisted a handkerchief in her hands. Another person she'd forgotten today, Daisy thought in chagrin. Helena had been indispensable, at Daisy's side since she'd heard about the wedding, helping her prepare for it. But precisely because everything had been done so efficiently and naturally, Daisy had taken her help for granted. Now she finally noticed that her companion had also dressed for the occasion, and looked very well. Helena wore a simple but well-cut violet-colored gown to the ceremony, and her hair, though neatly pulled back, as ever, had been allowed to curl around her face. Daisy realized how good-looking Helena was when she allowed herself to be. Unfortunately, she also looked very distressed.

"This is awkward," Helena said. "I ought to have brought it up before, but things happened so quickly . . . but the truth is that now you're married, my lady, my job is done. So I'll be leaving today. I just wondered, if you're so inclined, could you write me a letter of recommendation, please? Oh, not now, I quite understand you haven't the time. But if I leave you my direction, could you send on to me soon?"

"So inclined?" Daisy yelped. "Of course, I am, and will right this very minute, if you want, and if I can get some paper from the landlord. But there's no need to hurry; you don't have to rush off!"

"I rather think I do," Helena said, smiling for the first time. "A bride doesn't need any companion but her husband after her wedding."

"My home has more bedchambers than is decent, or so everyone has always said," Leland commented. "My lady is right; stay on with us until you find a new position."

Helena shook her head. "Thank you, but no, my lord. I've engaged my old rooms in London again. But I thought I'd go north and visit my children for a spell first." Her expression became wistful. "I always do, between positions. They look forward to it as much as I do. I need only take the stage from here tomorrow morning. There's one due, I know; I've asked."

"But you didn't ask for your wages, and you didn't remind me that they were due!" Daisy said. "That beats all! Please stay, I don't want you riding off alone just yet." She saw Helena's unhappy expression. "Oh all right, you must as you wish, I suppose. But I wish you wouldn't just leave like that."

"Thank you, I knew you'd understand," Helena said. "My job here is done. I never was companion to a married lady, you see, and a newlywed one will definitely not require my services. I go where I'm needed. So, I'll leave you now and visit my children. *I* need to see them as often as I can. If it makes you feel better, I thank you for this unexpected opportunity. But I will write to you, and if you know anyone in need of a companion, I'd be happy to meet with them."

Daisy felt terrible, and looked to Leland for advice.

But the earl spoke first. "We're all sorry to see you go," he said. "Leland will take care of your wages, and likely here and now if I know my man. But at least I can help you with your other predicament. No need to take the public stage, I'm going tomorrow morning, too, Mrs. Masters. I'd be happy to take you north. It's on my way to Egremont."

Leland smiled and looked at Daffyd, who shared his silent appreciation. The earl's estate was south of where they were, but Geoff hadn't even asked Helena's destination or knew how far north it was. But he was the sort of man who hated to see anyone left on his own.

"Of course I'll settle the matter of wages," Leland said. "But see what an expensive wife I've got! Married not ten minutes and already demanding my money."

They laughed. Daisy joined in, not because of the quip, but because it seemed to her that her new husband liked to use the word "wife." And for a wonder, for the first time, hearing herself called that didn't cause her heart to sink.

The guests began to toast them again, and they joined in the merriment.

After an hour, a servant in green and white livery ducked into the inn's common room, looked around, saw Leland, and went to him. Leland spoke with him for a moment, nodded, and sent him out again. Then he took his wife aside, and spoke quietly to her.

"This is amusing, but we shouldn't outstay our welcome," Leland told her. "So we'll stay on here, celebrating, for a little while longer. But then we must leave. A bride and groom who linger too long at their own celebration give rise to gossip just as surely as those who can't wait to rush off and be alone."

His eyes were grave and sincere as they studied her. "And you and I must begin this right. I want our marriage to be as little cause for gossip as my life was cause for it before we met."

"Then you shouldn't have married a convict," she said bleakly.

He turned so that his body shielded her from the eyes of the guests.

"Had I married a nondescript little nun of a girl in her first Season, with a bishop for a brother, they'd gossip more," he said in a low voice. "I don't mind that. It's you I'm thinking of. But as for your history? I'd wager that if we sat down, bared our souls, and compared our relative notoriety, I'd win, hands down. But there are much better things for us to bare and compare."

He smiled, and then shook his head at her involuntary start. "No, don't worry. It wasn't a threat or a promise, just a jest. I hesitated to take you back to my house until all the guests had been tossed out and we could be alone. I've just been assured that we will be—apart from my long-suffering staff, that is. Speaking of the staff, I've also been assured that they are ecstatic at the turn of events and eager to meet their new mistress. Who would have guessed that a wedding and the possibility of a quiet life in future would excite so many people so much?"

His voice gentled, and he smiled. "Including myself. Come with me, if you please, my lady. My pleasure palace awaits us, and so does our duty. We have to make it a home again."

Chapter 19

"This is it?" Daisy asked, astonished. "*This* is your little country home?"

"In comparison to my principal seat, where my mother lives, yes it is," Leland said. "It's small enough to be manageable, and it's entirely mine, alone. Not any longer, of course; now it's ours."

Daisy looked out the carriage window at his home as it came into view. She'd suspected something out of the ordinary after they'd turned from the main road and passed a gatehouse where a gatekeeper, goggling at their carriage, trying to see inside, let them in. Then they'd gone along a lane that curved and snaked so as to keep showing spectacular views of the grounds of some fabulous estate. But Leland only said they were nearing his humble home, so she assumed the estate was a near neighbor. She and her father had lived in a small manor house adjacent to a magnificent house and lands. It was this noble neighbor's lands that her father had poached until he'd overdone it, been charged, convicted, and sent far away.

Now they passed huge walls of rhododendron that Leland said he regretted were out of bloom, and she'd gotten glimpses of fountains and statues on distant green lawns, and glints of blue in the distance that was surely a lake. Daisy saw deer that stopped to stare at them and sheep that ignored them altogether as they grazed on long green meadows. She spied a waterfall that spilled into a stream that twisted beside the road until it ran beneath a bridge they crossed, and then rushed away. The coach went over an Oriental bridge, up a hill, and under an arch. And then she saw his home.

It was a sprawling red house with wings on either side, and it embraced a shining white oval of a front drive.

Servants in green and white livery stood on the white stairs to the house, and the big front door was opened wide. Leland got out of the carriage and turned to offer his hand to Daisy.

"Welcome," he said. "I hope you'll like it here."

She paused in the doorway of the carriage. "It's as big as London," she whispered in awe.

"Not quite. We lack a tower and a palace, although they say the ruler of this place is just as dissolute as our prince. But I hear this fellow's turned over a new leaf, taken a new bride, and promises to become as staid as anyone could wish. Come, meet my staff. They're yearning to be presented."

"I've never lived in a place such as this," she said as she came down the carriage stairs.

"You've lived with worse and survived, haven't you? I think you could get used to this, if you try. You will try, won't you?" he asked, his eyes suddenly solemn.

She laughed. "Oh, my lord, it will be a hardship, but I promise, I will try!"

She was as good as her word. The household staff stood in a reception line, and she accepted their well wishes, never letting them know how stunned she was by how many of them there were. She met the butler and the housekeeper, the cook and her assistants, footmen and maids, coachmen, stablemen, gardeners, and assorted outdoor workers. Daisy lost count of them and realized she wasn't that far off thinking her new home was as big as London. It was, in fact, a small city of workers, and though they all looked happy, well fed, and content, they beamed at Daisy as though she'd come to deliver them.

"They're delighted that I've taken a wife, and one with manners and dignity," Leland explained in an aside as they finished greeting the last of the servants.

When they were done greeting her, the assembled staff burst into applause. That almost made Daisy burst into tears.

"My lady is overwhelmed, as am I," Leland told his staff. "I know all will go well from now on. Thank you for your patience in the past, and for your well wishes today. I've asked Cook to prepare a special menu for you all today so that you can celebrate, too. Again, thank you."

After another bust of applause for his speech, the staff silently and swiftly dispersed. Soon Leland and Daisy were alone in the front hall.

"Your maid's already ensconced upstairs," Leland said. "I'm sure you'd like to change so I can show you 'round."

"Oh, yes, I would," she said.

"Good," he said as they began walking up the long, ornate staircase. "That gown *is* magnificent, but I worry that the trailing tulle will get caught in the rosebushes or dragged through the stable yard, or excite the chickens so much they'll stop laying. Yes, I do have chickens. I hope you're not appalled. I *know* gentlemen should have peacocks, but they're such idiots. Mind you, a peacock's intellect is a notch below that of a chicken's, who are no geniuses themselves, but at least I don't feel guilty about eating a chicken. They are rather dim, you know. Yet still it seems a pity to demolish a wonder like a peacock merely for one's dinner, as the Elizabethans did. Which is why, I suppose, being beautiful is always an advantage. Did you find it so?"

She laughed. "I'm not beautiful enough to answer that."

"Of course you are," he said mildly. "I might not keep peacocks, but I'm impressed by their beauty. I didn't marry for beauty, but I'm delighted to have a lovely wife."

"You flatter me after we're married?" she asked with a grin. "Now that's something wonderful."

"I don't flatter," he said in bored tones. "It's demeaning, at least for the flatterer. *I* merely comment."

"Then, thank you," she said, so pleased and surprised, she didn't know what else to say.

The room he showed her to was immense, and so opulently furnished that she caught her breath. But unlike most great houses she'd seen in illustrated magazines, for all its size and splendor the bedchamber was filled with light and seemed modern and airy. The great canopy bed, big enough for a family to sleep in, was hung with peach panels and covered with a sumptuous apricot-colored silk spread. The furniture was graceful and light, fashioned in the Chinese style the prince had made famous with his pleasure house at Brighton. Even the mantelpiece over the fireplace was made of rose-colored marble. The walls were covered with yellow and white stretched silk, and the paintings on those walls were of the sea and sky. The windows overlooked gardens, and it seemed they'd come inside as well, because everywhere there were vases and baskets of bright flowers.

Daisy peeked into an adjoining room to see a dressing room, and when she opened another door, found a second one. There were bathing facilities behind another door: a huge bath, fit for a Roman spa, and an indoor toilet. She swiftly changed out of the gown she'd been married in, and washed, admiring the beautiful marble water basin. She dallied only because she'd never seen a toilet that flushed before, but soon shook herself from the novelty of flushing, and dressed. She put on a simple yellow walking dress, comfortable slippers, and a straw bonnet. With a last backward glance at herself in a looking glass, she left her room. She couldn't wait to see what else lay ahead for her.

Leland was waiting at the foot of the stair. He, too, had changed, and was dressed like a country gentleman, or rather, she thought, like a London gentleman who had dressed as a country gentleman. Because though he wore a scarf tied carelessly around his neck, no squire had ever worn such a well-tailored green jacket, such immaculate linen, such tightly fitting wrinkle-free gray breeches, or such shining brown half boots.

She smiled. He'd be a paragon of fashion if he had to dress for mucking out a barnyard.

"Yes," he said, as though reading her mind. "Clothes *do* make the man, don't you think? Especially when the man isn't fortunate enough to command a lady's attention otherwise." He smiled. "I know, that's the past, there's only one lady's attention I want now. Even so, I suspect it would be hard to get out of the habit of dressing to suit the occasion. I'm afraid you'll have to put up with a fop. Unless, of course, it disturbs you?"

"No," she said, smiling. "I don't think that caring for your appearance means you're a fop." Especially, she thought, when one had endured a husband who bathed only when he felt too hot, and whose idea of fashion was to put on a clean shirt.

"Good," Leland said, offering her his arm, "Now let's go. I have so much to show you. My housekeeper won't bother you for instructions because it's our honeymoon and you haven't any duties until it's over. Let us hope it never is," he added. "The rest of the staff will also stay discreetly out of our way. So we must entertain ourselves. Shall we begin?"

They strolled down paths to see rose gardens and wisteria arbors, herb gardens and knot gardens and rhododendron walks. His gardeners paused to salute him and show her their prize blooms. Her new husband showed her statues and fountains, and then a huge gazebo that overlooked an artificial pond that suited the real carp in it to perfection.

"These fellows are all tamed, and looking for crumbs," Leland said, seeing her delight when the fish came to the edge of the pond and bubbled up their greetings to her fingertips when she touched the water. "They're ornaments, really. But we've streams that feed a larger lake on the grounds, if you care to see real fish or go fishing. It's too far to walk today, but if you like, we can ride there tomorrow."

"I used to go fishing," she said, her expression turning somber. "Remember, that's partly the reason I was transported. I helped my father as he helped himself to our neighbor's fish."

"I'm sorry to bring up bad memories," he said sincerely.

"I don't mind," she said, looking up at him. "I'd like to see the lake. I actually enjoyed fishing."

Her straw bonnet was a flimsy affair; the wide holes in the weave let in the sunlight. The sunlight brought out the gold in her ruddy hair, and had already begun to inspire a light dusting of freckles on the bridge of her nose. Her eyes glowed with pleasure. The sunlight also clearly delineated her form, because her gown was so thin. For once, that wasn't what held his attention. He studied her face instead. She was very beautiful, and very happy, which made her even lovelier.

"We'll go there tomorrow," he said. "I don't want to exhaust you today."

Her joyous expression vanished. She looked down at the fish again, her eyelashes shadowing her eyes. He frowned, wondered what had dismayed her.

"Oh," he said. "I see. The comment about not wanting to exhaust you today? Don't worry, it had no double meaning. It *is* our wedding night. But if you don't want to begin our marriage tonight in earnest, or in the marriage bed," he added, smiling, "we can wait. We have after all, forever. Or at least as long as it takes for you to invite me to join you in pleasure."

She looked up at him in surprise. Her first husband had taken her away with him the moment the prison ship's captain had finished reciting the wedding service. Tanner had laughed, grabbed her hand, dragged her to his cabin, tossed her on his bunk, flipped up her skirt, thrown himself on her, and done it. The act had taken much less time than the wedding ceremony and had terrified her even more. Leland expected her to invite him to do that? She sighed. She supposed she'd have to. But at least he was giving her time.

"Thank you," she said. "I would like to get to know you better."

"Now *that,*" he said, offering her his arm again, "is brave of you. Come, I'll show you the prize of my home."

He walked her down a path and up another, and then paused. She looked across a stream and another long lawn, and clapped her hands in glee. "A maze!" she cried. "How wonderful! I've read about them and never seen one."

"So you shall," he said comfortably. "I love it if only because it proves that my ancestors were just such frippery fellows as myself. My father was such a grim, dour, humorless man that I often wondered if my dear mama had got me off someone else, as she did Daffyd. But, alas, no. I resemble my late papa, in features, at least. He didn't care for the maze at all. Spending a fortune to erect and then maintain it down through the centuries? He considered it wasteful and unproductive. It didn't produce vegetables, fruit, or wood, and you couldn't hunt or graze animals on it. He didn't understand the reason for a maze because the word 'play' was alien to him. But luckily he was too conservative to destroy it. I'm very pleased that he didn't; it's the only living link I have to anyone in my family who remotely resembles me."

"Your mother didn't appreciate it?" Daisy asked.

"My mother didn't appreciate anything but attention, and though I suppose she could get that if she pretended to get lost in the maze with a handsome stranger, she had no use for it otherwise. My brother Martin is bored by it, maybe because he knows he's not heir to it and he's only interested in what is his. Daffyd's amused by it. Would you like to go in and see why?"

"Yes!" she said eagerly.

The maze was dark green, some twelve feet high, and made of ancient, thickly woven, manicured shrubs. Once they entered the doorway cut into the hedge, the air became closer and the heavy green smell of freshly cut vegetation was strong. The pebbled paths were so narrow, they had to walk close together, and it amused Leland to let Daisy decide the turnings they should take. After a while, she stopped, put her hands on her hips, and looked up at him.

"You are much too amused," she said crossly. "And I'm much too smart to keep walking in circles. I'll never find my way out without help."

"The point is," he said gently, "to find your way *in*," he said, as they began to walk again, taking what seemed like casual left and right turns at random openings in the hedges. "My ancestors would have parties and award prizes to whomever found the heart of the maze first. No one knows the secret path to it but the heir—and my brothers and your friend Geoff, of course. And no doubt, my mama. And the head gardener, and I suppose his helpers, and my butler and housekeeper as well.

"A secret just isn't what it used to be," he said, shaking his head in mock sorrow. "I can feel the weight of my ancestor's disapproval for sharing it so freely. But what if I came in one day and expired on the spot? It would take centuries for me to be found if someone didn't know the way in. Ah, here we are. What do you think?"

Daisy stepped through another doorway in the hedge and stared. The sun shone brightly on the center circle, a clearing of some twenty feet all around. The centerpiece was a larger-than-life-sized statue of a nude Venus being held by an equally nude and obviously passionate Mars. They were ringed and applauded by a host of nude cherubs. It was so grandly presented, it was hard to equate with the fact that it was positively pornographic.

The statue was framed by four curved marble benches placed at equal distances at the side of the circle, the perimeter was solid hedge, and above them, a clear blue sky.

"It is," Daisy said carefully, "certainly not conservative." And then she put her hand over her mouth to stifle her giggles.

"Yes," Leland said, sounding very pleased. "It drove my poor father mad, I understand. He wanted to take it down, but venerated his heritage too much to touch it. Lucky me. I mean, of course, lucky us. Would you care to sit down a while before we go on?"

He led her to a marble bench, waited until she was seated, and then sat beside her. He stretched out his long legs and gazed up at the sky. "The idea behind the centerpiece, of course," he said casually, "was that it would inspire whatever lovely creature my ancestor brought in here with him to romance, or a reasonable version of it. After all, she couldn't leave until he told her *how* she could. So I suppose he made it a forfeit. And I understand, from ancestral memoirs, that this was a very popular place. Well, but they were freer with morals in those days," he murmured. Then he turned his head and looked down at her. "Inspired?" he asked with interest.

He was so close that one of his lean, well-muscled thighs almost touched hers. She felt he was even closer. She smelled lavender and lemon, and something else, something intangible, something of sunlight and darkness, sweet and thrilling, which was his very essence. Her body thrummed, knowing he was so near.

He wasn't a handsome man, not remotely so. But he was compelling, which was fascinating. His eyes were truly beautiful, though, she thought irrelevantly: a different, darker, more intense blue than the sky, filled with intelligence and . . . desire. She'd recognize that anywhere. His skin was clear, his mouth was well shaped, and he was vital and real, and waiting here beside her. And now he was her husband.

She swallowed hard.

He looked at her lips, then her eyes. He hesitated, and then sighed. "No," he said with sorrow. "You're *not* inspired. Ah, too bad. I suppose you're listening to the cautions of the ghosts of too many foolish ladies who were lured here. So am I. It was a bad notion. Forget it and forgive me. I don't want to remember them, either. Well, rested? Ready to go on?"

"To what?" she asked nervously.

"*Not* to heights of sensual bliss, alas," he said with such mock sadness, she had to smile. "That's clear. No, we should go back to the house. The sun is sinking; it will be twilight before long. On the way I'll show you a lovely brook, and the home wood. There's a doe that comes to the edge of the wood at sundown; I confess I encourage her to. I carry a small block of salt in my pocket whenever I'm here, and the silly beast thinks it tastes better than anything in the whole wide meadow she grazes in."

He rose, and so did she. For a moment, standing there, looking up at him, she felt the urge to rise up on her toes and kiss him, so she'd know if what she'd experienced before had been real.

But a kiss could lead to unpleasantness, frustration, and the feeling of captivity she hated, and she found she liked him too much to dislike him so soon. So she simply put her hand on his arm and walked out of the maze with him, head down, watching her steps, thinking she was a coward, and then thinking she wasn't, she was a realist, and so she said nothing at all. But neither did he.

"Tell Cook she has exceeded herself," Leland told his butler as he rose from the dinner table. "She was inspired. I'd applaud, but I'm too full to exert myself."

"She'll be pleased, my lord," the butler said, bowing.

Daisy smiled. Dinner had been delicious, but it was just simple, well-cooked English food. Surely a world traveler and sophisticate like Viscount Haye had eaten better.

"I know," Leland whispered in her ear as they left the room together, "But Cook excels at simple country fare. She does it better than any French chef could. I don't ask swans to sing, or nightingales to be beautiful: to each his own expertise. A wise man shouldn't expect more than a person is capable of. The trick is finding that skill and appreciating it."

"You read my mind," she said simply. "You do that a lot."

"Good," he said. "See you remember that when you sigh over another gentleman, will you?"

"I won't," she said. "Sigh over another gentleman, I mean."

"Don't be so sure. I don't mind the sighing. I would, if it were anything more. Now, we could go to the salon, or the library, or wherever you choose. But it is past dinnertime, and our wedding night. I think the staff would be horrified if we didn't repair to our bed. I didn't mind one whit what anyone said about me before, but I find I'd be dismayed if we did anything to inspire gossip now. It's odd how one becomes a slave to one's servants, isn't it? Don't worry, if you're not sleepy," he said. "Neither am I. But never fear, I'll find something for us to do."

Daisy stiffened. She knew he would. Well, she

thought, better now than later. They could get it done, it wouldn't take long, and then she could act more naturally with him. It wasn't as if it was something she hadn't done hundreds of times before. In fact, she didn't have to do anything but endure it, and try to remember men were men, and so it shouldn't change her feelings about him forever. Because she did like him, very much.

It would be best to get it over with. She realized she was too on edge now, waiting for the moment, it made her nervous and her conversation stilted. She missed the way they'd been before they'd married. They'd certainly laughed more.

"Go on up," he said, pausing at the foot of the stair. "I'll follow, soon."

She trudged up the stairs, and then remembering the omnipresent unseen servants, raised her head, pasted on a smile, and went bravely to her bridal chamber.

Chapter 20

Daisy had brushed out her hair and braided it, when her maid, all a-giggle, held up a fine night shift for her to put on. It was made of the sheerest linen, so it was thin and transparent. Daisy hesitated. But she didn't want to be fully dressed when Leland came to her, because then there'd be the awkwardness of undressing. And she didn't want to disappoint her maid and cause more talk, because the shift really was quite suitable for a wedding night. So she put it on. She dismissed her maid as soon as she could, climbed up into the huge canopy bed, drew the coverlet up to her chest, and sat, waiting for her new husband to appear.

It was an awkward moment that would become

worse, and so she'd brought a book with her in order to be doing something when Leland arrived. She'd thought about it long and hard. She refused to just lie there like a sacrifice on an altar. Or sit up, rigid, tensing at every creak in the floorboards that might signal his approach. She plumped up pillows behind her back, drew the coverlet up again, and pretended to read while her every sense strained to hear his footsteps.

He came into the room a few minutes later, fully dressed.

She gaped at him. He smiled at her.

"Something amiss with my shirt?" he asked in surprise.

"No," she said, and couldn't say more, because she couldn't tell him she'd expected him to be in his nightclothes.

"Gads!" he said, stretching. "It isn't really late, but I feel as if I'd been up for hours. I suppose that's because it isn't every day that I'm up so early, and out associating with so many people. I might as well get ready for bed, too," he said, as he shrugged off his jacket. "You look so comfortable, you inspire me," he said, as he unwound his neck cloth. "Then we can find a pleasant way to while away some hours, because exhausted I may be, but I'm not tired. I never go to bed this early. I'm sure if I did it would be a tremendous shock to my constitution."

Daisy blinked, and then stared. Because now he pulled his shirt over his head, so his voice was muffled as he added, "We have some hours before I'm ready to sleep, but I never asked you. How rude. Are you used to such early hours?"

His head emerged; he tossed his shirt to the side, and looked at her.

She was staring.

"Oh that," he said, looking down at the thin red line on his chest. "My souvenir of London. Don't fret, it's just a lingering reminder of that night at the park; it doesn't hurt."

But that wasn't all she was staring at. His naked chest surprised her. He was so slender, she'd never have guessed how well formed he was: He had a broad, well-muscled chest, and his trim torso tapered to lean hips. There was a light fuzz of hair on his chest, and his skin was clear, except for that healing scar too close to where his heart was.

Then, as she stared, he sat, pulled off one boot and then the other. While she sat mesmerized, he bent and stripped off his breeches, as though it was the most natural thing in the world to undress in front of her.

Tanner had never fully undressed in all the years they'd been married, unless he had to take a bath. He always wore a shirt to bed. Tanner had been a chunky man whose fair skin had often been blotched, and he'd added more flesh around his middle with every year that passed. Now Leland stood up, and Daisy's gazed arrowed to his sex. She glanced away, embarrassed. Leland looked almost like a different species than Tanner. He was fit and firm and though very large, everything was in pleasing proportion to his long body.

Leland turned his back to her, picked up his discarded clothes, and strolled into the adjoining dressing room. Even his rear was taut and trim.

"I have a problem," Leland called from the dressing room. "I do hope you can help me with it. Of course, you're not widely experienced in such matters, but I want your admiration and approval. So I can't act on my own. I've something to show you, and then I'll ask your opinion."

Daisy tensed. The moment was almost upon her, even though it was arriving in weird fashion. Tanner never spoke to her when the mood was upon him. But his needs were obvious and simple. Now she wondered what an experienced roué like Leland expected of her.

For the first time, it wasn't just embarrassment or distaste she worried about. She'd heard about men who liked whips and chains and such. Was her new husband such a one? Was he so jaded that he needed pain or shame? Did he think that just because she'd been a convict she had no sensibilities? That explained much, and would ruin everything. She tensed.

He emerged from the dressing room holding two nightshirts. One was plain and white, the other was cream-colored with embroidery on the neck.

"Now this one," he said, holding it up in front of him, "is classic. Very simply, very tasteful. But this one," he said, switching hands and holding up the other, "is the latest word in France, or so I hear. Which do you like?"

"I don't know," she managed to say. "Either."

"Well, to tell the truth I don't care for either," he told her. "You see, I don't like to sleep in anything but my skin, but I am trying to be sensible of your sensibilities. Wait a moment, I think I have just the thing!"

He disappeared into the dressing room, and came out holding his hands out as though he'd just pulled a rabbit from a hat, like a magician on the stage about to take a bow. Now he wore a colorful red silk dressing gown, sashed in gold. *"Voilà!"* he said. He turned for her, head high, nose in the air, like a fashion model at madame's shop. "What do you think?"

She didn't know what to say.

"I agree," he said sadly. "Outrageously opulent, not my style at all."

He turned, very dejected, to go back to the dressing room.

"Wait!" she said. "Do you really think what you wear to sleep is important?"

He looked at her in shock. "My dear," he said, "a man of taste *never* slacks off, even in his slumbers. And, I remind you, I can't have you thinking your new husband is careless, can I? It's obvious this doesn't impress you, but I have a blue satin one that I thought was too simple. Now I think perhaps it will be the very thing."

She just sat and stared at him. That was how she saw his lips quirk. "Good God!" he said. "Your expression!" And then he began to laugh.

She joined in, as relieved as she was amused. He came over to the bed. "Well, I had to think of something to unknot you," he said with a tender smile. "You looked as though you expected me to come out with whips and chains. You don't, do you? I'd hate to disappoint, but I wouldn't care for that at all."

"Oh my," she said, between the giggles she'd subsided to. "That's exactly what I was thinking you meant."

"Hence the look of a trapped rabbit when I came out of my dressing room," he said, nodding. "*So* relieved to know it wasn't just my presence that made you freeze. Now, for some entertainment."

She stopped laughing.

"Daisy," he said patiently. "Please believe me. I won't touch you until you want me to. It's most unsettling to see you look at me like that. All I meant is that we can play some cards," he said, extracting a deck of cards from his robe's pocket. "Or dice, if you wish," he said, dropping a pair of dice on the bed. "I thought we could while away our hour together that way until it's time for bed. Is that all right with you?"

She breathed again. "Yes," she said earnestly.

Then she dropped her head to her hands and bent double. "Oh, Lord!" she moaned, "How can I ever be ready? What have I done? This is terrible, if only because the more I like you, the harder it will be for me to submit."

He put the pack of cards down on the bed, and came to sit beside her. He placed one large hand on her back; she could feel the warmth of it through her thin gown. "Daisy," he said softly. "That's the point. I don't want you to submit. I want you to enjoy."

She looked up, and he could see her misery. "I don't know if I can. I honestly do not know. I'm not a cheat. I never thought this would happen. I thought I could, but when it comes to it, I freeze, as you said."

He smiled. "We haven't come to it. Relax. I know your past, and you know mine. What we have here is a rake, and a lady who has been abused. If I can use my knowledge, and you can forget yours, we may yet come to *it*, as you say, and find all is well. I think we will. Now, ecarte, piquet, or whist?"

She sniffed, and dried her eyes with the back of her hand. "Piquet, I think," she said. "But beware! I'm very good at it."

"Good!" he said, and drawing his robe around his long legs, he sat on the bed with her.

They played piquet for an hour, and declared it a draw.

Then they played whist, and he won, by a wide margin.

She sat up on her knees, and studied her cards with such seriousness that he teased her for it.

He sat, legs crossed like a tailor, his robe correctly draped to spare her blushes, and himself from stray breezes, or so at least he claimed.

They laughed as they played. He told her the origins of the names of cards, how the jack of clubs was Sir Lancelot, and the queen of hearts was first Helen of Troy, now Queen Elizabeth. He told her how the games were played in gentlemen's clubs and in secret gaming hells. She told him about incidents at card games back at Botany Bay and the truly cutthroat way the games were played there. She sometimes forgot it was her wedding night, and the fellow beside her was the husband she was depriving of his rights. He didn't seem to mind.

He couldn't forget it for a moment. Leland watched his new wife with tender enchantment that made him ache as much with pity as amusement, and thought that if he could tame her and bring her to his hand, his would be the best marriage he'd ever seen, and this, a better relationship with a female than he'd ever dared imagine.

He was almost overcome with the urge to hold her close and tell her she'd nothing to fear from him. But he had to do it with quips and laughter, and hope the rest would follow, in time. She looked more beautiful than ever to him tonight, in her simple white gown. Her hair, in a night braid, made her seem younger and more vulnerable. Her beautiful firm, rose-tipped breasts, clearly visible in her thin gown, made him more vulnerable still. He yearned for her. And all he could do tonight was try to win her trust.

She looked up, saw his expression, and paused, cards forgotten, and stared at him. He held his breath, and leaning forward, touched her mouth with his. Her mouth was as soft and yielding as he'd hoped. Cards fell from her fingers like leaves in the autumn breeze. He put down his cards, put a hand on her waist, drew her closer, and she yielded, clinging to him as they kissed. He murmured a word to her, and that word was "love," and ran his free hand lightly down her neck, only letting his fingertips touch her. He felt her shiver. He kissed her neck after his fingertips had grazed there, and then kissed her lips again. She murmured something he couldn't hear.

He touched her cheek, and then lightly cupped her breast.

She shivered again, and then went rigid.

He stopped and looked his question at her.

She lowered her gaze. "I'm sorry," she said unhappily. "I'll try not to let it happen again."

"No," he said, drawing away. "I don't think so. It's like trying not to sneeze. If you can't help it, you can't. So," he said, sitting back. "Was it anything I did? Or something you thought? You can tell me."

"I don't know. What you did was lovely, but then I thought about what we'd do, and it happened."

"Well, then we won't do it," he said. "It's actually quite late now. Let's go to sleep, if not to bed."

He rose from the bed, went to the dressing table, and turned down the lamp. Though it was dark, she could see him in outline as he drew off his robe, and climbed into bed beside her.

"You're sleeping here?" she asked in surprise.

"Why yes, it *is* my bedchamber," he said as he laid his head down on a pillow. "I mean," he corrected himself, "*our* bedchamber now. I've always disliked the idea of a man and his wife having separate rooms. It leads to estrangement. Don't you agree?"

"I never thought about it," she said, honestly. Tanner would have murdered her if she had demanded a second bed, and anyway, it would have been foolishness in a house the size of the one they'd shared.

"We have this huge bed, and separate dressing rooms, and there are a dozen other bedrooms you can retreat to if I snore," he said on a yawn. "But I've never been told that I do. Excuse me," he added. "One is not supposed to talk about previous experiences."

"Oh," she said, as she lay back and made

herself comfortable beside him, wrapping herself in covers so they wouldn't touch, even in sleep. "Then I should never speak about Tanner."

"No," he said. "You could. I meant that one shouldn't speak about former lovers. I gather he wasn't one."

"Oh no," she said softly. "That he was not."

"Never a word of love?" he asked.

"No," she said. "Because he didn't love me."

He was still. She couldn't see him, but she could sense his interest as the silence between them grew. The statement clearly required more; she knew he was waiting for her to say it. The darkness made it easier for her to speak, and so she relaxed and spoke into the night, and found she could say things she'd never said before.

"He wanted me, but he didn't like me. He didn't even like the way I was with him in bed."

"I'd imagine even he didn't want to make love to someone who loathed him and merely put up with his embraces," Leland said.

He waited for her answer. The more he knew of what she'd endured, the better he could try to change the act of love for her. She wanted him; he knew that. Her past was preventing her. He wished they could have had this talk before. He supposed he'd thought a widow would know more. He scowled; he'd been a blockhead. He'd erred the way that some men who married sheltered virgins did, expecting unrestrained passion to immediately follow marriage vows after a lifetime of restraint. Enough past lovers had told him about that folly. Now he'd done the same thing, misled because she was a widow. He should have listened more closely to what she said before. He had. It was just that he realized he hadn't wanted to believe her.

"No," she said, finally answering his question. "Actually it was the other way around. You see, one night when I was asleep he came to me and didn't bother waking me. I suppose I was still dreaming, or maybe it was because he was drunk and it took him longer than usual, but I began to feel something I never had before, and I moved. He stopped, and slapped my face, hard. He said he didn't want whore tricks, and that if I thought he did, I could think again. He blamed it on other women in the colony, some of whom had been whores. He didn't allow me to talk to them after that."

"I'm very glad that he's dead," Leland said. "Or I would have had to kill him."

She hit the comforter with a balled-up fist. "I shouldn't have told you that. Oh God, Leland, you made such a mistake in marrying me!"

"No," he said. "I didn't. Whores *do* use those tricks to please men, because women are supposed to move, because passion *is* moving. Most men think of it as a compliment to their skill." He sat up, turned, and held open his arms. "May I just hold you?"

She nodded, and buried her face in his neck.

"Don't worry," he said, one hand making large circles on her back, the way he would comfort a child. "That's over and done, it will never happen again."

In time, he felt her relax. A little while later, she drew back. He had to let her go.

"Good night," she whispered, and lay back down on the feather tick.

"Good night," he said, and turned his back to her, so she'd never know how aroused he'd been. He'd had to keep that from her when he'd been comforting her. He stifled a groan, realizing it would be a long time until he got to sleep this night.

This could not go on, he thought, and not just for his sake. He spent the next hour thinking how to end it.

Daisy woke to find herself alone. She closed her eyes as the events of the past night flooded back to her. What had gotten into her, why did she talk about such shameful things? She wondered if Leland was out somewhere trying to find out how to annul this marriage. She couldn't believe what she'd said and what she hadn't done because she'd lacked the courage to do it. That shocked her. She knew it had disappointed him. She resolved to try harder. This was no way to keep a bargain. He had every right to be angry with her.

But when she saw him at breakfast, there

wasn't a trace of reproach in his face or a hint of it in his eyes.

"Good morning," he said calmly as he rose from the table to greet her. "Shall we continue our tour of the grounds today, after breakfast?"

"I'd like that," she said in a subdued voice.

"We can take a basket with us, and go fishing after," he said. He eyed her pretty new saffron-colored gown. "But not in that. Let's go up in the attics, and see if I can find some old waders and breeches for you. I don't want you enacting the role of Ophelia in the water, drifting away, beautiful, but drowned."

She laughed. "I can swim, and besides, fish are drawn to women, and if I wear breeches, they won't recognize me as one."

"Fish are drawn to women?" he asked, raising an eyebrow.

"So my father said," she said, smiling at an old memory. "Or at least so he said when he wanted me to go with him to hold the basket to put his pilfered trout in No gamekeeper ever suspects a little girl."

"I'm positive any sane trout would know you were female no matter what you wore," he said loftily. "They're *my* trout, after all."

They had a wonderful time that day. Less so, that night.

Leland didn't attempt anything but a brief good night kiss before he turned his back on her—to lie awake half the night knowing the only woman he'd ever desired body and soul was so close, and so distant, and wondering what to do about it. More than his resolve and her coldness separated her from him. There was a cocoon of satin bedcovers keeping her chaste. Still, he could smell her perfume and imagine he could feel her body heat, while he tried to subdue his own. It was a sort of penance, he finally decided, which he supposed he richly deserved for past sins.

Daisy lay equally awake, arguing with herself, wondering if she should just rise up on an elbow, wake him, and try to make love to him without hating him for it. She'd thought she could do that with Geoff, and been proven wrong, but maybe it would be possible with this man who was coming to mean more to her every hour she spent with him. She made up her mind in the middle of the night, and was going to wake him, but fell asleep before she could raise her hand to touch him.

"Now, here we are," he said the next day, as he helped her down from her horse. "We'll go into the maze, and you find the way to the center, because I've told you the secret."

"I'm to think of the sonnet you will recite, make out the rhyme scheme, turn to the meter, and *that's* how I get to the heart?" Daisy asked.

"Shhh," Leland said, looking around furtively. "You don't want anyone overhearing it."

"There's no one here but some birds in the

sky," she said crossly. "I can't do it anyway. I don't know the sonnet! I mean, I *know* it but I never memorized it."

"Oh, that," he said, as they went in through the dark hedge. "You don't have to. I only told you that story because it makes it sound so difficult. I'm not even sure it works that way. Listen, now we're absolutely alone, I'll tell you the whole truth of it. I'll sing you a song that I'm sure you do know, and you turn at the end of each rhyme, first right, then left and then left again and then right. If you start off on your right foot and start singing at six paces, you'll be there in no time."

He began to sing an old song in a clear pleasant tenor, a song she knew well enough. It was not one any lady would sing in mixed company.

"I don't believe it!" she cried indignantly, cutting him off. "You yourself said you told Daffyd the Shakespeare sonnet that was the key to this place."

"So I did. But that's not the only way. Am I to blame my ancestor's tastes?" he asked innocently. "They entertained both high and low, as they lived. They were less priggish in those days. Now, step out on your right foot, and at six paces, begin. And all the verses, mind."

She looked at him skeptically. He looked back, and shrugged. So she started to pace off her steps, and when she got to the sixth, began singing in a small, self-conscious voice, as much muttering as singing, because they were really very naughty lyrics. While she sang, she turned at the appropriate places, but when she'd repeated the song five times, now oblivious of how she sounded, she was still in one of the long dark green tunnels that made up the maze. She scowled and looked at Leland.

He was biting his lip, and his eyes sparkled.

"Wretch!" she cried. "You did that just to amuse yourself at my expense." She batted at his shoulder. He turned aside, and, laughing, captured her hands in one big hand. And then he looked at her and stopped laughing, as she stopped fighting and looked at him.

He drew her close, and kissed her. Breathless and surprised, she kissed him back, and found she had to have more of the taste of him. His mouth was sweeter than she'd remembered. She felt the strength of his long hard body against her own, and it dazzled her. He held her gently and deepened the embrace. She closed her eyes, leaned in, opened her mouth to his, and drank long and deep of his kiss.

They paused for breath, looked at each other, and he kissed her again. Or she kissed him; she neither knew nor cared. His hand on her breast thrilled her. She felt her nipple rising to the palm of that big warm hand, and the thrill of it was like shivering heat. He bent his head to run a burning kiss from her earlobe down the nape of her neck, causing her bonnet to fall back and away. She wanted to discard her gown the same way, because everywhere he touched felt on fire. She closed her eyes and gave in to the sensations he roused, breathing in the scent of him, of good lavender soap, clean lemony herbs, and Leland Grant.

She wasn't afraid of disappointing or displeasing him; she couldn't think to be afraid. His shoulders were hard under her hands; she could feel his heart beating hard against her own. She couldn't remember ever feeling this way and was overwhelmed, yet greedy for more.

But he was the one to stop. "Damnation," he said on a shaky laugh, as he looked around. "There's nowhere to go further right now. Why couldn't we have done this in the middle of the maze? You've got us so far from it, it will take time to get there."

Sense was returning to her, he could see it in how her eyes grew wide. She pulled her bonnet back on and tied its strings with shaking fingers. "You mean you want us to do that here and now?" she asked tremulously.

"No," he said on a long sigh of defeat. "It would be impossible here; just think of how we'd block the path. We don't want any wandering hedgehog to fall over us. And I don't fancy leaning back against the hedges; I doubt they'd support us and I'd think it would be far too prickly in any event. Daisy," he said in a softer voice, "don't worry. That was just a good omen of days, and nights, to come."

She nodded.

He saw her retreat from him as clearly as if she'd struck him. There'd be no further lovemaking now. She was too self-conscious.

"Come," he said gently. "We've been here too long. Let's go home. Would you like to sing our way out?"

That made her smile and she pretended to bat him, as he laughed and pretended to dance away. They both knew it was pretense, and were glad for the diversion as they walked back to their horses together.

They rode in silence, but as their horses neared the house again, she spoke. "Leland?" she said.

"Yes?" he asked warily, because there was something in her voice that alerted him.

"Can we make love together, today or tonight?"

He stared at her. A slow smile appeared on his lips. "I am your servant," he said, bowing from the waist. "Anything to please you. Would you like to join me on my horse?" he asked. "He's really faster, and we can get there straightaway."

Chapter 21

They raced back home, gave their horses to a stable boy, and arm in arm, went into the house. The butler met them at the door. Leland nodded to him, and led Daisy into the hall. A footman there told him the housekeeper had a question about the dinner menu, and then blushed scarlet. And two maids on the stairs paused to gaze at them round-eyed.

Leland stopped in the hall and sighed. "The look on my face gave me away," he whispered to his bride. "There were times when this home's hospitality was ill used," he explained. In those times, he thought, he'd have gone upstairs with a woman he desired despite how many of his servants saw him. But this was different. This was his bride. And the look on her face now told him it had to be different.

There wasn't any way that he could take her to their room now without the whole household knowing. He saw that knowledge in her eyes, and realized that must have been like cold water on the fire that he'd lit in her. Because she'd stopped laughing.

But she was obviously determined. She gazed at him with gravity. "Well, we're here," she said. "Shall we get on with it?"

All laughter had fled; she was sober, actually steely now. So she'd resolved to take him on, he thought. Gads! He'd assumed a difficult task.

Daffyd and Geoff had told him more about their experiences in the Antipodes than the woman he'd just married ever had done. He'd been content to wait for her to relax and trust him in time. One thing was coming clear, though. That brute of a husband had almost ruined her for lovemaking. The operative word was "almost." Her new husband was determined to change that, because he felt—he knew—he had to believe—she wanted to change it, too. He'd felt the hidden fire in her.

He'd never wanted a wife who would simply endure him. He could have married any number of well-brought-up young women who would do that. They were trained to. Not only had he met too many eager to learn more from other men after they'd presented their husbands an heir, but too often such women could never be brought to joy. Nor had he wanted a wife who was wildly profligate. He'd had a mother who had ruined too many lives with her appetites. Still, to marry a woman who dreaded the marriage bed because of what she'd experienced there? But he was ever a man for a challenge.

"Then let's continue this discussion upstairs," he said. He signaled to his butler. "What we'd like," he told the man, "is an assortment of Cook's cakes. I especially like the little ones, with currants. Can we have them brought upstairs? And bring up a few bottles of champagne from the cellar too. The '94, the ones without tax stamps, from France. We've been married three days, we wish to celebrate. Now," he told Daisy, as the butler, smiling, left. "We'll have ourselves a revel."

Her eyes widened, but she swallowed hard, and went up the stairs with him.

She was laughing in an hour. They'd had champagne, and Leland was telling her about some incident at a revel when he'd been at Cambridge. He'd changed to his silken robe, and seemed comfortable, sitting and spinning stories for her. He was a wonderful storyteller.

She sat on their high bed, cross-legged, her pink gown making a pretty contrast to the peach coverlets. When he finished his last story, she pummeled the coverlets with a fist and groaned with laughter. Her hair had come loose from its ribbon, and it framed her face with rosy gold curls. Her smile was radiant; she wasn't intoxicated, merely merry.

"No more," he said when she held out her glass for champagne again. "You're feeling too lovely."

"I am not!" she protested.

"Then get angry with me. See if you can."

She collapsed into giggles. "You're right! How can I be mad at someone who gives me such delicious cakes and wine?" She raised her head and peeped at him through errant curls. "I'm not tipsy, I'm just happy. This reminds me of the days before I was sent away, when I'd visit with my friends and sometimes stay overnight at their cottages. We'd tell stories and giggle until dawn. My friends," she said wistfully. "I wonder what happened to them. After my father and I were arrested, I never heard from them again."

She sat up straighter. "Too bad for them, right?" she said, tossing her head to clear the curls from her eyes. "I made friends back in Port Jackson. They call it Botany Bay, but no one can live there. We stayed at Port Jackson. And I did have friends there, too. But we never laughed so much. There are people with tales sadder than mine," she said seriously. "And now," she said on a deep breath, "I don't intend ever to be sad again."

"I'll try to ensure that you never are," he said. "That, at least, I can promise."

He rose from the chair he'd been sitting in, and came to sit beside her. He drained the last of his champagne, then paused and held up the empty glass, scrutinizing it. "They say that these were made from molds of the breasts of Marie Antoinette," he mused.

From the corner of his eye, he saw her eyes widen. "But I also heard they're modeled after those of Diane de Poitiers, mistress of our Henry the Second. I also heard that Paris took a mold of Helen of Troy's bounty, and that's where they come from. Odd, that so many lovely breasts figure in stories about one simple glass, don't you think?

She eyed the glass carefully. She took it from him, and suddenly clapped it over her own right breast. Now his eyes widened.

"Phoo," she said, looking down to see that the glass didn't encompass half of her breast. "That doesn't speak well for me. I couldn't fit in one of these. Or even two put together. Well, maybe two put together. What do you think?

"Oh! Your face," she exclaimed, laughing again, and clapping her hands. "I've finally done it! I've shocked you! And here you were, trying to scandalize me. Don't deny it. You've been telling warmer and warmer stories . . . why, that's what happens when *you* drink too much," she said. "Did you know that?"

"Possibly," he said, taking the glass from where she'd put it on the bed, and placing it on the nightstand. "But actually, I was trying to warm you up. Seduce you, that is. There are some who say that warm talk enlivens a woman wonderfully."

He traced one finger along her collarbone, then leaned forward and brushed his lips along it. His hand trailed down toward her breast, his lips following. "I wouldn't want to put this lovely article in a glass," he murmured against her skin, as his finger pulled down the neckline of her gown. "There are far better things to do with it."

He cupped her now exposed breast and brought his mouth to the puckered rosy tip. "Much better," he murmured.

She sat still, feeling too much to know what to say as he put his tongue to her breast, and then his lips again. Tanner had sometimes squeezed her breasts in lust, or pinched her there as a jest, but he'd never done this. This was extravagantly delicious, it overcame her; she couldn't assess her feelings.

He raised his head to see her expression.

"This is good, isn't it?" he asked.

"It's too good, I didn't know . . ."

He silently cursed the dead man who had obviously never treated her with any tenderness, even in lust. "Oh, it gets better," he said as he gathered her in his arms.

He kissed her gently, his palm over the breast he'd abandoned, so that the air couldn't chill her. They sat on the high bed and he stroked and kissed her, touching his tongue to hers. She sighed into his mouth. Her hands went to his head and she held him so she could drink deeper. Her skin warmed; he could feel her heart racing against his. She moaned, low in her throat. That was what did it. She heard herself and woke from the sensual spell he'd been weaving.

He felt her body stiffen. He drew away.

"What?" he asked.

She shook her head; he could see frustrated tears springing to her eyes. "Don't stop," she said angrily. "I can't help it, ignore it, go on."

"In a pig's eye," he said. "What happened?"

"I don't know. I just thought of what we'd do. Pay it no mind. I'll get over it."

"Get over what?"

"Dreading," she said, and then cursed in a way that made his eyebrows go up. He was impressed.

"It's fine when I *feel*," she said furiously. "But when I *think*, it all stops. It must be because I always had to think before, with Tanner. Whenever he came to me. Because I couldn't bear to feel. Now, when I want it the other way 'round, this happens. Damnation!" she swore, balling her hand to a fist and pounding the bed, "I didn't know it or I'd never have married you, or anyone! Do you believe me?"

"Oh, yes," he said. He thought for a moment, trying to rein in his senses, so he could make sense. "Well," he finally said, "there are several ways we can fix this. Believe me, it can be and will be remedied. Now, let's see the best way to do it. We can feed you a whole bottle of champagne and open another. Then you won't be thinking at all." He frowned. "But the problem is that if we get you drunk enough you won't remember how good it was with us, and we'll have to start all over again next time."

She smiled, but it was a small, sad smile.

"Or," he said, "we can put you in charge. That's it! You won't have to think of anything but what you want me to do next."

"What?" she said.

He cocked his head to the side. "Of course, there's the distinct possibility that you won't know what you want. But that can be sorted out, too. I'll tell you in advance. Or show you, and you can judge. How does that sound?"

She stared at him.

"Shall I tell you your options?" he asked, smiling.

She bowed her head into her hands "Oh," she whispered in an agony of self-loathing, "why do you put up with me?"

"Because," he said softly, "I love you. I thought you knew that."

She looked up at him.

He gathered her close in his arms. *"Nothing* could be worse than not knowing what's going to happen," he told her. "I should have realized that sooner. Sometimes talking about such things can be lovely. Did you know there are some people who would rather talk about it than do it? Well, not you or I, but I think talking can ease our way. Let me tell you what's possible. Remember, you will have your choice."

And then he spoke to her about making love, the things they could do together. He described those things in soft words, delicious words, wooing her with how he phrased them. Nothing he said sounded wrong. He punctuated each lesson with a kiss, and told her about things she'd heard of, but had been grateful Tanner never asked of her. Now, listening to her new husband's husky, entrancing voice, as he sat next to her with his arms around her, trying to seduce her into a deeper embrace, she found she wanted to try everything he spoke of.

Only once, she stopped him, her eyes wide. "*Good* women do that?" she asked in wonder.

"The *best* women do that," he assured her. "And I, of course, would do similar, only different, of course, for you. Would you like to hear about that?"

"No," she said.

He stopped breathing, and silently cursed himself for a fool, to think a woman who had been hurt by a man could be lured by words that told her about what she must think of as only further indignity. He was wondering how to repair the damage, thinking frantically of what to do next, when she pulled his head down to hers, and kissed him.

"Don't you want to hear more?" he asked,

when he could, though he felt that if he waited longer his heart would surely pound out of his chest.

"Show me *now*," she said against his mouth. "Please."

He did.

This time, she didn't pull away. Not when he kissed her mouth, or when his lips sought her throat, or her breasts. Certainly not when he finally helped her out of her thin gown, which she suddenly found too tight, too warm, and far too concealing.

She paused only once. "Take off your robe," she whispered. "I want to know what you were talking about, Lee. Oh, I do so want to know."

"At your service, my lady," he said. "So do I." He opened his robe and flung it away.

He cupped her bottom so he could hold her closer against himself, laid her against the pillows, and followed her down to the bed. She felt his excitement, and wasn't afraid; she was too busy learning how amazing kisses could be and reveling in his caresses.

She wanted to know what he tasted like, she had to touch him as he was touching her, not because it was only fair, but because she *had* to. He obliged her, as, body to body, they sought each other.

Only once did she startle, when he touched her as no man had ever done before. It felt too wonderful; she was as shocked as thrilled. His hands were gentle; she didn't even worry when she felt one long finger begin to explore her intimately. She only wanted more. But he stopped when he felt her body leap.

"No, no," she murmured disjointedly, her face buried in his neck, "Don't stop, don't. It's just that it's so good and I never knew."

"Know now," he breathed in her ear, and kissed her as he went on touching her.

She shivered with pleasure and then gasped for breath, as she felt a spasm of pleasure she'd never imagined. He waited until she realized she wanted even more.

It was more than he'd hoped. She was all fire, and now, all readiness. But she'd obviously listened to what he'd said.

She reached for him. "My choice," she breathed. "I want the same for you. Like this?" she asked as she finally gently measured his length in her hands. The size and power of him astonished her. He went very still.

For one second, before he answered, she wondered if she'd gone too far, or not far enough. She'd only touched Tanner when he'd been too drunk and unable; when he'd commanded her to ready him, and do it fast. She didn't want to mishandle this man.

"Any way you touch me is right," he breathed. "That's good, that's fine, that's perfect, yes."

He finally stopped her, and moved over her. "That's wonderful," he said. "But there's something even better."

She lay back, trusting him. He kissed her before he probed her intimately again. He couldn't believe his luck. She was ready, and she was, at last, greatly willing.

Slowly, carefully, though he was afraid he'd perish if he didn't hurry, he entered her. She sighed, and shivered, and stretched her whole body beneath his, accepting him, moving to accommodate him.

He moved with her, glorying in the heat and sweetness of her, murmuring love words into her ear, holding back because he'd be damned if he'd leave her before he satisfied her, even if his heart burst from the effort.

And then she finally rose against him and shuddered, gasped, then shuddered again and again. Only then did he allow himself to join her in ecstasy, crying out her name as he did.

They lay quiet. Her body still quivered from the vastness of the sensations she'd experienced. He was totally fulfilled, and yet, still yearning. His hand stroked her hair where she lay now, against his heart.

She was the one to speak first. "Thank you," she said. "I never knew how I could feel. This was nothing like . . . Oh, thank you."

He could feel her lips curl against his chest as she smiled.

"Now I don't wonder at your reputation of a seducer," she said.

His hand stilled in her hair. "No," he said softly. "In fact, I never seduced anyone before. What a revelation. What an oversight. I didn't know what *I* was missing. It was lovely. Thank *you,* my love."

She didn't answer, but he felt a drop of moisture fall from her eyes.

"Here now," he said, pulling her up so he could wipe that tear away. "No more of that! We can make love in the water, it's actually quite entrancing, or so I've heard. But not now."

She giggled, then she laughed.

He joined in. "Now," he said. "Shall we get on with our lessons?"

"You can?" she asked in wonder.

"Well, I think so. Care to help me try?"

"I'm so glad we came in from the maze," she said a moment later. "Imagine if anyone had stumbled on us doing *this*?"

"They wouldn't have," he answered absently. "I gave orders to keep everyone away."

She drew back. "Oh, you cheat!" she cried. She caught up a pillow to swat him, then she lowered it. "Thank you," she said, and stilled his laughter with a kiss.

Chapter 22

The honeymoon couple spent a week discovering each other's bodies, finding how gloriously they fit together. Then, the next week, they passed their time also learning how their minds did the same.

Daisy told her new husband about her trials from the first moment of her father's arrest to her arrival at Botany Bay. She tried not to talk too much about Tanner, but Leland asked, and so she did. One day he stopped asking, and soon she realized she'd almost forgotten Tanner, because she never had to think of him again. Her new husband had eclipsed him in every way, erasing bad memories, replacing him, until Tanner seemed like a person from a bad dream she'd had long ago and far away.

Leland listened to what his new wife said, and wondered at her courage and buoyant spirit. She'd survived the terrors of being a young girl imprisoned through no fault of her own, facing the horrors of Newgate prison and transportation, and then the consequences of being sold into marriage to a man so far beneath her that if the world had been run right, she'd never have even chanced to see him passing her in the street. Daffyd and his foster brothers and the earl had come through similar trials intact, but Leland couldn't think of any woman who could have survived with such spirit and grace.

They walked and talked, made love and talked; they danced and sang, rode and drove around the surrounding countryside. They fished in streams and swam in the lake, and slept locked in each other's arms in the night, even when they didn't make love. And daily, they thanked each other for being there.

Though Leland joked about it, Daisy heard how his childhood had been plagued by gossip about the adventures of his errant mama, and plagued by his cold martinet of a father, and his mother's continuing disapproval.

"I had the bad fortune to look like my father," he explained.

She wondered how he'd survived with such

decency and charm. Daisy came to understand at last how his sense of humor had saved him, and she silently vowed that he'd never have to use it for strength again, not if she could help it.

In short, she fell madly in love with him.

He came to respect her as well as continuing to adore her.

They were so happy, they didn't want to think about returning to London. But they remembered she had an enemy, and they knew they'd never really know peace until they discovered who had falsely accused her and tried to drive her out of the country again.

They returned to London on a sultry morning, and immediately wished they'd stayed in the countryside. An unusual bout of hot weather had settled on the Town, just before the end of the social Season, and it curtailed activity just as surely as a blizzard might have done.

As they drove in through the gate near the Bull and Mouth, they could see London's streets were simmering. The street criers and barrow mongers positioned themselves in the shade, no matter where their customers were. Business was off, because the streets were empty of everyone except for those drooping poor souls, servants, and travelers who had to be out and about. As they passed the park, they saw it wasn't particularly crowded, because shade didn't mean cool in such weather.

At least the front entrance to Leland's town house was relatively comfortable, because of its marble floors.

As Daisy went upstairs to wash and change into something light, Leland's Town butler presented him with the post and the messages that had piled up on a silver salver in the front hall since he'd left. He also informed his master that the *ton* were not very active these days. They sat in their parlors or back gardens fanning themselves. Evening parties were being poorly attended. No one wanted to be at a fashionable crush if it was also a truly suffocating one. Affairs held in the early morning were attended, though. Breakfasts and morning calls were substituted for soirées and balls for those who still hoped to get their unwed daughters married off before the premature ending to the Season. Plans were being made to return to their country homes.

"So we'd best see our old friend Geoff right away, and ready ourselves for some morning callers," Leland told Daisy when she came down the stairs. "I've sent a message to him, and word to Bow Street as well as some of Daffyd's old cronies on the other side of the law, to see if any new information is known. I want you not only to be safe, but to feel safe. That won't happen until we know who laid charges against you."

"And who knifed you," she said.

He shook his head. "No, I don't think that

matters. More and more I think that it was actually just a purse snatcher who got frightened when I lunged at him. We'll know soon. Then we can go back home. I'll have to take you to see my ancestral home, too. My mother will likely be there, but we won't have to stay long. As for now," he told her, "I just have to read all my messages; my desk is covered with letters and cards. Then we can sit somewhere cool and wait on events. Why don't you wait in the back parlor? I hear it's less hot there. I'll join you as soon as I can."

He came into the parlor a few minutes later, grinning ear to ear. He waved a letter in his hand. "Guess what?" he asked, grinning. "Daffy's had a boy! That is to say, his wife, Meg, has had one. A healthy, squalling little brat, Daffyd says. Dark as his father and fair as his mother, he says, with very blue eyes, and the fiend's own temper, just like his father, too. He's over the moon about it, and begs us to come see and admire him. I think we should. You'll like Meg very much. We can go there before I take you to my estate in the north."

He scanned the letter again, and his smile slipped. "He also asks if I know where Geoff is, because he hasn't heard from him, and he expected him to be there over a week past."

Daisy's head went up and she paled. "No word of him?"

"None," Leland said, scanning the letter again. His jaw tightened. "Don't worry yet. There are a thousand things that could account for that. He said he was taking your Helena to her mother's home up north. He could have gone anywhere from there. He may have stopped off at Egremont, to see how things stood at his estate. It's not good to leave a place without a master for too long. He has tenants there, and he is a responsible landlord. He may have visited with a friend. Sometimes a letter sent from the north can take days to reach London. Let me go through the rest of my mail to see if I can find the answer, and if not, I'll pay a call on the earl's house here. Then, if there's no word, we can be alarmed."

"*We'll* pay a call on Geoff's house," she said. "I can't bear to sit and wait."

He hesitated, and then when he spoke, there wasn't a trace of humor in his voice. "No, I think not. If something has happened to the earl, you are the *last* person who should be out in the streets right now. I can protect you. But I'd rather not have to."

She took a deep breath and nodded, once.

"We'll find out, it's likely nothing," he said. "Sit tight, and stay cool. It's murderously hot outside."

She shivered at his choice of words. And seeing that, he winced.

Viscount Haye returned to his town house at dusk, looking wilted and walking slowly, lost in thought. When he saw he'd arrived at his own house, he straightened and walked faster. That was what alarmed Daisy the most.

"What has happened to Geoff?" she asked him at once when he walked in, rising from where she'd been sitting on a window seat watching the street.

He ran a finger under his neck cloth and sighed. "What fiend made this fashionable? Sooner put a man in manacles and ask him to swim than to wear this torturous thing on a hot day. Ah well, at least there's no one around Town to notice that I look like a laborer. I didn't find out *anything*," he told her. "There's no ransom note. There's no hint of violence, no accident recorded in the past week going up or down the North Road. And no one from his old days in Botany Bay has heard a word of other violence, either. I met with Bow Street as well. No one knows where he is. That's good. Because wherever he is, it can't be because anything dire happened to him."

"But he is wealthy," she said. "One of the richest men in England. And he's kind, and trusting."

"Yes, he's wealthy. He's also more experienced with crime and criminals than most men in England. Don't forget that. He'll be fine, he is fine, I'm sure of it. We can't do more than wait on word from him. I'm sure there's a perfectly good reason for his silence. Even the men I paid to find out about him said that, and they've reason to hope for mischief, if only because they'd be better paid if there was any."

She felt relieved, until she noticed that he stood irresolute, unsmiling.

"But so many ears to the ground can hear anything," he said. "I learned something else, something that I must resolve."

"What is it?" she asked fearfully.

"I finally discovered who laid evidence about you. Oh, don't worry," he said quickly when he saw her grow paler. "It's utter nonsense. The powers that be know it. The information is ridiculous, and false. It was given by a fellow named Samuel Starr, recently arrived from Botany Bay."

"Samuel . . . Starr?" Her eyes widened. *"Old Blister Me?"* she cried. "We called him that because he said it all the time. He was an old pirate; I really think he was one. When he couldn't go to sea anymore, where he could sail away from his crimes, I suppose, he took up stealing in London. He was very bad at it on land. He was a burly, bald old man, with a tattoo on his cheek like a South Sea Islander, and . . . But he didn't dislike me! In fact, I thought we were friends. He had such good stories to tell." She smiled, remembering. "I always enjoyed talking to him. I didn't know he'd left the colony . . . "

She sobered. "Why did he do it? Lie about me, I mean? He knew Tanner died of an accident. He was one of the men who brought him home after it. He saw me then, and even tried to console me. He said I was well out of it, and I know he meant it kindly. Why did he change his mind?"

Leland had pulled off his limp damp neck cloth and now held it as though it were a dead rat, dangling from the ends of his fingers. He shrugged, and didn't look at her. "Why else?" he asked. "For the money. It seems he was starving. He was an exquisitely inept pickpocket. And someone offered him a sum of money he couldn't resist. Once he'd had a decent dinner, he began to regret his part. He's very sorry, he says. Never mind that, if you don't want to, we won't press charges against him. He *is* only a poor old fellow, and abjectly sorry to boot."

Now he looked at her. "More to the point, he told me who paid him to do it." Leland's eyes were stark and dark, haunted by some misery she'd never seen there before. "I'm going to change my clothes, and then go to speak with that someone. This time, if you like, you may come with me. *I* don't like it, but you'll be safe enough, and I do think it would be for the best for all concerned. Especially you. There's no need for you to be afraid of ghosts. Will you come?"

"Of course," she said.

He studied her with an unreadable expression. "Very well. Dress in something cool," he finally said, ". . . and beautiful."

* * *

Daisy's eyes grew huge when she saw where Leland stopped his carriage. She looked at him. "Here?" she asked.

In that moment, he looked infinitely weary. "Yes," he said. "I believe here is where it started, and I know here is where it will end. Nothing to feel bad about," he added in a soft voice. Nothing to fear. That I promise. But you should see this, and relieve your mind. *I* am the one who should be upset," he said. "If I refuse to be, then so should you. Come, let's get it over with."

He gave the reins to his tiger, the boy in livery who rode on the back of the curricle, and stepped down. He took his wife's hand to help her down from the driver's seat. "You look lovely," he said, admiring her new peach-colored muslin gown and matching bonnet. "And wasn't it delicious to feel the breeze as we drove? It's the only way to get one today. Let's drive 'round the park after we're done here, shall we? I want to show you off, as well as cool you off."

She smiled, but her hand shook in his, and not from fear of getting down from the high driver's seat. When she reached the pavement, she breathed a shuddery sigh. "Lead on," she whispered.

"What a pleasure to see you, sir," the butler who admitted them at the door said.

"A pleasure to see you again so soon, Fitch," Leland said. "You're looking in fine fettle, I must say. You don't change, someday you must tell me your secret. And here is my lady, Deidre, the new

Viscountess Haye. We were married a month past in the West Country, at a church near my country house. I'm planning to have a reception for the villagers and everyone at Haye Hall later this summer, so I can introduce my lady to everyone properly, as well as introducing my home to her."

The imperturbable butler blinked. "My lady," he said, when he recovered. He bowed. "A great honor to meet you. I had heard of your nuptials; it was in the papers. May I offer you my very best wishes?"

Daisy nodded. "Thank you," she said. She shot a puzzled look to Leland where he stood, his lips thinned, his expression impassive.

When the butler straightened, he looked at Leland, and much that wasn't said seemed to pass between them in that moment. "I will inform your mother that you are here, my lord," the butler said. "Please come sit in the garden. I'd ask you into the salon, but the heat is perishing there today."

"Thank you," Leland said. "Come, Daisy, Fitch is right. We *will* be cooler in the garden. My mother's salon is a welter of heavy furniture and heavier fabric. The furniture is priceless, and the fabric, museum quality. Fine for December, but not for today."

But Daisy only stood, white-faced, looking up at him.

"Yes," he said, putting his hand over hers

where it lay on his arm. "Unpleasant for me, but not out of character for her. At least the nonsense will end, here and now. I want you to hear it from her own lips."

He looked at the butler. "Fitch, please send to my mother. And there's no need to mention that my wife accompanies me."

"Certainly, my lord," the butler said, and led them through the stifling house to the garden in back. "I'll tell the viscountess at once," he said, and left Leland and Daisy on a terrace overlooking a neat square of a garden shaded by ancient lacy leafed elms.

Daisy couldn't sit. She stood by the stone balustrade and watched Leland prowl, pacing back and forth. She didn't try to speak to him. He seemed too preoccupied by his own thoughts to listen. Then she saw his head go up and his nostrils become pinched, as though he smelled something distasteful.

"Haye," the viscountess said as she came out on to the terrace. "How good to see you." She wore a white gown, and with her fair hair and skin, the only color she had was in her deep blue eyes, so like her son's. Except they were devoid of expression. That searching blue gaze found Daisy. "How charming. You've brought me a guest. Have we met before? You do look familiar. Forgive me for not remembering," she said to Daisy, "but at my age, one does tend to forget the names of new acquaintances."

"Really?" Leland said in cool amused tones. "How odd, considering how involved you made yourself in her life. You must learn to remember her name. This is my lady wife, Daisy, Mama. I'm surprised you don't remember what she looks like. You certainly did recall her name when you paid poor old Samuel Starr to testify against her. Oh, I see what it is. You paid someone else to ask him. Of course. You never would stoop to actually speaking with someone like him. You must recall his name, though. You got it from some seedy persons. And then you paid him to lay information against my wife in an effort to have her arrested for the murder of her husband."

She stood stock-still, staring at her son.

He waved a hand as though to bat away a gnat. "I haven't the time to play today, Mama. I simply came to you with the truth. Useless to ask why you did it. I can guess. I'm here to ask you to apologize to my lady. And to vow you'll never meddle in my affairs, or hers, again. If you do not," he said in a steely voice, "I must ask you to remove yourself from this house. I own it, if you recall. But you may stay on if you keep far from us. I'd ask you to leave England altogether, only I don't want more gossip. And, if you do ever return to Haye Hall, you can only take up residence in the dower house. I never intend to sleep under the same roof as you again, and would certainly not ask my wife to do so. I'm sure you understand.

My wife's comfort, peace of mind, and safety are paramount to me, you see. And your presence ensures that she won't have that."

He turned and paced a step, then wheeled around to face his mother again. "For shame, madam," he said angrily. "What a beastly thing to do. Not clever, not witty, just pure troublemaking. Whatever possessed you? Surely it wasn't done for my welfare? You've never concerned yourself with that before. And how misguided that would have been. You must have discovered that my wife is wellborn, and her transportation a travesty of justice, as all now admit. You also know that I could have married far beneath me, instead of being lucky enough to wed this beautiful young woman who foolishly consented to be my wife. It couldn't have been to protect the family name, either. Hers has *far* less scandal attached to it than ours. And not only because of my reputation. I remind you that yours is similarly sullied. So, why then?"

His mother stood tall, rigid. "I never meant the girl harm," she said haughtily.

"Nonsense," Leland said. "What would you call trying to arrange her arrest and deportation? And I remind you, madam, that she is not a 'girl,' she is my wife. Never forget that again. I can understand, if never condone, your attempting to have her deported. You didn't know her, after all. Hard as it is for me to believe, I concede it may have been misplaced and belated concern for me.

But why the devil arrange to have me skewered that evening in the park?"

Now his mother sneered. "I had nothing to do with the assault on you. I may not be a doting mother, but I do not want your death. In fact, I had it investigated. My sources tell me it was a random incident. The fellow who did it confessed as much to his friends, and then fled the city. He was only a petty criminal who lost his head when you frightened him. I may have done many things, but I would not harm you, Haye. You have committed follies yourself, but you are nevertheless a credit to your name: Your tenants thrive, the estate does well, you pay your debts and increase the family fortune. In fact, you uphold the title as your brother, alas, could not."

"*Which* brother?" Leland asked. "Martin, yes. I can see that. Though he may improve with time. But Daffyd is intelligent and well balanced."

"Don't be absurd," she said, her own nostrils pinching. "I meant your legitimate brother. But you likely know that very well." She turned her gaze on Daisy. "Understand please," she told Daisy, ignoring her son. "I bear you no ill will. In fact," she said, with a slight icy smile, "I congratulate you. You are exactly fit to marry him."

Leland gave a cough of a laugh. "Now *that* that was deftly done—an insult wrapped in a compliment, ambiguous, but offensive. And untrue. She is far above me, and leagues above you. Now tell her that you won't ever meddle in her life again."

"Done," his mother said. "I won't, my dear," she told Daisy. "Why should I? You have married my son, and with that, pleased me very well." For the first time, she showed emotion. She was smiling and seemed genuinely pleased.

Leland frowned. "I can't guess your game," he said slowly. "But wait!" he said. "Now maybe I can. You didn't want to harm Daisy. That I believe, if only because you wouldn't want to be blackmailed for it one day. Nor did you do it to save me, of course not. Why the devil did I keep trying to believe you care a jot for me? You only wanted her out of the way. So if we take that and spin it out further, realizing that you weren't considering me at all, not only because you never have done, but because I didn't seem to be courting her . . . "

His eyes opened wide. "Good God! It was *Geoff* you were trying to protect from Daisy! The earl! He was the one you wanted her to keep away from. Because—" He stopped and shook his head. "Lord, madam," he said ruefully, "you fly high. But he'll never ask you, you mistake your prey this time. He doesn't care for your sort at all."

Her chin went up. "Do you think so? I do not. Time will tell. You are clever, Haye. But you don't know everything. He is a gentleman born, and in need of a wife. You cannot know what *he* would consider a fit mate. I believe I can. Now, enough, if you please. I have apologized and I promise not to meddle in your affairs again. Your ban on me living with you doesn't concern me at all. I have no intention of doing so. You may save the dower house for whatever you wish. I will never set a foot there. I have funds, and friends on the Continent, and this house in London, which you say I may keep if I leave you alone. That, I can promise. So. What else do you want of me?"

"*I?* Nothing. Just as well, that's all I ever got from you. Good morning, Mama. My wife and I were just leaving."

"Go in good health," she said. "I never wished you harm."

"But you almost caused it," he said. "Because to harm my wife in any way is to do the same to me. But you never understood that, did you?"

"I have ever been unfortunate in my dealings with men," she said. "I wish you daughters," she told Daisy. "Because I cannot think to wish you better than that."

"I want to have your son's sons *and* his daughters," Daisy said, straightening her back. "Only know this: Do not disturb my husband again. Remember," she said coldly, "I own a pistol and can use a knife."

The viscountess's eyes widened, and she stepped back.

"Forgive me, my lord," Daisy told Leland with sincerity. "But I get very emotional when someone I love is threatened."

He laughed. "She does," he told his mother. "Remember that. Good day, madam."

Leland took Daisy's hand and they walked out of his mother's house together. He said nothing until his curricle was two blocks away. He spoke then, through clenched teeth.

"You're always apologizing to me because you were in prison," he told Daisy, without turning his gaze from the horses he drove. "I never wanted you to; now you understand why. On balance, my love, you now must admit that I had the worse upbringing, and it is *my* family who has the worst criminal. Forgive me, and let's end this here, shall we?"

"There's nothing to forgive," she said. "I'm so sorry."

"For what?" he asked, as he turned the curricle to enter the park.

"For you," she said.

They rode in silence for a while, going down green paths, not speaking because they both were thinking so hard.

"Do you think Geoff will ever . . . ?" she began.

"Fall victim to her? No."

"She is very beautiful," Daisy said doubtfully.

"So is a snowfall. And if it ever looks like he's

about to succumb, I'll speak with him, never fear. Did you feel that? The wind is finally moving. It looks like a storm coming. Good, it will clear the air. Let's go home."

They drove out of the park and returned to their home as the sky darkened and a brisk fresh breeze began blowing. When he got to his house, Leland handed the reins to his tiger. As thunder rattled, Leland took Daisy's hand, and they ran into the hall, laughing, racing the rain. They got inside just as the first fat drops began falling.

"I can't dry you off properly here," Leland said tenderly, his hands on Daisy's shoulders as he looked at her rain-spattered gown. "Shall we go upstairs and do it right?"

"My lord," his butler said from behind him, just as Daisy reached up on tiptoe to kiss her husband. "You've company. I've asked them to wait in the parlor."

"Indeed?" Leland said, his attention caught. His butler was smiling. He would never have asked anyone in without permission unless it was someone close. "You go change, and wait for me," he told Daisy. "I'll just see who it is."

"Thank you," she said pertly, "but I'd like to know too. A little damp won't kill me. Curiosity will."

He smiled. "Then let's assuage it as soon as we can, and get on with things, shall we?"

They walked, hand in hand, into the salon. When Daisy saw who was getting up from a chair, she gave out a whoop, and ran to him. "Geoff," she cried. "You're safe; you're well. Oh, I'm so relieved!"

"I'm safe, and better than well," he said with a grin. "I couldn't send word, and then when I could, I decided I'd rather bring the news in person. I was on my way up north with Helena, when something happened."

"What?" Daisy asked.

He smiled, and looking behind him she saw her old companion, Helena Masters, dressed in a beautiful russet gown, rising from a chair. She was smiling.

"What happened," Geoff said, "was that I realized I never wanted to let her go out of my life. May I present my new countess, Lady Egremont? We were married over the border at Gretna, and then returned to stay on awhile at her mother's house, getting everyone ready for the remove to London and then Egremont. Now I've a wife, a mother-in-law, and two more delightful children. You see, on our way up north, we talked, we reminisced; we found so much in common. I couldn't let her go. And luckily, she consented to stay with me. I'm very happy."

"As am I," Helena said softly. "I never dared hope . . . "

"She never dared anything," the earl said fondly. "Always trying to keep her 'place,' when her only true place is by my side. I was the one who had to make the push to get to know her. I'm very glad you two married or else I'd never have had the chance to be alone with Helena."

Helena smiled. "I never thought to be so happy again. We both loved and lost and yet found that we could love again."

The earl looked at her lovingly. "I couldn't find a soul mate in Botany Bay or in London. But sometimes life gives us a second chance, and when I saw I'd found one, I acted before Fate could intervene. Now, little as I enjoy the *ton*, I want the world to know! We'll have a more formal wedding here and then another reception at Egremont soon after. They will be the sort of gala affairs I always avoided in the past. Just exactly what I want now to show the world my great good luck. You must attend," he told Daisy and Leland. "For now, you may congratulate me."

"Oh Geoff," Daisy said, as she embraced a tearful Helena. "I'll do more than that. I applaud you!"

"Well done," Leland said, shaking the earl's hand. "We are both pleased." He exchanged a sparkling look with Daisy. "And *vastly* relieved. Now, shall we celebrate?"

"Gladly," the earl said. "And by the way, you two look happier than I've ever seen either of you before. I congratulate you, too, and hope you don't mind that the gossip about me may overshadow whatever anyone says about your marriage."

"We are stunned and overset to think that we

have been so thoroughly, deliciously upstaged," Leland said. "Thank you."

"No, thank you," the earl said.

"You're welcome," Daisy said. "Now, let's celebrate!"

They all laughed, and then they celebrated, and kept on doing both through all the many long and merry years that were to come.